Wild Wild Cowboy

Elizabeth Bright

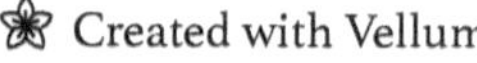 Created with Vellum

You do not have to be good.
You do not have to walk on your knees
for a hundred miles through the desert, repenting.
—Mary Oliver

The Painted Cat was the sort of place where a man could find himself in a whole heap of trouble, if he put his mind to it. I was in a mood to put my mind to it. It was a restless, ticklish feeling under my skin that still felt stretched too tight, a feeling that had been there ever since the day I found out life as I knew it was over. The only things that eased it any were drinking and fighting.

Which was why I jumped fists first into a fight that wasn't mine to begin with. I wasn't clear on the particulars of how it all started, and I wasn't in any hurry to end it, either. I doubted anyone in this bar had a claim to righteousness, me included, so I didn't land my punches with a whole lot of care or forethought.

The bar blurred into a haze of pain, grunts, and shouts. I gave slightly better than I got, or maybe it was the whiskey that made it seem that way. It was going pretty well until the unmistakable pump of a shotgun brought us all up short.

"Hands up!" Janie Belmont hollered from her usual place behind the bar. She had one hand on the barrel and the other near the trigger—but not touching it, I noted. She was tough, but she wasn't insane. "Asses in seats. The next man who tries anything uncivil is getting an extra hole somewhere on his body."

"Or woman," I said around a mouthful of blood. Someone had got me pretty good. Not knowing what else to do with it, I spit the blood out in the elbow of my flannel sleeve. "For equality and shit."

Janie cocked her head so her red hair tumbled over her shoulder and narrowed her eyes at me. "Don't you sass me, Zack. I'll call your brother and have him drag your ass out of here." I didn't ask which one, since either of my older brothers was more than capable of getting the job done. "I don't see a single woman in here asking for trouble, do you?"

It was the wrong question to pose, because right then a blonde woman outside the bar peered in through the window. The back of my neck prickled as her sharp gaze landed on me. Her chin jerked up, like I was exactly who she was looking for.

Trouble, in other words.

She came in with the wind as she opened the door. I felt the cold bite of it on my cheeks but that was nothing compared to the bite in her tone when she spoke.

"Mr. Hale, I presume?" She said my name like a reprimand.

I felt some kind of way about that. "Nope," I said. I grabbed a napkin from the bar and used it to sop up the blood leaking from my bottom lip.

That set her back on her heels a bit. She blinked at me through her round glasses like a suspicious owl. "No?"

"Mr. Hale is my father," I clarified. "I'm Zack. Which you know damn well, Hannah Bell, so you don't need to presume shit."

Until ten months ago, I had spent most of my time on the road, traveling and competing in rodeos, but I had been home to Aspen Springs, Colorado, enough that I had seen the town librarian a handful of times. Not at the library, since it was safe to say I hadn't set foot there since...well, ever. Mostly I'd seen her around town. Sometimes at Lodestar Ranch, the quarter horse training and breeding property my family owned. She was good friends with my sister-in-law, Essie Price, and my soon-to-be other sister-in-law, James Campos, who was also the head trainer at Lodestar.

Come to think of it, I couldn't recollect a single time we had actually been introduced, but I knew who she was, and she damn well knew who I was, too. Everyone did. It struck me as odd that she was pretending we didn't know each other, but then, Hannah Bell was a little odd in general.

I always looked twice at Hannah Bell. First to gauge that she wasn't for me. And then again to confirm it.

The women I gravitated toward could be summed up with one word: fun. Easy on the eyes, and easy on the brain. Not that any of those women had been dumb. They just knew better than to waste their deeper thoughts and dreams on a rough-and-tumble bronc rider only in town for the weekend rodeo. Honestly, they probably would have been disappointed if I had wanted anything but sex. I was a vacation for them. A fantasy.

Fun was not a word I'd ever use to describe Hannah. Maybe it was the ankle-length skirts she always wore or those oversized blouses and sweaters that left far too much to the imagination. Maybe it was the way she wrapped her blonde hair in a tight bun that suggested she wouldn't be happy if a man were to give it a little tug. Or maybe it was that she never looked at me the way I looked at her.

Whatever it was, I knew instinctively that Hannah was not for me. Still, every time we found ourselves in the same vicinity, I felt the need to verify the truth of it all over again.

Twice.

"Well, Mr. Zack Hale, I've been trying to reach you," she said crisply. "I've left several messages."

That gave me pause. I had received hundreds of texts in the month following my accident. Some of them from real friends and colleagues. Some of them with descriptive names meant to jog my memory, like Nice Tits Molly, Nice Tits Allison, or Nice Tits Tonya.

That system didn't work as well as I'd hoped, since apparently I was of the opinion that all tits were nice tits.

But the vast majority of texts were from anonymous nine digits, and considering the content of those messages, I highly doubted Hannah's was among them.

Frowning, I dug my phone out of my front pocket. "Did James give you my number? I don't recall seeing a message from you."

"Not your cell phone," she said. "I called the ranch phone."

Since the last person to sit in the Lodestar office and answer the phone was my mother, may her peaceful rest give her strength to raise holy hell, this came as a surprise. "The ranch has a phone?"

"It's listed on the website."

"The ranch has a website?" Now I was just fucking with her, for no particular reason other than I wanted to. As it had been a good ten months since I had wanted to do *anything* with a woman, much less fuck with them, I leaned into it.

She pursed her lips. "I left you several messages," she repeated.

"And I didn't receive a single one of them, but I'll let you tell me all about it over a beer. How's that?" I posed.

Her gaze fell to my mouth, where I still held the napkin to stem the bleeding. She looked at me like she was thinking unflattering things. "Is that wise?"

"Fuck no, it ain't wise," I said. "The Painted Cat is not a place people go to seek wisdom, Hannah Bell. However, I do have an open wound on my face, and it was put there by a man whose hygiene I have reason to doubt. So maybe it's not wise to add alcohol to injury, but at least it might kill some germs."

Every time I called her by her full name, her cheeks pinked up a bit. It made me feel inclined to keep doing it.

She scrunched her nose like a judgmental bunny. I figured that meant she was about to say no, thank you, she would rather not further partake of my company this evening. I didn't care. There were plenty of better ways to spend the night than conversing with a prim librarian about...well, what *did* she want to talk to me about, anyway? It couldn't be books. She wouldn't have hunted me down in an April snowstorm for a ten-second conversation.

"All right." She plopped down on a barstool. "What are you having?"

Her brown boots peeked out from under her skirt. She rocked her weight from one hipbone to the other and tugged at her skirt, loosening the fabric that had stretched tight over her thighs. I caught a glimpse of pale, slim ankles and my dick twitched to life.

I sent a baffled look to my crotch. *The stacked brunette who offered to suck you off in the bathroom did nothing for you, but a fucking ankle wakes you up?* Goddamn. My dick was every bit as broken as my leg.

With a shake of my head, I eased onto the barstool next to her. "Any beer on tap will do. I'm not picky."

Hannah waved to Janie, who was sweeping up a glass that had shattered during the fight. Janie dumped the shards into the wastebasket, rinsed off her hands, and faced us behind the bar, leaning forward on her elbows with a genuine smile. "Hey, babe. What can I get you?"

Hannah smiled. "Water for me, a beer for Zack."

Janie looked at me like she was suddenly realizing we were sitting next to each other on purpose. Her eyes narrowed suspiciously before she turned her attention back to Hannah. "Sorry, can't do it. He's already had three, and Brax made me promise I wouldn't let him get to four without a designated driver present. So unless that's you, I'm cutting him off."

Hannah blinked. "Oh. Um—"

"I'm not drunk," I protested. Maybe I wasn't entirely sober, either, but I knew the twisty mountain roads leading from town to the ranch like the back of my hand. Not that my older brother would care about either of those points, seeing as he was a stickler for rules and bossy as hell. "Anyway, just because Brax knows laws and shit doesn't mean you have to do what he says."

Janie smirked. "That's not why. Anyway, it's snowing, the road is hazardous, and you might be a pain in my ass, but I'd rather keep you alive a while longer." She patted my hand. "You're a good tipper."

Hannah sighed. "It would take me nearly two hours to get him to Lodestar and then drive all the way back to town." She chewed her lip. "I guess you could stay on my couch? Would that be okay?"

My leg ached just thinking about spending the night on a cramped couch. Not going to happen. "No, it would not be okay, Hannah Bell. Haven't you ever heard of stranger danger?"

"We aren't strangers, remember?" Cheeks pink, she pushed her glasses up her nose and stared at me. "Anyway, your reputation precedes you. Dozens of women have spent the night with you, and they all came out alive."

The way she said it all blunt like that, without the slightest hint of disapproval or embarrassment, caught me off guard. I was used to people having strong opinions about my sex life, thanks to that damn profile Sport Magazine did on me three years ago. People tended to be either appalled or...*interested*. Hannah was neither.

"I wasn't insinuating that *you* were the one in danger, darlin'." I leaned in, enjoying the momentary confusion in her blonde-fringed blue eyes as she worked through exactly what I *was* implying. When she blinked those pale eyelashes at me, my stomach did some sort of nonsense fluttering. "As for the other women, I want it on record that they came out alive and they came *happily*."

I said it to get a rise out of her. A reaction of some kind. Maybe a blush. But instead she regarded me with all the resigned patience of a kindergarten teacher.

"Good for you," she said.

Encouragingly.

Like she didn't quite believe me, but didn't want to wound my feelings.

That put me back on my heels a bit. I was of a sudden mind to slip my hand under that ridiculous skirt of hers and lay those doubts to rest. Maybe an orgasm would wipe that condescending look right off her face.

I wasn't going to do that. I wasn't going to even try. Women had never been something I had to *try* for, and I wasn't about to start now. Anyway, my skin was starting to itch again and I wanted another drink. And I was still curious what had brought her here to begin with.

"There's an empty cabin at Lodestar," I said. "You can stay there tonight and drive me back here in the morning to get my truck."

She wrinkled her nose again. "Or you could not drink," she suggested.

I smiled kindly. "Now, darlin', we both know that's not going to happen."

Her lips flattened as she considered. "Fine. I'll stay the night at Lodestar and bring you back to your truck tomorrow morning." She turned to Janie. "And when I show up to sewing club tomorrow unshowered and still wearing today's clothes, I don't want to hear a single word from you."

Janie, who had been leaning on the bar, eyes darting back and forth between us like she was fully engrossed in a tennis match, straightened. "No one will know. And even if they did, no one would care. It's Zack." She grabbed a glass and held it under the tap, filling it with amber liquid.

I didn't bother to take offense to that. "Sewing club?" I asked Hannah.

She nodded. "Ten a.m. at the library."

I ran the logistics in my head. Aspen Springs was a

forty-minute drive from Lodestar Ranch, and even longer if cows were in the road. She'd probably want an hour to shower and change. "All right. I'll be ready at eight."

Her eyebrows shot up in surprise. "Really? You could do that?"

"Of course I could do that. I grew up on a ranch. Not only that, but I'll have you know that in all my years in rodeo, I've never once missed my call time, Hannah Bell," I said, and watched her cheeks flush in response. Sexual innuendos couldn't make her blush but calling her by her full name was proving reliable. Odd, that. Even odder that I couldn't seem to stop testing it.

I took a long swallow of beer with a nod of thanks to Janie. "Now. What was it you wanted to talk to me about?"

"Right. The rodeo." She managed to pull another half inch of height from her already ramrod-straight spine. "You might be aware that the Aspen Springs library has had its budget cut—again—and quite frankly, the amount we've been given won't even keep the lights on. If we can't make up the difference, we'll have to cut hours of operation. So I thought we could hold a charity event to raise money—a rodeo. But I don't know the first thing about rodeos. I've never even been to one."

I nodded. "So you figured, why not ask the person in Aspen Springs with the most rodeo experience? And here we are."

"Sort of." She pushed at her glasses. "Lodestar Ranch would be the perfect location, so I went to your dad first. He agreed to host the rodeo at the ranch, and said he'd be happy to do whatever grunt work I needed, but he wouldn't be much help with the planning."

I nodded again. Dad was great with horses, but he had always left the business paperwork to Mom while she was alive, and then to Adam after she passed. "So he told you to come to me."

"No, he sent me to your brother, actually," she said.

"Which one?"

"Both."

Well, damn. I rubbed my thigh, which had a tendency to ache if I sat still too long. Or if I stood for too long. Or if I slept for too long. Basically, it always ached.

"But both Adam and Brax were too busy with the breeding program," she went on. "James—"

"James?" I interrupted, an edge to my voice. Because god*damn*. Just how far down this list was I?

"Right. Adam suggested her because she ran a horse show every year at her dad's stables. But she's swamped with getting clients ready for rodeo season. She sent me to Essie. Essie offered to help with the work, but she's pretty busy with clients now, too. She sent me to you."

I tallied it up. "So I'm your sixth choice. Gotta say, darlin', that hurts my feelings a bit." I said it with a long cowboy drawl, heavy on the charm, and a flash of my dimples to show how little I actually cared.

But she had the audacity to take me at my word, regarding me with serious blue eyes. "I thought of you. I wasn't sure you were an option, after your injury. But Essie said you were healed well enough and had some time on your hands."

Well enough. For fucking what? Not bronc riding, I knew that.

"I suppose that's right," I muttered into my beer.

"So you'll do it?" she asked hopefully.

"I'll think on it." But I already knew I was going to say yes. I always said yes. I drained my beer and signaled for Janie to bring me another. "You want anything?" I asked Hannah. "This round is on me."

"If we're going to be here a while, I'll take a pinot grigio. Thank you." She reached into the enormous slouchy bag she carried and pulled out a tablet. "Don't worry about entertaining me. I'll be fine. Let me know when you're ready to go."

Apparently our conversation was over. I paid for our drinks and took my beer to the pool tables, pool being something I could still do just as well after the accident as before. The next time I looked in Hannah's direction, she was happily engrossed in her book, sipping her wine, looking somehow both completely out of place and entirely comfortable with that.

Nope. Definitely not for me.

But I looked at her again, just to be sure.

Twice.

HANNAH

It was unfair that I woke up smelling like sins I had not actually partaken of. Cigarette smoke from the nicotine addicts who had huddled in the doorway of the Painted Cat, not bothering to avert their exhales as I passed. Stale beer from the guy who had jostled his mug against my back. Colognes both masculine and feminine. I sniffed my sweater and winced.

Ugh.

I did not believe for one second that Zack would be ready to go at eight a.m. Not after the six beers he'd consumed last night. Ranch chores and rodeo events were one thing, but I couldn't expect my sewing club to outweigh his hangover. He didn't even know me.

Except for my name, apparently.

And the way he said it, like he did actually *know* me. I was so used to people looking straight through the nerdy girl with her nose buried in a book or an embroidery project. That was fine. I was comfortable with being invisible. Even if it stung sometimes.

Zack Hale, the golden rodeo star of Aspen Springs who probably had so many notches on his bedpost there wasn't any wood left to notch, was the last person I ever expected to notice me.

But noticing was a long way from caring, and while I believed Zack was the sort of good-natured, golden-retriever type who always meant well, I wasn't going to stake my reputation on him dragging his hungover body out of bed just so I'd be on time for sewing club, which was why I was on his doorstep at precisely 7:52.

I still gave him the benefit of the doubt and knocked first, though. After a suitable pause, my ear pressed to the wood to listen for sounds of life and hearing nothing, I pushed open the door.

And froze.

Because there was Zack, very much awake, standing by the window in a puddle of spilled sunshine, black headphones over his ears, fuzzy pink bunny slippers on his feet, and not a stitch of clothing to be found anywhere in between. He cradled a white bowl in one broad palm while he shoveled ramen noodles into his mouth with chopsticks. He should have looked ridiculous, but with the morning light sliding over his sculpted muscles like liquid gold, he could not have looked more perfect if Michaelangelo had carved him from marble.

I could feel heat spreading from my cheeks down my throat, but Zack didn't seem at all bothered. He didn't yelp or move to cover himself. Instead, he glanced at the oven clock and slurped up another mouthful of ramen.

"Hannah," he said, a little too loudly, making me startle. He dropped the chopsticks into the bowl and tugged off the headphones, leaving them to circle his neck. "Want some breakfast?" he asked in a normal-volume voice.

I didn't fluster easily, but good lord.

Fuzzy pink bunny slippers.

"My eyes are up here, Hannah Bell," he said.

Mortified to be caught looking down—at his *slippers*, not *there*—my gaze snapped to his face.

"My feet were cold. The slippers were a Christmas present." He grinned. "Breakfast? It's my own personal hangover cure. Ramen and ginger ale."

"No, thank you. I'll grab something from Jo's on the way to the library." I glanced at the clock. 7:55. "If I have time. You said you'd be ready to go at eight."

"And I will be. Don't you worry your pretty little head about that, darlin'. I still have five—four minutes. Plenty of time."

My mouth fell open as he resumed his naked ramen eating. Calmly. Like he really and truly believed that four minutes was more than enough time to go from bunny slippers to fully dressed.

I started to twitch.

He eyed me curiously. "You all right there, sugar?"

"I'm fine," I lied as I fell apart inside. Not because an extra five minutes would ruin my day. It probably wouldn't matter much at all either way. And still the anxiety of whether he would make his self-imposed deadline made my blood pressure rise.

"If you wanted me ready at 7:59, you should have said so."

"No, it's fine." I showed him my teeth in what I meant to be a calm, carefree smile. Judging from the way his eyes widened, and his last bite of ramen went down with a sputtered cough, I did not succeed.

"I only need sixty seconds." He tilted the bowl to his mouth and slurped up the last of the broth. The lines of his throat bobbed in deep swallows. He wiped his mouth on the back of his hand and dumped the empty bowl and chopsticks in the sink. "Time me."

"What?" I asked.

It was hard to make sense of his words when ninety-nine percent of my brain was occupied with the way his body turned mundane tasks into poetry. Even the way he limped slightly, favoring the leg that had been broken several times over in a rodeo incident, was elegant. And in bunny slippers. It shouldn't have been possible.

"Time me," he repeated. His eyes glinted with challenge. "Sixty seconds."

Time him? The man was stark *naked* and he wanted to play games? The whole situation was absurd. Zack Hale was clearly a deeply unserious man and I...I had never been silly in my entire life.

It didn't bother me. I liked who I was.

But the way Zack looked at me made me want to test him. To see if he could do something I thought was impossible. I wanted him to prove me wrong. I wanted him to impress me. And somehow none of that seemed silly at all.

I pulled out my phone and swiped to the stopwatch on the clock app. "Go."

He didn't hesitate for even a millisecond—I had the stopwatch to prove it—before kicking off the slippers and tumbling over the back of the sofa. He landed on the cushions with a soft bounce that propelled him back onto his feet, now with a pair of black boxer briefs in his hand.

Convenient that he had a basket of clean laundry right there, I supposed, although I did wonder exactly how long it had been there.

Zack leaned against the armrest for balance as he pulled his underwear up to mid-thigh, then reached one long arm behind himself to grab his jeans. Both legs went on at once and he pulled his jeans and underwear up together.

My gaze stayed glued to the rapidly increasing numbers while Zack moved in a blur. "Twenty-five seconds," I warned.

He tugged a white t-shirt over his head. I spared a millisecond of pity for my future self, who would never have the opportunity to look at that six-pack again.

"Thirty-three seconds," I said.

He slipped his arms through a red-checked flannel. When his fingers moved at the neck like he meant to button the damn thing, I made a low keen of distress. He laughed. "Just teasing, darlin'."

He was already onto his wool socks when I said crisply, "Thirty-nine seconds."

He wiggled his right foot into one of the worn cowboy boots by the door, then braced his side against the wall while he went for his left. "Don't hit stop yet. I've got one more thing."

"Fifteen seconds left." My voice was sharp with nerves.

Zack pushed his hand into the mess of coats and hats that hung on the wall and pulled out a leather belt with a shiny red buckle. He threaded it through the loops of his jeans with a rough efficiency that made my mouth go dry. His fingers were so *nimble*. Metal clanged against metal as he buckled it. "Time."

I hit stop. "Fifty-eight seconds."

Zack's shit-eating grin could melt snow. "Well, would you look at that. And it's eight on the dot."

His hands went to his hips and my eyes went there, too, landing on the travesty of a belt buckle between them. It was a cherry-red enamel rectangle the size of my fist. RIDE, it proclaimed in shiny gold letters above a cowboy on a bucking bronco.

I wondered how many women had taken him up on that suggestion. Not that I cared. But I wondered.

"Let's go, darlin'," he said as he opened the door and motioned me to go through ahead of him. "You don't want to have to tell your sewing club you were late because you were busy gawking at my crotch."

"I'm not gawking." I marched past him with a withering stare. "I've gone blind. My eyeballs are so horrified by your belt buckle that they've mutinied."

He chuckled. "I'd take offense, but given what you're wearing, I think it's safe to assume you don't know what you're talking about."

I unlocked my car, frowning down at myself. "What's wrong with what I'm wearing?"

"Nothing at all. Just tell me where the portal is to 1852. I don't want to accidentally fall through."

"I like my clothes. They're comfortable."

I hiked up my skirt to mid-calf so I could get into the car without dragging the fabric in the dirt. Zack tilted his head sideways, his body following, like he was trying to see what I had on underneath. But that couldn't be right. For one, he couldn't see anything more than my ankle from that angle. For another, Zack might be the only man in Aspen Springs who knew my name, but he had a very obvious preference in women, and I was not it.

"What are you doing?" I asked bluntly.

He jerked upright. "Trying to figure out what's so comfortable about a skirt you constantly have to tug at just so you can sit down."

I rolled my eyes. "It's a lot more comfortable than being constricted by jeans."

The truth was, when I left the Nevada compound at fourteen, I had been so excited to wear jeans and tank tops, like every other girl I saw at gas stations and highway diners on our way to my brother's ranch in Wyoming. They all looked so carefree. So *normal*. But I couldn't shake the feeling that I looked *weird* in normal clothes. I was sure people were staring at me. I was so uncomfortable.

So now I wore the long skirts every girl wore at the compound. The funny thing was, even though I knew my clothes made me stand out, I wasn't uncomfortable with it at all. I felt like myself.

I pulled onto the dirt driveway, which would eventually turn to a gravel road for another couple miles before we finally reached actual pavement. Lodestar Ranch was maybe a third the size of what it once was when Zack's great-great-great-great grandfather bought the land in the gold rush of the eighteen hundreds, according to old maps and deeds we kept on microfiche at the library, but it was still a few hundred acres. Its pastures stretched all the way to the mountains.

"Right there," Zack said as we bumped past a pasture on the outskirts of the property. "That's where we'll set up staging."

"What staging?" I asked distractedly, all my focus dedicated to getting my twelve-year-old Subaru out of here in one piece. "Parking and all that."

"For your rodeo."

That got my full attention. "You'll do it?" I squeaked. "You'll help me?"

He grabbed the steering wheel and steered us around a sharp dip, then leaned back with an easy smile.

"Yeah, Hannah Bell. Let's do the damn thing."

ZACK HAD GIVEN me plenty of time to shower, change, and feed my cats before I was due at the library. Annabelle, Lillian, Evie, Daisy, and Lord St. Vincent—named after characters in my favorite book series—were clearly confused that I had spent the night elsewhere, but they happily wrapped themselves around my ankles to show they were glad for my return. Except for Annabelle, my old gray tabby, who would rather die than show unearned affection.

My little bungalow was a two-mile walk from the library. Aspen Springs was a very car-centric—or, to be precise, *truck*-centric—town, but I liked to be on foot anytime the weather would allow it. It had taken two years for people to stop shouting offers to give me a ride out their windows. Now they rolled on by with a honk or a wave.

Today was gorgeous, perfect for a brisk walk, despite last night's sudden snowstorm. People around here liked to say, *if you don't like the weather, just wait five minutes, it will change.* That change wasn't always for the better. Aspen Springs was nestled in the Rocky Mountains, between the Front Range and the San Juan. The weather tended to be as wild as the scenery.

There were patches of snow on lawns, and some deeper drifts where the shadows were darkest, but the street was clear, and so was the sidewalk—when there was one. The Colorado sunshine was a force to be reckoned with.

My stomach was in danger of cannibalizing itself from hunger by the time I reached Jo's, the only coffee shop within a twenty-mile radius. Chain restaurants had been banned decades ago, which sounded like a quaint, darling idea until it was three a.m., you're muttering *one more chapter* for the tenth time, and would do murder for a bean burrito with globs of cheese or hot, salty fries.

The good thing about Jo's was the pastries were baked fresh every day and she kept a decent selection of teas. Jo Ramirez—whom no one ever called Josephine—was somewhere between the age of fifty-five and seventy-five. It was hard to tell. She had salt-and-pepper hair she kept short, smooth brown skin without a line to be seen anywhere, and a wiry frame that reminded me of a ballet dancer.

She also had no sense of humor. I knew this because the first time I met her, I pointed out how fortuitous it was that her name was slang for coffee, given her chosen profession. She had stared at me like I was speaking Latin.

Exactly how I had stared at Zack this morning, probably.

It was possible she had heard that joke before.

I indulged in a cranberry-orange muffin and a nice Earl Grey tea. I didn't have time to sit down for a decent breakfast, so I ate it as I walked the block from Jo's to the library. After a quick stop in the ladies' room to wash the muffin oils from my hands so I wouldn't stain the fabrics, I found everyone waiting for me in the sole multipurpose room.

"You're not wearing yesterday's clothes," Janie said as I walked in.

James, Chloe, and Essie stopped sorting their embroidery projects. They looked at me and then at Janie.

"Why would she be wearing yesterday's clothes?" Chloe asked. Her head tilted and I could practically see the gears turning. She knew where Janie worked Friday nights, so those gears didn't have to turn far. "Ohhh, was this a walk of shame situation?" she squealed.

"I gave Zack a ride home, that's all." Not that I had anything against one-night stands, for other people. I had tried one, once. It hadn't been a good fit. "You promised you wouldn't say anything, Janie."

Janie arched an auburn brow. "That's not how I remember it. You said, *if I show up to our sewing club tomorrow in yesterday's clothes, I don't want to hear a word about it.* And you didn't. So..." Her voice trailed off with a grin.

"You drove all the way from town to Lodestar Ranch and back again?" James asked. I couldn't tell if she looked suspicious or concerned. "In the snowstorm?"

"No, I stayed in Brax's cabin," I said.

"Huh." Essie bared her teeth in a grimace. "I *think* we washed those sheets recently?" She said it like she had doubts.

I wrinkled my nose. Ew.

"You should have stayed with Zack," Essie said. "Had

that one-night stand. He's like the Statue of Liberty or Paris. Something everyone should do once."

"I've never been to Paris," I said. "Or seen the Statue of Liberty."

"Yeah, well, no one in this sewing club has fucked Zack, either, and that's a crying shame, quite frankly." Essie tossed her hair—she had recently traded rainbow ends for bright pink highlights framing her pretty face, a purposeful, defiant clash with the deep red lipstick she always wore—and thumped her fist on the laminate table. "Someone needs to fact check his reputation, dammit. For *science.*"

All four of them were staring at me now with amused, knowing smirks. I had seen those looks before, always directed at another member of the sewing club when she found herself entangled with one of the infamous Hale brothers. First James, when she started sleeping with her boss, Adam Hale. Then Essie, when she went from hating Brax Hale to marrying him.

I knew that look. They wanted gossip. Entertainment. Things no one had ever looked to me to deliver, and with good reason. Fitting in never came naturally to me. These women—James, Essie, Chloe, and Janie—were the first real friends I had ever had, and even so, I was still on the outskirts of the friend group, watching wistfully as the others formed tighter bonds that I simply didn't know how to forge.

I wanted to. I wanted to so very badly.

Obviously, I wasn't going to agree to sleep with Zack as

a science experiment just to have something to bond over, but I wanted to give them *something*.

"I saw Zack naked," I blurted out.

The smirks immediately shifted to gaping jaws.

"Details!" Chloe demanded.

James laughed. "What she means is, how did that happen?"

"No, what I mean is, how big was his dick?" Chloe clarified.

"Oh, um..." I faltered. Wasn't that private? On the other hand, so many other people had seen Zack naked and talked about it that he probably wouldn't care. "Well, he wouldn't be popular in ancient Greece, that's for sure." I laughed at my own joke.

James, Chloe, Essie, and Janie did not laugh. They stared at me blankly.

"Because the ancient Greeks preferred men with small penises?" I tried. When they kept staring at me like I was speaking, well, Greek, I explained, "Like Aristophane said. The ideal man had a strong butt, small tongue, and little prick. Big dicks meant big dick energy, and the ancient Greeks saw that as a bad thing. Men should be rational, intelligent, and not guided by passion."

"Huh." Janie blinked. "But I've seen *Troy*. They literally fought wars because they were all thinking with their dicks."

"I think that's Aristophane's point," I said.

"Huh," she said again.

"Alright, we've established that the Hale brothers

would not have been model Greek citizens, due to their penis size," Essie said. "Now, *how* did this happen? Were you naked, too?"

"No, I was not naked," I said.

I told them the whole story. They hooted with laughter at every new detail. The earphones. The ramen. How he had told me to time him getting dressed, and how I had actually agreed. The god-awful belt buckle.

But I didn't tell them about the bunny slippers. It seemed too intimate, somehow. Which was ridiculous, because I had told them all about his dick size, so why should slippers be a bridge too far?

Maybe it was that he hadn't seemed at all bothered that I'd seen his penis, but he felt the need to explain the slippers.

He probably didn't care, and I was just imagining him to have depth he didn't possess. A hundred other women had seen him in those slippers, probably.

But still, I kept it to myself.

issy heaved a sigh, thinking she had won, and I took the opportunity to tighten her girth another notch. She gave an annoyed toss of her head, but a loose saddle wouldn't be safe for either one of us. I patted her neck and slipped the bridle over her ears. She took the bit easily. Missy never minded the bit, so long as I took care not to clank it on her teeth.

In truth, she didn't mind the saddle, either, despite her nonsense about the girth. She had jogged eagerly to the gate when I called for her, and only part of her excitement had to do with the apple she knew I'd give her. My girl enjoyed our rides. We'd been a pair for the last fourteen years. Even though I was away from Aspen Springs half the year, I always made time for her when I was here.

Sliding into her saddle should have felt like coming home.

It did not.

Maybe it never would again. But I wasn't going to let myself dwell on that thought, because if I did, I might just decide to find the edge of a very tall cliff and then keep right on walking.

"Business or pleasure?" Dad's words pulled me back. He had ambled over while I had been feeling sorry for myself, and now he squinted up and me from beneath the wide brim of his tan Stetson.

"Business. Adam told me to make myself useful, so I figured I'd check the fence after last night's storm," I said.

Missy chose that moment to lift her tail and manure tumbled out. I stood in the stirrups to take the pressure off her back. Fuck, that hurt.

"Looks like you're getting your strength back. Didn't I say you'd be back to normal before you knew it? Feels good, right?" He said it like there was no alternative.

Back to normal. I thought about that cliff again. About finding the edge of it.

"Sure," I said. My lips tilted up. "Feels great."

Dad nodded and gave Missy a brisk pat on the neck. That was what he wanted to hear.

"If you don't mind waiting a minute while I tack up Xander, I'll join you." He grinned up at me. "I'm feeling pretty good today, too."

Waiting was probably my least favorite thing ever, but of course I said, "I don't mind."

At seventy-five, Dad was in better shape than most men

twenty years younger, but he had the occasional flare up of arthritis in his knees that made riding uncomfortable. If this was a good day for him, I wasn't going to stand in the way of him spending it on horseback.

Three years ago, deep in his grief from losing Mom to cancer, he would have spent the day with a bottle of whiskey. He had sobered up when Adam told him he couldn't be around his grandson, my nephew Ben, while drunk, but it had taken him another year after that to want anything to do with Lodestar or the horses. Mom had been by his side when he started the training operation, and it was too painful for him to be there without her.

Seeing him take pleasure in riding again was good. I might not know what the fuck I wanted for myself, but what I wanted for other people hadn't changed. I just wanted everyone to be happy.

Missy got antsy as we waited, and I shifted my hipbones. My seat felt all wrong. My skin felt too tight. I was a little worse for wear this afternoon. Last night's barfight might have had something to do with that. But I suspected it had more to do with this morning. *Time me*, I had told Hannah, and then proceeded to throw my body around like it hadn't been trampled by a nine-hundred-pound animal ten months ago.

And she had done it, too. That prim little librarian had surprised me. Not just because she did it. It was the *way* she did it. The second she had hit that green button, she was all in—and she was on my side. It wasn't me against her. It was me against the clock, and she was rooting for me to win.

Maybe I should have taken more care with my battered body, but I couldn't bring myself to regret it now, sore though I was. Those sixty seconds were the closest to normal I had felt since the eight seconds that had changed everything. I had given our stupid game everything I had, holding nothing back.

All or nothing.

It was how I lived my life.

Giving my all was easy. Having nothing left to give turned out to be a lot harder.

Maybe giving my all to a race against the clock was stupid, although there were probably plenty of people who would argue that bronc riding wasn't exactly smart, either. Anyway, my leg was going to ache regardless. What did a little more pain matter?

Hannah's squeal of victory was worth every extra ache.

"It's good to see you smiling again," Dad said, joining us by the fence. He swung onto Xander's back with careful ease.

"What are you talking about? I smile all the time." I knew this was true. I made sure of it.

Dad's blue eyes travelled over my face. "Not like that. Not lately."

With a nudge of his heels to Xander's belly, he took the lead. He headed west where I had planned to turn east, so I could ride into the sun rather than let it beat down on the back of my neck. I was wearing a baseball cap today rather than a cowboy hat, and anyway, I liked catching the sunset. If I said that, though, Dad would have something to say about my choice of hat. He didn't care if cowboy hats were not as common these days as they had been back in his youth and younger generations preferred a ball cap. He'd wear a Stetson to his grave.

"James said you're going to help the library with their rodeo," Dad said as we moved at a slow walk, checking for downed rails and loose wires as we went. "Seems the topic of conversation came up at her sewing club this morning."

"That's right." I wondered what else had come up. My dick, probably. Not in the fun way, either, although there had been a moment where she was getting in the car and I had definitely felt...interested.

I needed to stop thinking about that woman's ankles. This was how people developed embarrassing kinks. Not the standard butt plugs and ropes stuff, either. The kind that brought shame to your friends and family.

"You don't have to, you know." Dad's head was tilted down toward the fence, his face obscured by the shadow of his Stetson. But I knew he wasn't minding the fence at all. He was watching for my response. "No one would blame you if you backed out."

How he could possibly think that after spending even five minutes with Hannah Bell, I wasn't clear. She would absolutely blame me if I backed out. That disapproving frown of hers was a fearsome thing, and I wasn't in any hurry to be on the receiving end of it again. The way she had looked at me last night at the bar, like when I wiped the blood from my lip, I took her last hope with it.

And still, she had wanted me to win our stupid little game.

I wondered about that. The audacity to believe in someone despite all the evidence that she shouldn't. I shook my head.

"Your body took a beating, Zack," Dad pressed, misreading my thoughts. "That accident was traumatic. It takes time to recover from something like that."

I scratched the back of my neck, which was already starting to feel the effects of the afternoon sun. "I always knew the risks, Dad. A broken leg, a fractured spine, some busted ribs...I've been hurt before. This ain't my first rodeo, you know." My smirk came easy despite the sharp twist in my gut.

Dad kept pretending to study the fence for damage when he was really looking for signs of damage in me. Hale men weren't known for their ability to handle big emotions real well, and that was an understatement. Kindergarteners were more well-adjusted than a heart-broken Hale. And it didn't last days or weeks—it could drag on for months or *years*. Dad tumbled down a whiskey bottle for over a year after Mom died. When Ben's mother left Adam, he swore off women for a solid decade until he met James.

Heartache had a way of bringing life to a standstill, in my experience. And if there was one thing I fucking hated, it was standing still.

I didn't do big feelings. I did big things instead.

Used to, anyway. *Used to.*

And there was that cliff again.

Needing to move, I squeezed Missy's belly with my calves, urging her forward. Her body swayed as she ambled along. My hips didn't quite catch the right rhythm, but I felt slightly less stiff than I had twenty minutes ago. It took a while for my body to warm up these days.

I got to work on a rail that had rotted through. It should have been dealt with months ago, but we didn't get out to this part of the property often. These pastures had been at rest since Mom passed, which was why it would make the perfect staging area for Hannah's rodeo.

"I'm thinking we could use this field for parking. Competitors hauling horses in from out of town." I surveyed the area, then pointed toward the far fence. "And outhouses over there. Close, but not too close."

"Outhouses?" Dad repeated.

"Yeah. We're going to need outhouses. Can't have people hanging out at the ranch all day, drinking beer and water, with nowhere to relieve themselves. And I know you don't want to invite them all into the big house."

"Right." Dad frowned. "I guess I hadn't considered that."

"Then it's a good thing Hannah meandered her way to me," I said drily. "Despite your best efforts."

Dad gave me a sheepish grimace. "We all care about you, you know."

"As I said, this ain't my first rodeo. Hell, it's not even my first injury. I've been thrown before."

"You always were a tough one." Dad was at the fence again, checking my work, and this time he gave it his full attention. "You got hurt, but you got right back on that horse. Nothing keeps you down. You have guts, son. I spent many long nights worried about rodeo breaking your body, but I never once had to worry it would break your spirit."

I grinned. "You know me, Dad. I'll always be okay."

The lie sat lightly on my chest, even as the bracelet on my left wrist felt like a goddamn shackle. It was what they needed from me. Dad, Mom, my brothers. And it was something I was good at giving them. A bright spot when things were tough—and, fuck, things were always tough, weren't they? There was always *something*, waiting there in the shadows, ready to drag you down if you let it. They wouldn't be able to handle the truth, that sometimes the shadows pulled at me, too.

So I lied.

Get right back on the horse. That was the rule, but it was so much more than that. It was a way of life. Obviously, no one was climbing back into the saddle with a broken bone or a concussion, not without proper medical attention. But the second you healed it was time to try again. Waiting too long gave fear an opportunity, and once it settled in, it was hard to shake.

Over my decade riding broncos in the rodeo, I had broken several bones, bruised every part of my body, and had a couple concussions. But I had always gone right back to the rodeo the second my doctor gave me the go ahead. This time, I couldn't do that.

For the first time in my life, I couldn't get back on the horse.

And I was fucking terrified.

Ilifted the book to my face and gave it a deep, giddy sniff. E-books were convenient, but there was something about the scent of ink and paper that thrilled my soul.

Today was a book day.

Books were my favorite thing in the world. I loved the musty smell of the paper. I loved the promise in their pages. Some books were a discovery. A new viewpoint, a new world, a new emotion. Other books were a warm hug. Plenty of books were both. And you never knew what it was going to be, even when you thought you did. You never knew when you were going to open a book and find a word, a sentence, a thought that made your heart thrum.

So it was no surprise I was a librarian, even though only a small part of my job had anything to do with books. The Aspen Springs Public Library was the hub of the community. Whatever the community lacked, we tried to provide. Internet access, after-school activities for kids, classes on everything from computers to yoga, and sometimes we were simply a safe shelter. We put those tax dollars to work and, quite frankly, the community got more than their money's worth out of us.

But with another budget cut looming, that could all change.

I really, really needed this rodeo to bridge the gap between government funding and grants that we had applied for and would hopefully receive in the next year.

And this community needed it, too, even if they didn't realize how much.

As the Director of the Aspen Springs Public Library, and the only full-time employee, my day had started at seven a.m., a full hour before we opened. We also had two part-time employees, Janice and Yvette, who ran the circulation desk, shelved books, and assisted with the after-school programs. And for eighty hours over the next three months, we also had Silas Moore, who was paying off his DWI debt to society with volunteer work. A couple of people like him showed up every year. People who couldn't afford the DUI or DWI fines were often assigned community service. The only thing that surprised me anymore was how many people signed up to pick up trash along the road instead of fulfilling those hours at the library.

I got some paperwork out of the way and made sure we had all our classes and programs ready for the week. Most of my work days had very little to do with books but today was special. I had been looking forward to it all month.

Today was a book day.

Twice a year, I culled the library inventory. Books that were falling apart, smelled like pee or vomit, or had suspicious stains were all thrown in the garbage. Books that had served their purpose to the community and were no longer useful were set aside for our annual used book sale that we held every June. This made space for at least a fraction of the thousands of new books published every year.

Supposing we could afford to purchase any of them.

But I wasn't going to let anything ruin my good mood today. Especially not thoughts of doom and gloom.

By the time I unlocked the library doors, I had a printout of the circulation report in my hand, a list of all the books that hadn't been checked out in thirty-six months.

"Good morning, Mrs. Spencer," I greeted the elderly woman who entered as I grabbed a rolling cart.

"Good morning, dear," she replied before heading to her usual corner.

Mrs. Spencer was always our first visitor, October through April. As a retired widow on a fixed income, she used the library as a way to keep her heating bills manageable. She liked to sit in the red stuffed chair by the window, usually with a romance book that she never brought home. She'd read a book all in one sitting and check out another one when we closed for the evening, which she'd bring back the very next morning. She was a voracious reader, and it was always romance.

Goals, honestly.

Although I did worry about her on extra-cold nights.

I scanned the report. A good chunk of the books were history and reference books. Most of those would stay put on our shelves for students doing research papers and whatnot. They hardly ever checked out the books, but I knew they were well-used. I hoped we could clear out the five-year-old SAT study guides and replace them with new editions this year, but I wouldn't toss the old ones until I knew for sure.

I started with children's books, which tended to get damaged faster than any other genre. Once I tossed out anything gross, I made my way down the list. I decided to keep books I knew were still loved and read during story time on Saturday mornings, like *The Bear Snores On* and *Llama, Llama, Red Pajama*. I removed ten from the shelf, thanked them for their service, and placed them in the book sale pile.

By mid-afternoon, I had moved to the last—and hardest—genre on my list: adult fiction. These shelves were my heart and soul. Thrillers, general and women's fiction, fantasy, romance—I loved them all and I hated to let go of any single one of them, but it had to be done. I comforted myself with the reminder that if anyone requested one of the culled books, I could help them find it at another library or maybe order the e-book.

There was an older historical romance that hadn't been checked out in over three years, although it was hugely popular when it came out. I pulled it from the shelf and traced the outline of the man and woman in a passionate clinch. It was the kind of cover no one did anymore, but I still loved them. It was like looking at a painting.

This one happened to be one of my favorites. I had a copy on my shelf at home, although I hadn't picked it up in years. I flipped it open to a random page near the beginning and read the words *"You just plugged your soon-to-be husband"* and just like that, I was sucked into Regan's misadventures as a mail-order bride. Without realizing what I was doing, I sank down onto the blue carpet and turned the page.

Sometime later—who was to say how long, really, but it wasn't a great sign that I was sixty pages deep—I was interrupted by an exasperated voice saying, "Hannah. Bell."

I blinked the visions of an Old West cowboy from my brain and found myself staring into the bemused face of a modern one. I adjusted my glasses. "Zack?"

He huffed and straightened, putting us face to crotch. RIDE, commanded that atrocious belt buckle. I blinked again, then slowly dragged my gaze to his face.

His lips curled in a smirk. "Darlin', you sure do make a pretty picture on your knees like that, but I'm gonna need you to stand up so we can have a proper conversation."

"Oh! Right." It always took me a minute to pull myself from a fictional world into the real one. I started to scramble to my feet but apparently I wasn't fast enough because Zack scooped me up by the armpits and stood me in front of him.

"I said your name three times," Zack accused.

"Well." I looked down at the book still in my hand. "It's a very good book. What can I do for you?"

His eyebrows went up like I had amused him. "*You're* the one who asked *me* for a favor, as you might recall."

My brain finally switched back on. "The rodeo!"

"That's right. The rodeo. We should start making plans, don't you think?"

"Absolutely. I get off work in—" I craned my neck to see the clock. Good grief. Today had flown by. "Thirty minutes. If you don't mind hanging around for a bit, you could come to my place and we can discuss it over dinner."

He squinted down at me. "You want me to come home with you?" he asked slowly.

"For dinner and rodeo planning," I said. Firmly, so he wouldn't think it was a pretext for something else. I knew Zack had plenty of women throwing themselves at him, and I wanted to be very clear on what I was offering, and what I was most certainly not. "I'm not even going to cook for you. We're having leftover green chili chicken soup and cornbread." My stomach growled at the thought of food. I had an hour-long lunch break, but as usual, I had forgotten to eat and worked right through it.

His lips kicked up again. "Sounds great." He took the book from my hand and glanced at the cover, then back at me. "Go on and finish up. I'll wait."

I went back to culling books and Zack took my book to the chair cattycorner to Mrs. Spencer, who wouldn't leave until we closed.

Five minutes later, I heard him laughing.

"I HAVE FIVE CATS," I warned as I unlocked the door to my sweet little bungalow and Zack followed me over the threshold. I should have thought to ask if he was allergic before inviting him over. I kept a clean house, but sweeping, vacuuming, and dusting could only do so much against five cats.

"Five?" he echoed. "Isn't that a lot of cats?"

I sniffed. "Only compared to some. Others hold themselves to a higher standard."

He grinned.

"You won't see most of them," I said. "They don't like strangers."

Evie took that moment to pad toward us, her plumy tail waving high, and proceeded to wind herself around Zack's ankles.

He promptly dropped down to rub her head. No one could resist all that white fluff. Everyone who met her cooed over her pretty blue eyes, but I personally thought her best features were her brown ears and the matching tip of her tail, like she had been dipped in chocolate sauce.

"This one seems to like me," Zack said, running his hand down her back in a way that made her arch and purr.

"Yes, well, Evie likes everyone," I conceded. "She's a slut."

His head jerked up. "That's not very nice."

"It's not a criticism. It's a fact." I scooped Evie into my arms and cuddled her against my chest. "She can't stand to be alone and she's happiest when someone is petting her. Plus she is forever trying to get St. Vincent to mate with her, despite the fact that they are both fixed." I rubbed under her chin right where she liked it the most. "Probably because she wasn't spayed until she was three years old. I didn't know that when I adopted her, so their names are fortuitous."

"Why's that?" Zack asked. He moved closer so he could pet Evie, who was still in my arms.

"They're named after book characters who fell in love," I explained. "All my cats are named for characters in my favorite series. Annabelle was my first. You won't meet her, even if you do see her, because she doesn't have a high opinion of people in general and men in particular. Then I adopted Lillian and Daisy from a litter that was abandoned here at the library a couple years ago. Lord Vincent came next, and Evie joined us last year."

"Do you plan on getting more?" he ventured.

I gave him an exasperated look. "A person does not *plan* to have more than two cats. They just happen. If you're lucky."

Evie jumped from my arms and padded away. Off to find St. Vincent, probably.

"I hope you're hungry," I said as I lead the way to the kitchen. "There's plenty of food." I tended to cook large batches of things and then lived off it for the next week. Cooking for only one person involved too much math.

"Starving," he said. "Anything I can help with?"

I shook my head, already pulling the container of soup out of the fridge. "It will only take a minute to get everything together, and five minutes or so to reheat the soup." I nodded toward the table. "Sit down."

He sat. I could feel his eyes on me while I turned on the stove and dumped the soup into a pot. I removed the tinfoil from the cornbread pan and put three squares on a plate—two for Zack and one for me—to heat up in the microwave.

"Do you like butter or honey with your cornbread?" I asked.

"Butter," Zack said, so I put some on the table. "So, the rodeo. Do you have a date in mind?"

"I was thinking early June, before rodeo season gets busy in Colorado. Is that enough time to pull it together?" I glanced over at him while I stirred the soup. The smell of green chilis and salsa verde wafted upward, making my stomach growl again.

"Eight weeks?" His head tilted as he considered. "We could make it work if you don't try to get fancy with all eight events. I suggest you stick to the ones where contestants bring their own horses. The roping events and barrel racing. It will be easier to get insurance if you're not including the real dangerous events like bull riding and bronc riding."

"That makes sense. Could we also include performances? Like the high school equestrian drill team? They have their own horses."

"That's a good idea. James is working with a vault rider now at Lodestar. Maybe she'd like to perform, too."

With the soup bubbling, I turned off the stove and ladled it into porcelain bowls, then pulled the cornbread from the microwave. Zack was immediately on his feet. He somehow managed to balance both bowls on one hand and took the plate in his other. Having nothing else to carry, I grabbed spoons and a knife for the butter.

"Do you want anything to drink? I have water and white wine. No beer, sorry." I had the occasional glass of wine, but mostly I stuck to water and lots of tea.

"Water is fine, thanks."

I filled two glasses from the tap and joined him at the table. "So, what do the roping events entail? Do they bring their own rope or is that something we have to provide?"

He froze in the middle of buttering his cornbread and stared at me.

"I've never been to a rodeo," I reminded him. "I don't know what any of the events look like."

He set his knife down. "Well, darlin', we're going to have to do something about that."

ZACK

ZACK:
Polish up those cowboy boots, sugar. We're going on a road trip.

HANNAH:
Where to?

ZACK:
I found us a rodeo. It's two hours from here, so we'll leave early. I'll pick you up at eight.

HANNAH:
Two hours? I'll bring a book.

ZACK:
But then who is going to keep me entertained? I have needs, Hannah.

HANNAH:
I'll read you the good parts.

I leaned against the tail of my truck as Hannah proceeded to slather every inch of her exposed skin with sunblock. She was wearing a short-sleeve t-shirt, and even with the neckline that came right up to the base of her throat, it was more skin than I was used to seeing from her and my dick was having thoughts about that. Between the sharp sunlight and whatever was in that sunblock, her skin sparkled like one of those dumbass vampires.

"I feel obligated to warn you, darlin'," I said. "It might cause a ruckus, me being here."

Hannah's pale eyebrows rose a fraction.

I grinned. "I'm kind of a big deal on the rodeo circuit. And since buckle bunnies have been deprived of my company for the past ten months, they might be a hair feral."

She scrunched up her nose. "Buckle bunnies?"

"Rodeo champions take home a belt buckle, and bunnies take home the prize underneath." I canted my hips for emphasis and of course her eyes went there. I smirked. "It's a time-honored tradition."

She glanced around the half-full lot. No one was paying us any mind as they ambled about, greeting friends and heading into the fairgrounds. She looked back at me dubiously.

"Just wait," I assured her. "Buckle bunnies don't tend to be early risers. They'll show up eventually, and when they do, I'm counting on you for protection."

She stared at me for a beat, then heaved a sigh as she slipped her bare, sunblocked arms into some shapeless brown sweater thing, which made no fucking sense in this world and also made my dick sad. And *that* made no sense, either, because there was no shortage of bare arms and bare ankles right here in this very parking lot, some of them even attached to attractive women, but no. My dick didn't care about any of *those*. Apparently they had to be Hannah's bare arms and bare ankles to be of any interest.

"All right," Hannah said at last. "I'm no use in a physical altercation, but I think I could hurt someone's feelings if I put my mind to it."

I burst out laughing. "Hannah Bell, I *know* you could."

When her cheeks pinked up a bit, I shook my head and took her by the hand. This woman. She had no inkling that I'd only been teasing—teasing being my preferred method of flirting. I had expected her to giggle and tease me back, but no. This confounding woman continued to do the last thing I expected of anyone.

She took me seriously.

It wasn't what I had wanted. But damn if it didn't feel like exactly what I needed.

It was mid-morning, and the rodeo was still slowly coming to life. We had driven two hours south, which was about ten degrees warmer than Aspen Springs. Seventy-two and sunny, perfect rodeo weather. It was going to be a good day.

"What do we do first?" Hannah asked.

"Barrel racing starts in an hour," I said. "Until then, we wander around and enjoy ourselves."

"Well," she said. "All right."

She dropped my hand. That was fine. I barely even noticed. When was the last time I had held hands with a girl, anyway? Eleventh grade, maybe? It had to be, because that was also the last time I'd had a real girlfriend, the kind where handholding was something we did without thinking much about it. Shit, that was over a decade ago. A decade ago, and now Hannah for thirty seconds—

"What's mutton busting?" Hannah asked. She stood by the sheep pen, frowning at the sign that advertised mutton busting at ten a.m. "It's not...people don't punch sheep, do they?"

I chuckled. "No, nothing like that. It's a kiddie event. Five-year-olds ride the sheep for as long as they can hold on."

She looked downright horrified. "That doesn't sound better."

"They wear helmets, sugar. No one's putting a bunch of babies on an animal without proper protection."

"Did you ever do it?"

"Hell, yeah, I did." I smiled, remembering. "It was the closest I could get to the real thing. Mom wasn't thrilled about it, so one day I hopped right onto a neighbor's ewe to show her I could do it. The ewe wasn't too pleased about that and took off. Mom hollered, Mrs. Anderson hollered, but there wasn't anything they could do to help me. It was about twenty minutes before the ewe decided I wasn't worth the trouble and stopped to eat some grass. By the time I slid off, my arms were numb. Mom figured there was no point in saying no after that, and at least the rodeo would have some safety precautions, and I'd only be expected to hang on for a minute."

Hannah looked at me like she was imagining it, her lips curved into a wry smile. "Five years old, and already a wild, wild cowboy."

"Damn right," I agreed.

AFTER BARREL RACING, we grabbed lunch. There were a few women who glanced my way with recognition in their eyes, and I was quick to pull Hannah in front of me like a shield. Not out of necessity, but because I liked it. Only one of those women seemed to take it as a challenge. She tossed her hair with a smile that suggested we had seen each other naked and reached for my bicep, but Hannah shifted against me, blocking her hand.

"No, thank you," she said firmly.

The woman paused and looked at me with confusion in her eyes. She looked familiar, and I tried to recall when I had last passed through this town, but for the life of me, I couldn't remember her name. I shrugged.

Her gaze dipped to Hannah's, and whatever she saw there had her backing right on out of my personal space. I grinned. I couldn't see Hannah's face, but I had the feeling I knew the expression.

"You might as well hold my hand." I twined our fingers together as I pulled her along to the bronc event. "Safer that way."

"You realize you could just tell them no?"

"Of course I realize that. I also realize that I like it better when *you* tell them no."

She scrunched her nose at me. "You just want me to do your dirty work."

But she didn't let go of my hand.

"You're going to love this," I told Hannah as we took front-row seats in the arena.

She settled onto the hard plastic seat with a swish of her skirt. "You might be biased. This is your event, so of course you think it's the best one."

"It *is* the best one," I insisted. "Rodeo events are micro-tests of real-life cowboy skills. So you've got the roping tests and the riding tests. Roping events test a cowboy's relationship with a well-trained horse. It's about how well they do a job together. Bronc riding is different. It's a test of how well you can ride when a horse wants nothing to do with you. It's not about controlling the animal. It's about instinct. It's about the ride." I stared out at the empty arena. I could almost feel the sweat on my neck, taste the adrenaline in my mouth. "But that's not why I think you'll love it."

She pushed up her glasses. "Then why?"

"Eight seconds." The memory of her twitching while I raced to get dressed made me grin. "It's a timed event. I have a feeling these eight seconds are going to make you lose your mind, sugar."

The way she looked at me, I knew she was remembering, too. It was an odd thing to share a memory with someone, to know what was on her mind, and know that she knew the same thing was on mine. It felt like the space between us dissolved, even though neither of us moved.

"We'll see," she said, but she didn't say it like she doubted it. She said it like she hoped for it.

At the ding, the first pair sprung out of the chute. The horse, Badlands Betty, didn't waste a millisecond before throwing out her hind legs. Betty was a fantastic ride. She bucked hard and true and rarely changed direction. Before every buck, she went airborne, bounding forward with all four hooves off the ground, before landing on her front legs and shooting her back legs higher than her rider's head.

At second four, Hannah moved to the edge of her seat.

At second six, she brought her hands to her cheeks.

At seven-point-six, she covered her mouth and let out a muffled shriek.

When the buzzer sounded at eight seconds, she didn't

move, didn't holler or clap like the rest of us. She stayed just as she was, her hands on her face, for another ten seconds or so, then slowly let her breath out in a big whoosh and lowered her hands to her lap.

"My goodness," she whispered. "My goodness."

I grinned. Yep, my fussy librarian had lost her damn mind, all right.

My grin faded slowly as it hit me hard how much I loved this. The rodeo. The cheers, the smells, the excitement and energy of it all. But most of all, I loved the ride.

And that was the thing I couldn't have anymore.

"Do you miss it?" she asked.

"Yeah," I said. "I miss it."

She chewed her lip, thinking. "Are you...done for good? Your leg won't ever heal well enough for you to bronc ride again?"

"It's not only my leg," I said. "I don't know if my leg will ever heal enough for me to be a top bronc rider again, but that's not what forced me out. It's the conglomerate of issues, I guess. I fractured my spine, too. That actually healed the fastest, but there's a big risk of breaking my back even worse. And then there's my spleen. I don't have one anymore. I took a hoof to the chest and it ruptured my spleen. Doctors had to take it out. That means I'm more likely to get an infection, and if I get an infection, I'm more likely to die." I held up my wrist. "That's what this bracelet is for. So if I end up injured, the doctors know what to look out for."

She looked out at the arena, where the next rider was

bucked off the horse in under five seconds. "And you're fairly likely to get injured bronc riding, I suppose."

I cracked a smile. "It's pretty common, in my experience. I've had my fair share of surgeries even before the big one. Without a spleen, every surgery has a high risk of infection." I looked down at my leg. "I nearly lost my leg from infection this time around. I'm not interested in losing limbs or dying of sepsis in a hospital bed."

Her head tilted. "Wasn't that always the risk with bronc riding?"

"Maybe. I never thought of it that way though. To me, it was all or nothing."

"What do you mean?"

"I..." I swallowed. "I didn't plan on getting maimed. Bronc riding...it's the sort of thing that takes everything you have to give. Anyone who ended their career wounded, I figured they just weren't trying hard enough. It should have killed them. It should have killed me. I never considered I'd make it out alive." Which meant I'd never considered what I'd do with the rest of my life. What the hell was supposed to get me out of bed every day? I'd never had a Plan B.

"You never wanted to? Make it out alive, I mean?"

I looked at her, mildly shocked that she'd even ask me that. No one else would have. But then, no one else would have wanted to hear my answer, either. I had the notion she *wanted* to hear it, without any preconceived idea of who I should be or how I should feel. She wanted to know what was inside me, and she would patiently sit there forever, as long as it took, for me to tell her.

It felt like a hug, the way she looked at me. Like something I wanted to burrow into.

I blew out a breath. "No," I said. "No, I never wanted to."

And she nodded, like that made sense.

I KNEW a couple of the cowboys in the bronc riding competition, so we headed to the back to say hello. I knew some of the horses, too, and I gave them each a pat as I introduced them to Hannah.

"They don't bite?" she asked nervously as I stroked the white blaze on Cactus's dark face.

"Not if you don't give them a reason to. Despite how it looks in the arena, these horses aren't wild. They were trained for this. Starting when they're two or three years old, they learn to wear the surcingle and a dummy weight. Bucking feels natural to them and they get rewarded for that because after they buck a few times, the dummy falls off. These horses are athletes. They know their job."

Hannah gave his cheek a tentative pat and he snuffled her. She laughed. "And their job is to buck off the rider?"

"Their job is to buck off the rider," I agreed. "It's the rider's job to stay on. The score is a result of how long and how well they do that together. Both the horse and rider earn scores on a scale of zero to fifty, for a combined score up to one hundred. For the cowboy, they're judged on control and technique. The horse, though…" I grinned. "The horse earns points for bad behavior. The meaner the bronc, the higher the score."

"Is Cactus mean?" she asked, rubbing his cheek. "He doesn't seem mean."

"He's not so mean anymore. We had a few rides together a couple years back, when he was younger, stronger, and meaner." I gave him an affectionate tickle under his jaw. "We had some good times together, didn't we, boy?"

"You remember a horse from an eight-second ride a couple years ago?"

"Every horse. Every ride."

She looked at me for a long moment, her expression soft. "Well, how about that. The wild, wild cowboy is sentimental."

I laughed and took her elbow to move her along to the next horse. "Cowboying is a hard, dirty life. You need sentiment to spruce it up a bit. Now, this here is Barracuda. I rode him, too. Most of the horses you see here today have been around awhile. They don't do the big, hard competitions anymore. Eventually they'll retire, hopefully to a pasture or training facility."

I moseyed over to a brown-and-white Paint mare and rubbed her nose. "Hey, pretty girl."

Hannah took notice of the name on the stall and served me a look. "Navajo Princess? Really?"

"The whole cowboy-versus-Native lore still runs deep here. They probably meant it as a compliment." I paused, considering. The Hales had arrived in Aspen Springs, dirty and penniless, a decade after it had been taken from the Arapaho tribe who had lived there for ten thousand years. We might not have done it ourselves, but we sure had benefitted from it. There wasn't a speck of land in this country that didn't have a similar history. That was the kind of debt that could never be fully repaid, but the very least we could do was stop romanticizing it. "I can see how it wouldn't be taken as such, though."

We moved on to a bay I didn't know, but gave him pets too, just to be fair about it. Horses had a tendency to notice injustice and not take kindly to it. There was something about the look in his eye that struck me, so I checked his name and looked up his stats on my phone.

"He's a young one. If he proves himself, he'll work his way up to the bigger rodeos. Same sire as Hurricane Red."

"Hurricane Red?" Hannah looked at me quizzically.

"My last ride." I rubbed his brother's nose. "He'd clear a solid three feet of air before every buck. We won that round, you know."

Hannah pushed her glasses up, blinking at me. "How? How could you win after—" She stopped abruptly.

"After he stomped me?" I supplied with a smirk. "I stayed on for all eight seconds. Whatever happens after the buzzer sounds doesn't count."

"Is Hurricane Red here?" she asked, looking around like he might materialize out of thin air.

I hooted. "You wouldn't find Hurricane Red in a small rodeo like this, honey. They save him for the big rides. He'll go down in history as one of the greatest broncs of all times, you mark my words."

"Won't see him anywhere no more," a familiar voice cut in, and I turned to see Will Stevenson, another bronc rider. "How you been, Zack?"

"Hey, Will." We did that half-handshake, half-hug thing and ended up clapping each other on the back. "They tell me I'm doing great, and they wouldn't lie about that, would they? This is Hannah Bell. She's putting on a charity rodeo for the Aspen Springs library. Thought I would take her to one so she could see what it was all about."

Will smiled at her, though the look he sent me was quizzical. "Nice to meet you, Hannah. I'm Will. Zack and I have been through a lot of rodeos together."

"What did you mean about not seeing Hurricane Red anymore?" I asked. "Did they retire him?" That would surprise me. He was at the top of his game and running me over hadn't hurt him any.

Will shook his head. "Nah. He's too young for that. But he's out of the rodeo circuit now. That accident of yours wrecked his mind up good. He won't get in the chute anymore. Can't drag him, can't force him, can't bribe him. Word is, he's going to auction."

Auction.

The word hit me like a sucker punch.

I knew what auction meant for a horse like Hurricane

Red. He'd been trained to buck any rider off his back and convincing him to try something new would be damn near impossible. He was gelded, so keeping him for stud wasn't an option, either.

But he was a big warmblood, a cross between a Clydesdale and a quarter horse. There was a lot of meat on his bones.

Hurricane Red was going to slaughter.

WHEN HANNAH OFFERED to drive us back, I didn't protest. It had been a long day, and the thought of folding my aching body into the driver's seat did not appeal. That was part of the healing process no one had warned me about. Lifting your foot back and forth between the gas and brake pedals, even just keeping constant pressure on the gas, used a shit ton of muscles from your abdomen all the way down to your toes. Driving fucking hurt.

With Hannah in the driver's seat—looking fucking adorable and completely out of place, I might add—I pushed my seat back as far as it would go and took the opportunity to stretch my body and massage sore muscles. Hopefully it would be enough to keep me mobile tomorrow.

I tucked Hurricane Red to the back of my mind, even though I knew he was going to poke back out again at three a.m. We spent the two-hour drive talking about the rodeo for the library, what events we would include—barrel racing and mutton busting seemed to be her top priorities, but reining and roping events would be the headliners—and what permits and insurance we would need. Brax was handling that part of the rodeo, but I told Hannah I'd check in with him to make sure he had everything he needed to keep us out of trouble.

And then suddenly we were pulling into her driveway after what felt like maybe thirty minutes. I hustled out of the truck so I could open the driver's door for her and help her down.

"You don't have to walk me to my door," she said.

"It feels good to move," I countered, and it was true, but I would have seen her to the door even if I'd had to crawl on my hands and knees behind her. Not because I doubted her ability to make it the twenty feet from my truck to her porch, but because I had manners. Some traditions were worth keeping, even when they didn't make a whole lot of rational sense. She could drive my truck anytime she wanted, but she sure as fuck wasn't walking to her door alone.

She unlocked the door and stepped just past the threshold. A white ball of fluff made a beeline for her ankles. With a laugh, Hannah scooped Evie into her arms and plopped a kiss between her ears, then turned back to me. "Do you want to come in for coffee?"

I leaned against the doorframe, half in and half out, not entirely committed to either course of action. "It's coming up on eight o'clock, darlin'. If I have coffee now,

I'll be wide awake until it's time to feed the horses at dawn."

Her glasses slid down a fraction. With her arms full of cat, she couldn't do much about it besides scrunch her nose. I had the oddest inclination to take care of it for her, to slide my finger up the slope of her nose and gently place her glasses back where they belonged, but I crossed my arms instead. Fuck, those blue eyes would be the death of me.

"I assumed a man of your experience would understand that by coffee, I meant sex," she said.

I stared at her. It shouldn't have knocked the wind out of me like it did. I had been propositioned hundreds of times, but never quite like this. Never so bluntly and never without so much as a kiss to warm things up. Never by a prim little librarian so deeply buried in yards of extra clothing that I had no idea what I would find under there.

I was fucking *charmed*.

Charmed, and horny.

I hadn't had sex since the accident. Hadn't even made use of my own hand. Before Hurricane Red stomped all over my body, nine months without sex was as unthinkable as nine years. Hell, I had never gone even nine *days*. But to be honest, I hadn't missed it. I'd missed *wanting* it. But the actual act itself? No interest at all.

Now, I was interested.

"Hell, yes, I want to come in for coffee, Hannah Bell."

HANNAH

There were very few things I loved more in this world than a well-thought-out plan. When I'd left the compound, I'd had a plan. The first time I'd stepped into a library and realized it had all the answers to any question I could ever ask, I'd determined the plan for my career. My first experience with sex had been *someone's* plan, but it hadn't been mine, and I had rectified that every time since.

Until now.

Because now, with Zack Hale filling my doorway and looking entirely too large for it, like a giant in a ginger-bread house, his lean, muscular body backlit by the porch-light, and that ridiculous belt buckle gleaming richly in the shadows, it could not be said that there was a single rational thought in my brain, much less anything resembling a plan.

Thirty seconds ago, I had intended to bid him good

night and send him on his way. Instead, I'd invited him in for sex.

Zack stepped fully inside, then gently kicked the door shut behind him with his heel. He came toward me until I had to tilt my head back to look at him. That delightful mouth of his tipped up at one corner as we studied each other.

"You changing your mind, darlin'? Because you can, you know."

I gave that due consideration, then shook my head. "No, I'm not changing my mind." Evie, cuddled against my chest, decided my affections weren't enough, and rubbed her forehead against Zack's abdomen. Honestly, who could blame her.

He glanced down at Evie, gave her head a slow, circular stroke with his thumb, then looked back to me. "You sure? Because you're holding that cat like a shield."

"Oh." I supposed I was. I stepped back a little, just enough to encourage Evie to jump down. "I'm sure."

I expected him to *do* something then, kiss me or touch me or something, but he kept right on watching me with an intensity that made me wish I still had Evie between us. But I wasn't a coward, so I took his hand and tugged. "Bedroom is this way."

He didn't budge. I might as well have tried to move an oak tree. I raised an eyebrow. "Zack?"

His gaze was locked on our hands. Slowly, slowly he pulled me to him.

"Zack?" I tried again.

He pushed my cardigan sleeve up to my elbow and sucked his bottom lip between his teeth with a sharp intake of breath. I looked down at our hands, perplexed. What the heck was he looking at? It was just a wrist. There were a million others exactly like it.

"It's been a while for me. I haven't done this since the accident." His thumb traced the blue veins in my forearm, then rubbed feather-light over the tendons of my wrist before nestling in the notch of my palm.

"It's all right." The words came out all wispy. I couldn't seem to catch my breath, and all he had done so far was play with my wrist. My *wrist*. "I'll be gentle."

He made a sound like I had amused him, but then he brought my palm to his mouth and scraped his teeth over the sensitized skin there, and when his eyes met mine over our joined hands, all I saw was fire.

"I wasn't asking you to be gentle, Hannah," he said. "I was warning you that I wouldn't be."

"Oh," I said. "*Oh—*"

But then his mouth was on mine and who needed words, anyway.

I had long ago accepted that romance books took a lot of liberties with things like kissing. The world didn't *really* catch fire or melt away. Kissing was…fine. I liked it well enough, but if it went on too long, my mind drifted to things like work or my grocery list.

Right now, I couldn't have found my way to the library with a map. But I had never been kissed like this before, like he needed my mouth more than his next breath. He kissed me like it wasn't a precursor to anything, like it was the meal itself.

This wasn't kissing the way I knew it. This was a devouring.

He backed me up, using his hips and legs to guide me while his hands unbuttoned my cardigan and slid it off my shoulders. The wall met my shoulder blades. I couldn't get my bearings. We might have been in the living room or the hallway, I didn't know. Everything was hot and liquid: his tongue sliding against mine, the swishy feeling in my belly, the sudden wetness between my thighs.

It was going to happen. This time, it was really going to happen.

But somehow just the thought of it, of orgasming with a man when I had never done that before, made the feeling recede like the tide pulling back the ocean. Frustrated, I balled my hands into fists and thumped them against his chest.

Instantly his mouth left mine.

He was breathing hard as he looked down at me, his mouth damp and swollen. "Do you want me to stop?"

That was the last thing I wanted. "No, I want—" I broke off on a huff. Explaining wouldn't do any good and would put too much pressure on both of us. I didn't need an orgasm, anyway. Not from him. I could take care of that myself. "I want to look at you. I want to touch you."

"Yeah?" He raised an eyebrow and gave me that cocky little smirk of his. "Go on, then."

I dragged my fingers down the front of his torso, feeling

the curve and indent of each muscle beneath the thin fabric of his T-shirt as I went. When I got to the hem, I fiddled with it a moment, my knuckles ghosting against his skin above the waistband of his jeans. His breathing shallowed, his muscles fluttered, and it made me want to touch him even more.

"Hannah," he gritted out.

"Hush," I said. "Be a good boy and let me look at you." With that, I pushed his shirt up and over his head.

Good lord.

I blinked, adjusted my glasses, and blinked again. I had seen him naked before, but the bunny slippers had distracted me, and he had been too far away for me to see the scars that crisscrossed his torso. Now he was right in front of me and I could see every violent, magnificent line. Most of his scars were silver from age, but a couple were still pink. The largest one curved under his left pec in a red swoop.

"My goodness, you're beautiful." I glanced up at him to find him staring down at me with an odd expression on his face. "Is something wrong?"

"Something is all kinds of wrong, Hannah," he said on a half-laugh, half-groan. "Do you know what you've done to me? I see a lifetime of inappropriate wood in my future. Someone will be talking to a dog or a small child and say *good boy*, and that's it. I'll be hard. Fuck."

I laughed. I couldn't help it. He looked so perplexed and...god, I wanted my hands on him. "Will it hurt if I touch you? The scars?"

He made a strangled sound. "It can't hurt any worse than you *not* touching me."

I took him at his word and let my hands roam wherever I liked. Scars, muscles, the short, sparse hair that covered his chest, then picked up again below his belly button. I bit my lip as I trailed my index finger down the happy trail that disappeared into his jeans.

"Hannah," he said roughly. "That lip is *mine*."

He captured both my wrists in one large hand and pinned my arms to the wall above my head. His other hand dove into my hair, scattering the bobby pins that held my bun intact. His mouth came down on mine with a savage intensity that made me gasp. And then he bit my lip, just as I had done a second ago.

It felt different, though, the way he did it. It felt like something I needed.

And it was back, that hot, slick feeling.

It could happen this time. It could actually happen.

I pushed the thought down. I didn't want to hope for it. That would only end in frustration, and right now I just wanted to feel good.

And I *did* feel good. I felt so amazingly good.

With my arms immobilized, all I could do was push my hips to his. So I did that, grinding my body against the hard bulge below his belt. Again and again, desperate and frenzied.

He tore his mouth from mine, panting. "This is going to go fast now. You ready?"

"Ye—" was all I managed to get out before he had my

T-shirt off over my head and my skirt pooled at my ankles. I was left standing there in my white cotton underwear and bra, but only for a moment while he shucked his jeans and that ludicrous belt, and then he wrapped those strong arms around my waist and took us to the sofa.

It amazed me how easily he maneuvered both of our bodies right where he wanted us. He reclined lengthwise on the couch with me on his lap, my thighs straddling his hips. I could feel his cock, hot and hard, through the thin, damp cotton of my underwear. Experimentally, I rolled my hips in a slow circle. I liked it so much that I did it again.

"Christ!" he bit out, jackknifing upwards, his fingers digging into my hips.

I whimpered and he kissed me again, hard, then and unclasped my bra behind my back. Despite his promise that this was going to go fast, he leaned back and took a long look at me. My heart was beating a thousand times a minute, my body starting to shake, but I sat there on his lap and let him look. No one had ever looked at me like that, like I was the answer to everything.

And then he smiled, took my glasses, and gently set them aside. "I don't want them to get broken."

"All right," I said, only slightly miffed because dang it, I wanted to see him.

He squeezed my hips, moving his hands leisurely up my body to cup my breasts, and I thought I might die from anticipation. My nipples ached, my clit ached, every part of me desperate for a touch of his rough, callused fingers.

His thumbs skimmed the undersides of my breasts and

I gasped, my breath coming in short, shallow bursts. He was so close to where I wanted but he kept deliberately taunting me, circling my nipples with slow, lazy touches. I was going to die...or murder him.

And then suddenly his mouth was there, his tongue, his teeth, the hot, sweet suction of his mouth. I cried out and dug my fingers into his scalp, holding him there like I thought he might change his mind. My internal muscles clenched in response. *It might actually happen.*

He growled, wrapping an arm around my waist, his mouth still on my breast, and flipped us over so I was underneath him, keeping one hand under the base of my skull to protect me from banging my head on the armrest, then hooked a finger under the waistband of my underwear and tugged them down my legs to my ankles. I kicked them off my feet, sending them god knew where.

"Zack," I whispered, because he was looking at me again, and I needed him to stop looking and start touching. I grabbed his hand and brought it where I wanted. I had never been shy about directing. My problem had always been that my directions never got me where I wanted to go. *That's okay*, I reminded myself. *An orgasm doesn't have to be the goal.*

His breath hissed as he dragged one finger through my folds. "Fuck, you're wet."

I rocked up against his hand. It felt good. It felt so damn good that I almost dared to hope again. He pressed the heel of his palm against my clit and worked his finger in and out of my body, first one and then two.

He shifted slightly to fish his wallet from the pocket of his jeans on the floor and pulled out a condom. I watched through half-shut eyes as he sat on his heels to roll it over his length and swallowed hard. He was big enough to make me a little nervous.

Like he was reading my mind, he said, "I promise I'll fit. I haven't ripped anyone in half yet."

I nodded, sucking my bottom lip between my teeth.

He pushed my thighs wider and positioned himself at my entrance. He pressed forward slowly, his eyes focused on my face. My vision blurred at the edges and I gripped his biceps. He was thick and perfect and it felt so good it bordered on pain. He paused for a moment, half inside me, then withdrew, and pushed forward again. He made it further this time before pulling back and sliding in a third time. And this time he didn't stop, not even when my breath hollowed out, not until he filled me completely.

"I need you to breath, sweetheart," he said, his voice tense, his body rigid.

I breathed out and tried to relax around the feeling of being stuffed full of him.

He moved. Faster this time, and with much less gentleness. And then he leaned back, hooked one elbow under my knee, and widened the angle as he stroked into me again and again, ruthless and desperate.

The room closed in around us until all I could see was him, me, us. My hands on his shoulders. The cords in his neck standing out with the effort to keep himself in check. His furrowed brow, the sweep of dark eyelashes against his cheek as he looked down at where he disappeared inside me.

Pleasure built, pushing me toward the precipice. *Oh, god, it might actually happen.*

And then suddenly his blue eyes were on mine. Looking right into my face, right into my soul. *Danger.* I faltered, there on the ledge. *No. I can't—*

But I pretended I could. Squeezing my internal muscles as hard as I could, I pretended I wasn't broken.

With a groan of *oh fuck*, Zack buried his face in my neck and thrust into me one last time, freezing as he pulsed inside me, his big body shuddering as he came inside me.

For a moment, we lay there, breathing hard. Then his arms shifted around me.

"Hold on tight, honey," he whispered.

He pushed to his feet with me still clinging to him. I wrapped my legs around his waist as he walked us to the bedroom, every step sending a ripple of pleasure to my sensitized clit.

"Wait here," he said, lowering me gently to the bed. Then he disappeared into the hall bathroom—I assumed to take care of the condom and clean himself up a bit.

My body was still strung tight with need. He would be back in a moment, but that was fine. I didn't need more than a couple seconds. I closed my eyes, slipped my fingers against my aching clit, and sent myself flying.

Two seconds later, the bathroom door opened. I heard the soft pad of his footfalls as he went in the opposite direction from the bedroom. A moment later Zack returned with my glasses.

"You want something to drink?" he asked. He set my glasses down on the nightstand. "Water?"

"I can get it," I said. "You don't know where anything is."

"Don't get up. I'll figure it out—" He turned to leave but then stopped and did a double take, his narrowed gaze sweeping over me.

I swallowed. He couldn't possibly know. He couldn't—

"Hannah," he said. "What did you do?"

Hannah started guiltily. She scrambled into a seated position against the headboard and dragged a pillow against her torso, like that was something that could keep me from her.

"What do you mean?" she squeaked.

I didn't answer, just strolled toward her, her eyes widening with every step that brought me closer. When I was right next to her, I picked up her right hand and brought it to my mouth. Gave her fingers a long, hard suck. The sweet taste of her pussy on my tongue woke my dick right up again.

I raised my eyebrows at her, my gaze locked on hers as I slid her fingers from my mouth. "You should have told me you wanted another orgasm, darlin'. I would have been happy to oblige."

Her eyes darted sideways, her fingers twisting in the pillowcase, and my world went sideways with it.

Because she didn't look like a woman who had been completely satisfied by a man.

"I need you to give me the truth, Hannah," I said slowly. "Was it *another* orgasm?"

She bit her lip. *Fuck.*

"Aw, hell." I raked my fingers through my hair. "Why didn't you tell me? I would have made it right for you. What did you need? More pressure? My tongue?"

"It wasn't your fault," she blurted.

I tilted my head. "Who said anything about fault? This is a collaboration. We get you there together."

She had already started shaking her head before I was done talking. "It doesn't work that way. Not for me. I can't—"

"I know you're not about to tell me you can't orgasm because I just tasted yours on your fingers," I interjected. "I was gone for what, twenty seconds?"

The flush that had given her away deepened. "I only needed ten."

"I would have given you ten seconds," I said. I would have given her as much time as she needed, and it fucked me up a little that she didn't realize that.

"No, *I* needed ten seconds," she clarified. "You would have needed..." Her voice trailed off like she couldn't think of a number high enough.

Now that was just mean. I played it back in my mind, that moment her hips had tilted and I swore I felt her pussy clench around me. The sounds she had made. She hadn't even given me a real chance to give her whatever it was she'd needed. She'd faked it.

I was fucking *offended*.

"Show me," I demanded.

She laughed like she thought I was joking, which I sure as fuck was not. "How can I show you? I already did it. It's done."

"Let me be clear on this. It's not done until we're both done. Are you really done, Hannah?" I rubbed my thumb over the back of her hand, then slipped my fingers in a V on either side of her middle finger. "I don't think you are."

She shifted restlessly, rubbing her thighs together. She wasn't done. And this time, I wasn't going to let her do it without me.

I stretched out next to her, tugged the pillow from her arms, and propped it behind my head so I could look down at her. "Show me," I urged. I kissed her shoulder, then nuzzled the crook of her neck. "I'll be such a good boy, Hannah. I won't touch. I'll just watch and learn."

Her chest rose and fell on rapid breaths. I felt her throat move beneath my lips as she swallowed.

"Can I keep my eyes closed?" she whispered.

"Do whatever you need to do to get yourself there."

She swallowed again. "It might not work. I've never—"

I covered her hand with mine, both our palms facing down, my fingers interlocked with hers, and slid it down her soft belly to the honey-gold hair between her legs. "You're still so wet, sweetheart," I murmured. She shivered as our fingers brushed her clit. "One more time. That's all."

Slowly, slowly, I withdrew my hand, leaving hers there between her legs. And fuck, I wanted it to be mine. My fingers sliding through all that wet heat. My hand bringing her pleasure. But I wanted *this*, too. I wanted to watch. Maybe even more than I wanted to touch her.

On a deep breath, her hand started to move. She pushed one finger inside her entrance, then brought it out and swirled the wetness around her clit. I leaned closer to get a better look at those slim, pale fingers playing with her pretty pussy.

"Fuck," I groaned. "You're perfect. God, you should see yourself, Hannah. So fucking wet and pink. I want to put my mouth there. Tasting your fingers wasn't enough. It just made me hungry for more. You're so sweet and soft."

She whimpered and her fingers went faster, harder.

"Yes," I hissed between my teeth. My dick was hard again even though I had come maybe ten minutes ago. I took it in hand and squeezed the base. "That's it, baby. You're doing so good. I want to see you come like this, giving yourself all the pleasure you deserve."

She dug her heels into the mattress and her hips bucked, grinding her pussy against her hand. She cried out and froze like that, hips arched forward, for one beat and then another, before lowering limply.

Her eyes opened and she turned her head to look at me, a dazed expression on her face.

"Fuck, Hannah." I didn't bother trying to keep the awe out of my voice. "That was gorgeous."

She watched me stroke my cock, her gaze still slightly

unfocused. Having her eyes on me like that, somehow looking sated and hungry at the same time, made my dick so hard it almost hurt. My grip tightened, my stroke roughened.

"You don't look done, either," she noted.

Usually I needed a good thirty minutes to recover from coming before I was ready to go again. Watching Hannah get herself off had cut that time in half. "I'm close. Look at my cock, Hannah. Look what you did to me."

She felt behind her for her glasses, her eyes never leaving my cock, then fumbled them onto her face, and fuck. *Fuck.* That damn near finished me right there. A bead of pre-cum leaked out and I spread it around the crown with my thumb.

It wasn't enough. I needed more.

Her tongue swiped over her bottom lip and I groaned. God, that fucking mouth. More pre-cum leaked imagining it on me.

"What do you need?" she asked, her tone crisp and almost business-like, despite the rosy flush on her cheeks and chest.

I liked it. I had the feeling I could ask her for anything right then, and she would simply do it. There was nothing squeamish about her.

"I need you to make it wet." I groaned as she licked her lips again. "Spit on it, Hannah."

She pushed her glasses up her nose for no other reason than to wreck my self-control, I was sure, then leaned forward. I stopped pumping and wrapped my hand around the base like an offering.

But she didn't spit. Instead, she licked the shaft from my hand to the crown, then swirled her tongue around the head and pulled me inside. She swallowed me down with enough suction to hollow her cheeks. My eyes crossed. My hips bucked.

Then she did it again, sucking me down, then slowly slid me from her warm, wet mouth. Our eyes caught as she spit on the head.

"Fuck, honey." I stroked her saliva over my dick with brutal pulls. "I'm gonna come—"

She didn't even blink. "Do it."

My balls pulled tight and I shattered, painting her chest with ropes of cum.

When I was wrung dry, I laid back, panting, and looked at her. She looked down at her chest, at my cum shimmering like a pearl necklace against her flushed skin, and then back at me, her lips curved into an impish smile.

"*Now* are we done?" she asked.

I laughed. "Now we're done."

A fucking lie if there ever was one.

I wasn't done with Hannah. Not by a long shot.

I slept like the dead. Between the long drive, the rodeo, and the double orgasms, my body and brain finally shut down. For a couple hours, anyway. An hour or so before dawn, I awoke aching and stiff, Hannah curled into my side, still fast asleep.

For a moment I didn't move. Just lay there and matched my breaths to Hannah's.

I wasn't one of those dipshits who had rules about spending the night with a woman after sex. If you could put your dick in a woman, you could damn well lay your head down on the pillow next to hers. It was a few hours of shuteye, not a binding marriage contract. Most times I had been too drunk or tired to make it back to my hotel room, anyway. So, this wasn't the first time I had woken up next to a woman.

But it was the first time I didn't feel a pressing need to get gone.

More than that, even, it was the first time I woke up wanting to stay.

So I lay there, breathed, and considered.

The way my muscles ached and my skin itched, I couldn't lay there much longer without losing my goddamn mind or waking Hannah up with my twitching. But I didn't want her to wake up and find me gone. Last night had been...different. Like nothing I had ever experienced before. The idea of walking away without a word felt all kinds of wrong.

I slid from the bed as quietly as I could, careful not to shake it and wake her up. I headed for the living room, where I grabbed my boxers from the floor and tugged them on. I didn't bother with my jeans or T-shirt. Hannah kept her house toasty warm and I tended to run hot anyway.

I flipped on the table lamp and looked around. Last night I had been much more interested in seeing Hannah out of her clothes than taking stock of her decorating choices. Honestly, it was about what I expected. It could have been my grandma living here instead of a twenty-nine-year-old. There were embroidered throw pillows on every cushion and some on the floor. Apparently the wall-to-ceiling built-in bookcase on one wall wasn't enough, because there were also books stacked on the end tables and on every random surface.

With nothing better to do, I wandered over to the bookshelves to investigate. There didn't seem to be any kind of rhyme or reason to the order of it, which was an interesting choice for a librarian. I caught sight of the one I had started reading at the library the other day, about a mail-order bride who accidentally shot her husband in the Old West. Fucking hilarious. I had never been much of a reader, but I had ended up taking that one home with me, figuring it would give me something to do when insomnia hit.

I looked for something else. There were a few biographies tucked here and there and what looked like mysteries or thrillers, but most of the books were romance.

Romancing the Duke.

A Duke in Shining Armor.

The Duke's Wicked Wife.

Gabriela and His Grace—wait, was that about a priest?

Kinky. I flipped it over and read the back. Nope, still a duke.

Damn. Hannah definitely had a thing for dukes. Everything I knew about dukes was from *Bridgerton* on television, but I figured it was safe to say they were all rich, stern, and stuffy. The exact opposite of a rough and dirty bronc rider. I didn't entirely know how to feel about that.

But I grabbed one of those damn duke books, anyway. Just to see what it was all about.

Something soft tickled my ankle. I looked down to find Evie winding her fluffy body between my legs. She yowled pitifully at me, and I scooped her up.

"Hope you're not wanting breakfast, darlin', because I don't know how to feed you. But you can come read a book with me."

We settled lengthwise on the couch so I could stretch my legs. I grabbed one of those embroidered pillows for my head and then did a double take. Roses, lilies, and violets twisted and bloomed, forming the words *oh, for fuck's sake*. I couldn't recall ever hearing Hannah swear before, but somehow I didn't have any trouble imagining her saying those exact words with dry exasperation, pushing her glasses up her nose.

I burst out laughing.

"Your mom is something, isn't she?" I murmured to Evie. So prim and proper on the outside. But on the inside? She was fucking *funny*. A little filthy, in the best possible way. And she was kind. I liked her. I liked her a lot.

Evie didn't answer, being too busy making biscuits on my abdomen. Trying to, anyway. My six-pack didn't offer a whole lot of give. Finally, with a look of deep disapproval that rivaled her owner's, she settled into the crook of my elbow instead. Within seconds, her eyes were closed and she was purring like a motorboat.

"You don't care that I'm not a duke, do you, darlin'?" I rubbed her little head, and her brown ears drooped to give me more space. "Of course you don't. Because you know cowboys do it better."

Everything was fine until I walked into the living room.

I had woken up to sharp sunlight cracking through the curtain. Zack was gone but I hadn't really expected him to stay, so after the smallest, silliest sinking of my stomach, I very firmly told myself that was fine. I would have to see him soon anyway to talk about the rodeo. And *that* was not going to be awkward at all, even though he had shot cum all over my chest. It would be perfectly fine. Really and truly.

Today was Sunday, my day off, and that was better than fine, and I had the whole day planned precisely to my liking, so it absolutely did not matter that Zack had rolled out of bed after *that* and left without saying a single solitary word. I didn't care in the least. That hollow feeling in my stomach was simply a lack of food. I wrapped myself up in my thick, cozy robe and headed for the kitchen to make tea and breakfast.

And that's when I realized everything was not fine.

Because Zack had not left. He was still here, naked except his boxers, his bare feet dangling off one end of my sofa, reading one of my books while he usurped the affections of four of my cats. And I did not feel fine about any of it. The sight of his bare chest and little Evie snuggled beneath his chin knocked me off kilter. Even St. Vincent, who was actually quite large and had been mistaken for a fox on more than one occasion, looked small curled up under one of Zack's knees. Lillian and Daisy had made a black-and-white cuddle pile on his stomach.

A gorgeously made, mostly naked man was sprawled out on my couch, covered in cats and reading a romance book. It was as though a fantasy I'd never even known I'd possessed suddenly came to life in my living room.

How was I supposed to function? Form coherent sentences, have intelligent thoughts, be a contributing member of society? All I wanted to do was lick him like an ice cream cone.

"You're awake," he remarked in the exact same voice he had used to tell me *I'll be such a good boy*, soft and rough all at the same time.

Honestly, how *dare* he.

I draped over the back of the couch, leaning on my elbow with my chin propped on my palm, and looked down at him in all his naked, cat-covered glory. "What are you doing?"

"Waiting for you, Hannah Bell." His voice was still rough-soft, his smile slow and teasing. My stomach swooped. I was in danger of being very silly about this man. "Your cats were kind enough to keep me company. Except for that one." He jerked his head in the direction of my gray tabby, Annabelle, who sat two feet away, her back turned to us and her tail flicking back and forth in high outrage. His eyes narrowed. "She doesn't like me."

He said it like he was annoyed about it, and I smothered a grin. "That's Annabelle. I told you, she doesn't like anyone."

"Hmm. Now that's a shame."

He cupped his large hand over Evie's small body in a long stroke down her back. She arched into his touch like a wave and I moved too, like I could feel his calloused fingers against my own spine.

"I'm not used to pussies giving me the cold shoulder. You think I can win her over someday?" He all but winked when he said it. His hand kept stroking, Evie kept purring, but suddenly I felt a lot less silly.

My spine snapped straight and I full on *vibrated*. "I am not frigid."

Shock replaced all the teasing humor in his eyes. "I didn't say—"

"I know what you *meant*, Zack," I said crisply. I spun on my toes and marched into the kitchen. "I have an English degree. I know a metaphor when I hear it. You weren't talking about cats. You were talking about my vagina."

I banged open a cabinet, grabbed a frying pan, and

banged that onto the stove. I reached for a bowl so I could bang that too but instead found myself hauled backward against Zack's hard, broad chest, his arms wrapped around my belly. His low laugh rumbled in my ear.

"*I* don't have an English degree. I don't have a degree at all. Fuck, darlin', I've had two concussions and if you ask either of my brothers, I didn't start out with a whole lot of brain cells to begin with." He laughed again, but I heard it this time. The anxiety that skirted along the edges. He used humor like a shield, but if he truly didn't care, he wouldn't have trapped me against his body so he could whisper every word into my ear.

"I was talking about your vagina, you're right about that, but I wasn't talking about its temperature. Hell, I don't even believe in frigid, as it applies to women, and it damn sure doesn't apply to you, either. I watched you come from fucking yourself with your fingers. I watched you spit on my cock. Frigid is the last thing I would call you. You're a goddamn volcano."

I wanted to believe him, to see myself the way he saw me, but his words couldn't drown out all the voices in my head, of the men who had been personally offended that my body didn't work the way they thought it should. "All right," I said, mortified to be having this conversation at all, much less in the bright light of day before breakfast. "I'm going to make us omelets."

I pressed forward and his arms gave way. I didn't have to turn around to know he was still standing there, watching me. I could feel the heat of him against my back. The man was a self-sustaining furnace.

"You know, a lot of women can't come from penetration alone," he said easily, as though that was a perfectly normal conversation to have while making breakfast. "Most women need clit stimulation to get there."

I shot him a baleful glance over my shoulder as I pulled eggs, milk, mushrooms, and spinach from the fridge. "Oh, really? Thank you," I cooed. "I had no idea how my body worked, having only been living in it for a mere twenty-nine years. Thank goodness I have a man to explain it to me."

"Yeah, okay." He laughed ruefully and held his arms up in the universal *I surrender* pose. "I'm just saying, you don't have to be shy with me. It's a privilege to be naked with you, and there's not a damn thing you could ask for that I wouldn't say yes to. Tell me how you want to be touched and I'll learn. Or hell, touch yourself while I'm inside you. That's fucking hot."

If only it were that easy. I shook my head and got to work cracking eggs. "I've tried that. More than once. It doesn't work for me. I wish it did. You can't even imagine how badly I want that. Do you know how it feels, to touch yourself with someone watching, to know that they're depending on you to make it happen, and then you can't? Even though it's your own body, you just can't? I'll tell you how it feels, Zack. It feels awful. It's humiliating. It's—"

To my absolute horror, my eyes burned with tears. I turned away quickly, swiping the sleeve of my robe across my face. Then I took a deep breath and whisked the eggs together with a splash of milk. I was *not* going to break down.

"Hey." He took the whisk from me and nudged the bowl aside, then turned me around to face him. "Hey. You don't have anything to feel bad about. I want to help you feel good, that's all. However that happens for you is perfect. Okay? I'm sorry."

"Oh, it's not you. It was—" I waved a hand, not wanting to waste my breath on his name.

"I see." Zack braced against the counter, bracketing my body with his muscular arms, and regarded me with narrowed eyes. "Darlin', I'm going to need a name and his last known address."

I snort-laughed in spite of myself. "That won't be necessary. Really. He's not in my life now, and it wasn't really his fault, either. It's me. I'm the problem."

"You're a lot of things, Hannah, but a problem isn't one of them, and whoever made you think otherwise is an asshole."

I fiddled with the belt of my robe, then sighed. "He was a jerk about it, but he wasn't wrong. I can't orgasm with another person. And it's not because I don't know how my body works, or because I'm too shy to ask for what I want."

I didn't know how to explain it, the overwhelming fear that took hold every time I became too aware of a man's proximity to my body. My fight or flight instinct was broken, because I didn't fight and I didn't fly. I simply froze.

I chanced a peek at him and found his gaze intent on

me. No judgment, just concern. It gave me the courage to keep going.

"It's not for lack of trying, either. I've tried. Really. Different positions, different men. Relationships, a one-night stand. None of it worked. Sometimes I got close"—*like last night, with you*—"but then something would happen. We'd make eye contact or I'd feel his breath on my neck and..." I looked away again. "Suddenly I wasn't safe. I mean, I was, of course. In reality, I wasn't in any danger. But I didn't *feel* safe."

"Safe," he echoed. His eyebrows drew together. "Hannah..."

The way he looked at me, I knew what he was thinking. What he was fearing. I'd had this conversation before with the therapist my brother, Jeremiah, sent me to while he was my guardian, and then again with another therapist I saw after I graduated college. I knew there was a connection between what had happened to me and how I felt during sex now, but *knowing* it didn't seem to help me *fix* it.

"I wasn't assaulted, Zack. It wasn't like that." Although it kind of was, but even with therapy, I never felt I had the right to claim it. I had never fought it. I had simply accepted it as uncontroverted fact that it was God's plan for me. "I was married. When I was fourteen years old."

ZACK

DAD:
The drain in the training barn is clogged.
Can one of you get on that?

ADAM:
Not it

BRAX:
Not it

ZACK:
Dammit

ADAM:
It works out better this way. You have the
longest arms.

ZACK:
Yeah, it goes with having the longest dick.

BRAX:
Doesn't matter how long it is if it's only
the width of a pencil.

DAD:

I don't need to be here for this.

Dad has left the conversation.

ZACK:

Hey, don't worry about it, Brax. Essie seems like the type who knows how to help herself.

BRAX:

Keep my wife's name out of your mouth, asshole.

ZACK:

No :)

The urge to smash my fist into someone's face was overwhelming.

Fourteen fucking years old.

Hannah had dropped that bomb, and I'd responded with the stupidest thing possible. *Are you sure?* Jesus fucking Christ. A day later, the memory still made me flinch. She should have kicked my ass out right then and there and thrown my clothes after me. I would have deserved that. But she'd just smiled and told me to sit down. *I'll tell you everything,* she'd said, *but I need to keep my hands busy. Just sit there, okay? It will be easier for me to get through it if you don't talk.*

Which, yeah. Fair enough.

Fuck.

So I'd sat there like a useless piece of shit while she made us breakfast and told me all about her childhood trauma.

And then I'd eaten the whole damn omelet because I couldn't *not* eat it, right? Not after that. But I didn't taste a single bite.

Hannah had grown up in a polygamous compound, one of the offshoots of the Mormon religion that had broken with the main church after they abolished polygamy. They didn't call themselves Mormons, though, Hannah had explained with the wryest little smirk and scrunch of her nose. They called themselves saints.

The fucking *audacity*.

She'd grown up in a desert town in Nevada, in a house with her mother and two other women who had married her father, and a pack of kids. There had been no connection with the outside world. No phones or television. No one came into town, and even high-ranking men needed permission to leave. The town had its own grocery store, but mostly each family had grown their own food and raised livestock. They'd been homeschooled in basic reading, writing, math, and scripture. No history. No science.

It was fine, Hannah had said with a careless shrug. *I didn't know any better. I loved my mom and the other women. I loved my dad. I loved my brothers and sisters. I knew my future would look like my mom's and that was fine, too.*

She just hadn't expected the future to come quite so soon.

At fourteen fucking years old.

He hadn't been fourteen, of course. He'd been fifty-two and looking for a fourth wife who was still young enough to give him more children. Because apparently three wives and seventeen kids weren't enough for him.

I really wanted to hit something.

Hannah had glossed over the three weeks she'd been married. She hadn't wanted to be a fourth wife, much less to the man she'd been given to, so she'd managed to sneak a message to an older brother who had left the compound years before. He came and got her, and he brought her to his ranch in Wyoming. She'd lived with him until college, when she got a full ride to the University of Colorado at Boulder.

And now I'm here, she'd said.

Like all that shit was over now, and everything was fine.

But it wasn't fine, was it? If everything was fine, we wouldn't have been having that conversation the morning after sex. She didn't think she was fine. She thought there was something wrong with her. That *she* was a problem.

The only problem I could see was that somewhere in bumfuck Nevada was a man who needed his balls shoved down his throat, and I wanted to make that right.

But instead of putting my fist down his throat, I was going to stick my hand in a drain clogged with horse feces, horse hair, and who knew what else but my guess was bubble gum and dip because there was *always* bubble gum and dip, and clean it out.

Fuck that guy, and fuck Adam and Brax, too.

I made it over to the training barn late afternoon. From the smell of it, cleaning it out was going to suck. Since there was no way I was going to stick my bare arm in that death trap, I headed to the supply cabinet in the tack room to grab a pair of breeding gloves.

Before James had come to Lodestar Ranch as the head trainer, the cabinet was a disaster. Expired medicine, unraveled leg wraps, sticky bottles of fly spray were shoved on shelves without any real order. Hell, even opening the door was a hazard, as something was likely to fall out. But a month or so after her arrival, things started shifting into place at Lodestar. James had a system for everything.

And right now, her system was telling me that we were out of breeding gloves.

Because right there on the shelf where the breeding gloves belonged was a note taped to an empty box, telling Adam to order more.

I slammed the cabinet door shut with a metallic clang that reverberated through the tack room.

Fucking Adam.

I found him in the old barn we used for hay and feed storage, tidying up with the old push broom. Whistling. Adam had been a grumpy, non-whistling asshole before James came into his life. Normally I'd take his whistling as a good thing because it meant my oldest brother was finally happy again. Right now, I took his happiness as a personal affront. People who forgot to order breeding gloves didn't deserve happiness. Fuck his whistling ass.

Adam paused with his back to me, leaned his weight against the broom handle, and surveyed the barn with the air of a man proud of his work.

So I kicked that broom right out from under him.

"Hey!" He fell forward but caught himself before hitting the ground. Dammit. "What the hell, Zack?"

"You didn't order breeding gloves, jackass."

"Breeding gloves? Sure I did. I…" His voice trailed off as he tilted his head, eyes sliding to the left, remembering. "Oh. Shit."

"Yeah. Shit is exactly what I'm going to have to put my bare hand into, thanks to you."

"I'm sorry. James put that note there a month ago when she opened the last box. I meant to order more, but I got sidetracked by something or other. I didn't think we'd go through them so fast." He looked sincerely apologetic, but I wasn't having it.

"That's the thing about breeding gloves," I said, my voice dripping with sarcasm. "See, they're called *breeding* gloves because they protect you when you need to stick your arm into a pregnant mare, but because they're disposable gloves that go up to your elbow, they're actually used for all kinds of nasty barn chores. Like cleaning out floor drains."

Adam's eyes narrowed. "Yeah. I know. Unlike you, I didn't get out of chores by running away to the rodeo. I've worked on this ranch damn near every day of my life, and

I've been running it for the last four years. So don't fucking lecture me on how to do my damn job."

"How about you do your damn job so I don't have to fucking lecture you?" I smirked, standing with my arms spread wide, all but daring him to throw the first punch.

He gave me a long, calculating look like he was actually considering it. But then he shook his head and turned away. "You've been a real ornery son of a bitch ever since that horse stomped you, you know that?"

I laughed. Then I shoved him into a hay bale.

It didn't take him long to recover. With a string of curses, he grabbed a flake of hay by the twine and smacked me in the head with it. I wrestled him down to the ground with every intention of making him eat that fucking hay, when I felt myself hauled off him.

"What the hell is going on here?" Brax demanded, keeping his arms between me and Adam to hold us back from each other.

"He didn't order breeding gloves!" I shouted, still mad enough to consider fratricide a viable outcome.

Brax caught on immediately to the significance of that. "Dammit—"

"Like you never screw up?" Adam asked me. "I do the work of three people around here. You didn't even show up today until after noon."

"Shut up, both of you," Brax snapped. "It's not worth fighting over. Zack, tie a garbage bag around your arm. You won't have as much movement with your fingers, but you should still be able to get the job done. And, Adam. For fuck's sake. You can't hit him. You need to be gentle. He's still—ooof!"

His words ended on a shout as I dropped my shoulder to his ribs and used his body as a battering ram to push both my asshole brothers into the hay. We all fell together in a heap of kicking limbs and curse words.

And then it was *on*.

I didn't have a clue who I was hitting or who was hitting me. Frankly, I did not give a shit. There wasn't a damn thing I wasn't pissed at right then.

Hurricane Red, for stomping me.

Every goddamn person in the rodeo circuit who didn't protect Hurricane Red from the repercussions of stomping me.

The piece of shit who dared to call a fourteen-year-old girl his wife.

Adam, for not ordering breeding gloves a month ago.

Brax, for telling Adam to be fucking *gentle* with me.

I couldn't do anything about Hurricane Red or the shithead who married Hannah—I refused to call him her husband, even in my head—but I could damn sure make my brothers hurt as much as I did.

Voices floated through the red haze of rage, sounding far away and close at the same time.

"Should we do something?" James asked.

"Like make popcorn, you mean?" Essie said. "Oh, my *god*. We should make this a rodeo event. Three hot brothers wrestling in the hay. Do you think we could convince them to do it shirtless? Maybe oil them up a little? People would pay good money for that, I guarantee it. What do you think, Hannah?"

Brax snickered, the sound of his wife's voice making him lose focus and miss an easy shot, which I took full advantage of. *Pussy-whipped sucker.*

"Boys." Hannah didn't even have to raise her voice to get my attention. My whole body froze instantly. She clapped her hands three times. "Stop that right now."

I pushed through my brothers and rolled to my feet with a smile. Hannah was flanked on either side by James and Essie, but she was the one I greeted. "Hey, there, duchess."

She blinked like I had caught her off guard, but then she adjusted her glasses and pursed her lips. "You're bleeding."

"You should see the other guys," I drawled.

"I'm looking right at them," she said crisply. "No one else is bleeding."

But she wasn't looking at them. Her eyes never strayed from me. All that red-hot rage that had set my blood boiling a moment ago eased to a warm, friendly simmer.

"*I'm* bleeding," Brax protested. "I think the hay scraped up my cuticle."

Essie sniggered softly. "Poor baby. Come on, husband. Let's get you patched up."

James gave Adam a quick once-over and then, apparently satisfied, turned to me with concern in her big brown eyes. "Are you okay, Zack?"

I laughed, already steering Hannah out the door.

"What, this? Brothers roughhouse, honey. See to your man, and don't you worry about me. Hannah has me in hand."

Hannah gave me an adorably befuddled frown. "You have *me* in hand, actually."

"Exactly, duchess. Now take me to my cabin so I can get cleaned up."

"This is the second time you've bloodied your lip in less than two weeks, and both times it was for a stupid fight that wasn't worth it." Hannah's voice was sharp, but her hand was gentle as she held a paper towel to my lower lip.

"Now, that's not true," I said. "Adam won't ever forget to order breeding gloves again, so I'd say that was worth it."

Unimpressed, she arched her brows. "And the first fight? The one at the Painted Cat?"

"Who's to say? For all I know, a great injustice had been done, and I was doing my part to rectify that."

"Hmm." She pursed her lips.

With a lazy grin, I leaned back against the counter and widened my legs so she pitched forward between my thighs.

"Zack!" She huffed, exasperated, and pushed against my chest with one hand, her other hand still occupied with stemming the bleeding. "Your belt buckle is—"

I grabbed her hand and turned it to kiss her wrist. "I'm not wearing a belt, duchess."

"Oh." She looked down at the unmistakable bulge in my jeans. "You're...hard. How are you hard right now?"

I laughed. "Fighting with my brothers got my blood up, and then you wearing that librarian costume moved that blood down south."

"It's not a costume," she huffed. "It's my clothes."

"My point is that the combination of violence and women makes a powerful aphrodisiac."

"Even after yesterday?" The way she made eye contact with my throat made my chest feel tight. "Even after...what I told you?"

"Darlin', I would give you the title to my truck and the keys to my cabin if you let me in your pussy right now. Hell, I'd give you almost everything I own. Last night only made me more desperate for you. Now I don't have to wonder what it would be like to fuck you. I already know." I pressed my jaw to her temple. Let my unshaved stubble scrape against her silky skin. Felt her unsteady inhale of breath. "Heaven, Hannah. You feel like heaven."

She pulled back slightly, still not meeting my eyes. I had left a smear of blood behind when I kissed her wrist, and now she slowly rubbed it away with her thumb. I don't know why that turned me on even more, that she had rubbed my blood into her skin instead of washing herself clean of me, but it did.

And then she raised her chin, meeting my gaze with

flushed cheeks and blown-out pupils, and I realized she was every bit as turned on as I was.

"Don't try to make me come," she warned.

"Wouldn't dream of it, duchess."

I wrapped my hands around the back of her thighs and hoisted her up, then spun us both around and set her down on the countertop. Her dark blue skirt draped loosely around her legs, the hem hitting the top of her ankle boots.

"Look at you, so prim and proper in that skirt, but underneath you're soaked for me, aren't you? Mmm." I bit my knuckle. "Are you going to show me?"

"If you want me to," she whispered, looking up at me from under her pale lashes.

"Fuck, yes, I want you to," I groaned. "Please, Hannah. Lift your skirt for me."

She went slow, lifting her skirt one excruciating, delicious inch at a time, because my prim and proper librarian was a fucking tease. First her shins, then her knees, then her thighs. I was damn close to exploding in my jeans by the time she gave me the smallest glimpse of her white cotton panties.

"Spread your legs," I begged. "Show me."

She opened her knees, then slid two fingers inside her underwear. When she pulled them out, they glistened. "Wet," she said.

I growled, hooked my hands behind her knees, and dragged her to the edge of the countertop. "Condom is in my wallet. My left back pocket."

I unsnapped my jeans and pulled down the zipper while she fished out the condom and tossed my wallet to the floor. She paused, about to rip it open, and watched me free my cock from my underwear. I gave myself a quick, rough tug and she licked her lips.

"Hannah, if you don't stop licking your lips, I'm going to fuck your mouth instead of your pussy," I gritted out. I was so hard now it hurt. "Condom. Put it on me."

"Oh! Right."

She rolled it over my length and I bit the inside of my cheek to keep from coming from the pressure of her hand.

The second we were both protected, I pushed her panties aside and slammed into her so hard her ass slid back an inch on the slick laminate countertop. I looped an arm around her waist to keep her where I wanted her and stretched my other arm to the far side of the counter.

"Hold on to me, honey," I murmured against her lips, and she did, wrapping her legs around my hips and her arms around my neck.

I fucked her hard and rough. Sweat beaded on my forehead, my thighs shook, and all I could hear was the sweet little moans Hannah made and the sound of flesh slapping against flesh. Pleasure crested fast, but I didn't even try to fight the wave of it. I let it take me, stifling my shout against her neck.

It took me a second to catch my breath after that, and when I did, I realized Hannah was still clinging to me, every muscle in her sweet body strung tighter than a guitar string.

"You want a little more, duchess?" I nuzzled her neck. "I'll stay just like this. And if you want to, you can put your fingers on your clit and give it a rub. Wouldn't that feel nice?"

She didn't say anything, but I felt her shift. She left one hand on my shoulder and slid the second down to where we were still joined. I remembered what she said about she said about eye contact and feeling breath on her neck so I held mine in tight. I needed Hannah to feel good more than I needed air.

It only took a second before her nails dug into my shoulder and her body shuddered. I let out the breath I'd been holding in a slow exhale and pulled fresh air into my lungs. Then I did it again.

It felt like the first full breath I'd taken in months.

HANNAH

ESSIE:

Did you visit Zack's Eiffel Tower, Hannah?

JAMES:

Ignore her. But seriously, is everything okay? No one has seen you in an hour. Where are you guys?

ESSIE:

Don't ignore me! It's for SCIENCE.

Also, Ted wants to know if you're staying for dinner.

HANNAH:

Everything is fine! Just taking care of Zack's mouth.

ESSIE:

I bet you are.

"You want something to drink?" Zack asked as he tucked his dick back in his jeans. "A glass of water? Beer? Ginger ale? That's all I've got."

I blinked at him. Zack, aside from a slight flush on his tanned cheeks, looked perfectly respectable, while I had the feeling I looked wrecked. My legs were still spread wide, my glasses askew, and locks of hair that belonged in my bun hung in my face.

"Um, water?" I suggested.

He smiled, righted my glasses, and reached over my shoulder to the cabinet behind me for a glass. I refused to melt into a bewildered puddle of gooeyness, but it was a *struggle*. Sex had always been fraught for me, in part because of my determination that it *not* be fraught. I wanted so badly for sex to be easy, and with every new relationship, I had tried so hard to prove that this normal, human experience hadn't been stolen from me. That I could give and receive pleasure on my own terms.

And I could...to an extent. Sex was enjoyable. But orgasming with another person remained right out of reach. And eventually, my inability to get there tore my relationships apart.

It was different with Zack. I still felt tendrils of fear curling around my limbs like ivy strangling a tree, but somehow the sound of his voice helped me hold on to reality. That I was here, with him, and I was safe.

Not safe enough to let him make me come, but safe enough to get there myself if I was already teetering on the edge.

And that was a freaking miracle.

Zack handed me a glass of water, then filled a second one for himself. His phone buzzed and he pulled it out of his pocket, side-eyed the message as he gulped his water, then sighed and wiped his mouth. "You hungry? Dad says you should stay for dinner."

I was hungry, but I hesitated. "Is that okay with you?"

He looked surprised. "Sure. Why wouldn't it be?"

"Because they might think..." I looked down at myself, made a face, and shook my skirt out over my knees.

"That you're my girlfriend?" he supplied. He hooted with laughter. "Duchess, ain't nobody going to think that."

"Because wild cowboys don't date mousy librarians?" I knew his reputation, after all.

"Because you're too smart to date a broke-down cowboy like me, and they know it." He laughed again. "I suppose I should count myself lucky that I'm not a horse. At least they can't ship me to Canada or Mexico and ground me up for dog food."

Like Hurricane Red. He didn't say it, but I knew that's what he was thinking about. What he was *feeling* about. This man made everything a joke, but I didn't believe his act for one second. He had laughed when Will had told him about Hurricane Red, too, but I had seen the anguish in his face for that brief second when he turned away. He *cared*.

And I wasn't going to laugh at his stupid joke.

"That's not funny," I said. When his lips parted, I had an awful feeling he was about to laugh again or tell another joke, and I clapped a hand over his stupid smirking mouth. "Say something real, or don't say anything at all."

His eyes twitched as I stared him down, and somehow I knew he wasn't smirking anymore. Slowly I lowered my hand.

"I hate that Hurricane Red did his job, and now it's going to cost him his life. I hate feeling helpless to stop it. It makes me want to hit something." He stepped back, crossed his arms over his broad chest, and glared at me. "Is that real enough for you?"

I tilted my head, studying him. "Is that why you picked a fight with your brothers? Because of a horse?"

He turned his head like he was more concerned with the view outside the kitchen window than our conversation. His throat moved as he swallowed. "It wasn't *only* the horse. Lots of shit makes me angry these days. In my defense, if my brothers don't want to get hit, then they shouldn't be assholes." When he looked at me again, that smirk was back on his face.

This time I let him keep it. "All right. Let's go save your horse, then."

He shook his head. "If it were that easy, I would have done it already. But there are dozens of auction pens west of the Mississippi, and they could have dumped him at any one of them. If he's not already in Canada or Mexico, that is."

I already had my phone out and Jeremiah's text conversation open. "My brother is great at finding things. Alive or dead."

Zack grasped my waist right above my hip bones, lifted me off the counter, and set me back on my feet. "I appreciate what you're trying to do for me, but don't get your hopes up. Looking for a horse in an auction pen is like looking for a needle in a haystack."

Now it was my turn to smirk. "You don't know my brother. He'll find him."

Hopefully alive. I had the feeling Hurricane Red's death would hurt Zack more than his stomping had.

"Hope you like tacos," Ted Hale said as Zack led me into the kitchen.

"I love them," I said. The smell was making my mouth water.

"Good." Ted's blue eyes crinkled at the corners when he smiled at me. "Because that's what we're having."

Ted's way of saying ordinary things that made you feel like it was an inside joke just between the two of you that reminded me of Zack. He looked like Zack, too, or what I imagined Zack would look like in another thirty-five years.

His hair was thinner and a whole lot grayer, and he was a little thicker in the middle, but he was still tall and leanly muscled, and his smile was open and easy. We had met a few times before, but this was the first time I'd seen him standing next to Zack, and the similarities were astounding.

"Wow, you really said copy paste with your sons, didn't you?" I said. "Zack is your spitting image."

Ted chuckled softly. "You haven't seen Jenny. All our boys look a little like me, but Zack takes after her in ways I can't put my finger on."

"I'll show you her picture after dinner," Ben, Zack's nephew, piped up. "We've got lots of photos. There's some of Uncle Zack, too."

"Hannah doesn't want to look at our photos, bud," Zack said. "She doesn't know any of those people."

"I do want to look at your photos," I said. "I absolutely do."

"Yes!" Ben shouted, with more enthusiasm than I expected.

"Ben's been looking through the family photo books for a project for his history class," Adam explained. "Now he's obsessed with the history of Aspen Springs and the Gold Rush."

"Really?" I said. "We've got tons of resources at the library. Stop by sometime, and I'll show you some old newspaper articles I found."

Ben's face lit up. I had the feeling he was going to show up sooner rather than later.

"Did you get the drain figured out, Zack?" Ted asked as we gathered around the dinner table.

I froze halfway in my seat and my gaze skittered to Zack. *Do not start World War Three*, I silently compelled him with my eyes.

But Zack just grinned. "Had a minor setback, but I'll take care of it right after dinner."

Apparently the thing that had brought the Hale brothers to blows not even two hours ago was no longer a big deal. I glanced around the table to James and Essie, then Adam and Brax, but no one seemed to think anything was amiss. Maybe this was just how things were with the three brothers. They fought it out and then got over it.

Maybe.

Zack was his usual self through dinner. Charming, mischievous, always ready with a teasing smile or joke. But I had seen through the cracks in the humor he wore like a shield. Maybe he didn't care about that stupid drain anymore. Maybe he really was over it.

But...

Every horse. Every ride.

There were some things Zack never got over at all.

TRUE TO HIS WORD, after dinner Ben pulled me to the couch and settled next to me with a big stack of leather photo albums. Zack also kept his word, disappearing with a big black garbage bag to go take care of the drain. Adam and Brax, I noted, slipped out after him.

"Should we go chronologically?" Ben asked. I had the feeling that even though he had lured me here with photos of Zack's mother, he was most interested in the photo album on top labeled "1800-Something."

"Sure," I agreed. I pulled the photo album into my lap. "We'll start in the past and work toward the present."

"The oldest one is from 1859 or so, best we can figure," Ben explained. He pointed to the first photo, a sepia-toned black-and-white photograph of a group of old men with bushy mustaches standing in front of a mine entrance. "That's when Thomas Hale came west to Colorado from Vermont looking for gold. He's my great-great-great"—Ben paused, his eyes darting sideways as he counted up the generations in his head—"great grandfather. I'm not allowed to touch those photos, because they're so old."

I nodded. "That makes sense. Paper is fragile, and the oils from our fingers could make them disintegrate even faster."

Forty minutes later, when Zack and his brothers returned from cleaning out the drain, we had made it through the great-grandparents and had just started in on Ted and Jenny. I glanced from the photo of his mom smirking at Ted, her golden hair blowing in the wind, and then at Zack.

"You were right, Ted," I said. "Zack looks so much like her." I leaned over the pages, peering closer, then up at

Zack again. "It's not so much your features. It's your expressions."

Ted smiled, looking a little wistful. "That's exactly it."

"Scooch, duchess." Zack swatted my thigh. I wiggled closer to Ben, and Zack sat down next to me. He looked over my shoulder, then pointed at their wedding photo. "You know that rose garden out front? That's where they got married. It looks different now, because they built up the house and added a driveway, but that's the spot."

"It's beautiful," I said.

"The next few pages are pretty boring," Zack said. "Just baby pictures of Adam and Brax, mostly. Skip ahead to where I come in. That's when it gets good."

"Uncle Zack! We have to go in order!" Ben protested.

"Hannah lives all the way in town, bud. If we keep her out too late, she'll have to sleep here."

"Are you offering to take the couch, Zack?" Essie's wide blue eyes were the picture of innocence. "Brax and I are staying at Lodestar tonight, so his cabin isn't available. Hannah will have to stay with you."

Zack draped an arm along the back of the couch. His fingertips grazed my ear and I broke out in goosebumps. "Of course I'm offering Hannah the bed. I'm a gentleman, darlin'."

He did not, I noticed, say he would be taking the couch.

I also took note of the endearment. *Darlin'*. He used that a lot. Sugar, too. Me, Essie, random acquaintances. If a woman wasn't his relation, she was his darlin', sugar, or honey.

Duchess, though. That one was new. And, so far as I could tell, reserved for me alone.

I wasn't sure how to take that. Was it a compliment or an insult? Maybe he thought I was an uppity snob.

"Skip ahead, Ben," Adam urged. "Show her the photos of my baby sister."

My head jerked up in surprise. "Sister?"

Adam, Brax, James, and Essie burst into laughter.

"What?" I asked, looking between them. "What am I missing?"

"The story of how Zack got his name," Brax said, smirking. "Do you want to tell it, little sis, or should I?"

"*I'll* tell it," Ted said. "You tell it wrong."

I looked at Zack to see how he was taking the teasing, but he didn't seem at all perturbed. "Go for it, Dad."

"It's like this," Ted said. "Jenny always wanted a big family. We settled on the idea of five kids, if we were blessed. Jenny had this idea in her head that we'd go down the alphabet, A through E. All through her first pregnancy, she insisted she didn't care if we started with a boy or a girl, but deep down she had strong feelings about it. She wanted a boy first so we could name him Adam, and our fifth baby would be a girl named Eve." He paused, staring into space, remembering. "It's funny, isn't it? She was rational about everything else, but she dreamed about this the way most folks dream of winning the lottery."

"Everyone has a little crazy in them," I said. "That's what makes us interesting."

Ted chuckled. "That we do, Hannah. That we do. Anyway, Brax was next. Another boy. Jenny loved our boys more than anything on this earth, but they were also a handful. Not enough to scare us off adding a third baby to the mix, but enough to hope that we'd be blessed with a girl. Jenny prayed for her every night. Had a name picked out and everything. Charlotte. She was so sure the baby would be a girl that she refused to let the doctor tell us the gender. She just went right on ahead and bought girl clothes."

Zack nudged my arm. "Turn the page, duchess. See for yourself."

I turned the page. And there he was, baby Zack, wearing a pink onesie embroidered with rainbows and ruffled pink socks on his tiny feet. It was just about the sweetest thing I'd ever seen. My ovaries ached.

"Oh, my gosh," I breathed. "You were *adorable.*"

Zack grinned. "I've always thought so. Mom did, too, and I promise, there wasn't a single moment I felt unloved. But the day I came out of her womb a boy, it crushed her. She saw the writing on the wall and had no intention of being a mom to five rowdy boys. She put a stop to it right then and there. Skipped C and went straight to Z."

"And that's how Zack got his name," Ted said with aplomb.

I smiled and kept turning the pages, watching the boys grow from toddlers to big kids. The pink onesies disappeared after the first three months and Zack wore regular boy clothes. And then, when Zack was about seven, there was a picture of him and his mom on the couch, a blanket over their laps, fuzzy pink bunny slippers on their feet.

Fuzzy pink bunny slippers.

Next to me, Zack drew in a sharp breath, then let it out on a quick laugh. "That's the year Adam and Brax found the old photos of me as a baby and realized I was supposed to be a girl. So for Christmas they got me pink bunny slippers. The card said, *to our sister, Charlotte.*"

Adam and Brax grinned at each other.

"Charlotte was so sweet," Brax said. "I miss her."

Zack rolled his eyes. "Anyway, joke was on them, because I fu—" With a quick glance at Ben, he cleared his throat. "I freaking loved them. When Mom got sick the first time, I used my allowance to buy her a matching pair. We would wear them while we watched movies together when she felt bad from chemo." He ran his thumb over the photograph like he was stroking his mother's hair. "She always complained her feet were cold."

The room fell silent for a moment.

And then Zack's warm laugh permeated the sudden sadness that hung over his family at the memory of Jenny's cancer, scattering the dark clouds with his sunshine. "Dang, I was cute."

His shield was back up.

No, not a shield. It was more like a force field. Because it wasn't about protecting only himself. It was about protecting his family, too. He laughed to make them feel better. And it worked.

"We love you no matter what, Zack, but anytime Charlotte wants to pay us a visit, we'd be happy to have her." Adam grinned. "And take pictures."

The slippers were a Christmas present. That's what he'd told me, the morning I'd found him naked and eating ramen. But there was no way they were the same pair his brothers had given him. The slippers he'd worn as an adolescent wouldn't fit his feet now.

His mother had given him those slippers.

I shifted the photo album so it lay across both our laps, half on him and half on me. Underneath the spine, in the narrow valley between our thighs, I found his hand and squeezed.

Because I knew he didn't find anything funny about those slippers.

ZACK

Hannah did not spend the night at Lodestar Ranch. She fed me some line about needing to be up early to get to the library on time, and she'd rather do the hard part now instead of getting up even earlier tomorrow. It made sense, and I should have been relieved because it had been a long day.

But I wasn't.

Mom used to say I had a brain like a two-year-old. I thrived on physical movement, but it was easy for me to become overstimulated by too much emotion, regardless of whether that emotion came from myself or others, and when that happened, my brain threw a tantrum. Like an overtired toddler, it refused to do the one thing it needed and shut the fuck down.

So I wasn't relieved when Hannah didn't spend the night, because all I wanted was to roll her sweet body beneath me and fuck her until I couldn't feel a damn thing anymore. Instead, I lay there wide awake, my body itching like a molting snake, my brain replaying the events of the past forty-eight hours like a movie.

I was married at fourteen.

Are you sure?

Grappling with my brothers.

Pink bunny slippers.

Hannah squeezing my hand.

Hannah squeezing my hand.

Hannah squeezing my hand.

HANNAH TEXTED me mid-morning and asked me to meet her at Jo's for lunch. By then I'd already been up for five hours taking care of the animals, and I was fucking tired. I'd managed to fall asleep somewhere around three a.m., an hour and a half before my alarm went off at 4:30. Before I got her text, I'd had lofty goals of sneaking back to my cabin and stealing a nap.

And then she texted, and my priorities shifted.

She was already at Jo's when I arrived, occupying a corner booth in the back. I wasn't late, but she was early. Watching Hannah was becoming one of my favorite things, so I allowed myself a moment to do that. She had her embroidery project with her. I had the feeling she didn't go anywhere without either a book or sewing. Like me, she needed to keep her hands busy to let her brain sort itself out.

Then she looked up, caught sight of me, and she...well, she didn't smile. Her expression did something funny, like she was girding her loins. Steeling herself for a hard conversation. It made my stomach tumble a bit, but I sauntered on over with a smirk.

"Hey, there, duchess. Did you order yet?" I asked.

She looked up at me and I swore she gulped. She shook her head. "Not yet."

"What are you having? I'll take care of it."

I put in our order at the counter with Chloe—a grilled cheese sandwich for Hannah, a grilled chicken salad for me, because the last thing I needed was clogged arteries that led to open-heart surgery and then germs would invade my bloodstream and my spleenless body wouldn't be able to fight them off and I'd die, pathetic and weak, in a hospital bed.

A better option would be to find that cliff.

I knew I wasn't going to do that. I felt like an asshole for even thinking about it, but I wasn't going to *do* it. Except even now, when I told myself I wasn't going to do it, when I *knew* I wasn't going to do it, something whispered in the back of my brain. *Maybe.*

No, of course I wasn't going to do it. Instead, I ordered the salad.

I waited at the counter for our orders because Jo's wasn't the kind of establishment that brought food to your table, and while I waited, I watched Hannah some more.

She tucked her embroidery into her slouchy bag, stared out the window for a moment, then sighed and took her embroidery back out.

Something was definitely up.

Was it Hurricane Red? Had her brother managed to find him, and now she had to give me the bad news? Shit.

Do not cry.

Do not put a hole in the wall.

Do not break that stack of plates.

I carried our tray of food to our table with the same smirk I walked in here with. "Here we go," I said as I slid into the booth across from her.

"Thank you." She put her embroidery away again, then pulled her plate closer to her.

I waited for her to say something else, something bad, but she picked up her sandwich, took a bite, and chewed silently. *Say it. Let's get this over with.* I speared a tomato wedge with my fork and angrily shoved it into my mouth. Fucking salad. This is what I had been reduced to, and somewhere Hurricane Red had paid an even worse price.

And then she set her sandwich down, folded her hands in front of her, and said, "Zack, I would like to discuss the nature of our relationship."

Suddenly I didn't want to hear another damn word come out of that rosebud mouth. This wasn't about Hurricane Red.

I leaned back and wiped my mouth on my napkin. "Are you breaking up with me, duchess?" I teased, but I forgot to smile.

Her head tilted as she studied me, and when I remembered to push my lips up, she sighed. "No, I'm not breaking up with you. That wouldn't make a whole lot of sense, would it? We're not dating."

"We're fucking," I said bluntly.

I said it to get a reaction from her, make her mad, maybe, because I was feeling a little mad myself. But instead her eyes lit up like I had said something right.

"Yes! Exactly. We're fucking."

I stared at her. I couldn't recall ever hearing Hannah curse before, and my dick made it known that it had very strong feelings about my prim little librarian, with her tidy bun and excessive sweaters, saying those words without a hint of shyness about her. I subtly adjusted myself under the table and wondered if I could somehow convince her to whisper that exact phrase in my ear. Preferably when we were, in fact, fucking.

"And you want to discuss that?" I asked.

For the life of me, I could not wrap my brain around this conversation. Normally, I didn't have this problem with women. Of course, most of my conversations with women had more inuendo than substance. The only thing we really *discussed* was her room or mine. A nice babbling brook of a conversation, never too slow or too deep.

With Hannah, that babbling brook had a tendency to plunge straight into a waterfall I never saw coming.

"I think it's going pretty well. Do you?" she asked. *Hopefully.* And the crazy thing was, she looked at me like she wasn't sure how I would answer.

I leaned forward. "I think it's going so well that if you asked me to join you here in the bathroom, I'd do it."

Her eyes darted to the bathroom door like she was actually considering it. Then she shook her head. "Chloe's only pretending to read her psych book. She's watching us."

I glanced to where Chloe stood leaned over her book that lay open on the counter. Jo's didn't tend to be very busy on weekday afternoons, so there was nothing keeping her from getting some studying done. As I watched, she looked me dead in the eyes and flipped a page, not even trying to hide the fact that she was spying on us. I smirked back at her.

"All right," I said. "Your place, then?"

She shook her head. "There isn't time. I have to be back at the library in forty minutes. That would give us only fifteen minutes for...stuff."

"Plenty of time. You'd be amazed at the *stuff* I can accomplish in fifteen minutes."

"I *am* amazed. That's the thing." She gave me a perplexed smile, then took another bite of her sandwich. "How is this so easy for you? And how do you make it so easy for me?"

"How is *what* so easy?" I asked, honestly baffled.

"Sex."

"Because it *is* easy."

"Not for me, it isn't. And usually not for my partners, either." She paused. "When they're with me, I mean," she corrected herself softly. "Sex isn't easy for people when they're with me."

Here came that waterfall.

I wasn't cut out for this, for heady waters tossing me about so I couldn't get my footing. I wasn't the person people came to for deep feelings. I was the person they came to so they wouldn't *have* to feel those deep feelings. But I couldn't walk away from her just because I was swimming out of my depth. I had to white-knuckle my way through it.

"Hannah," I said in all seriousness, because if she kept looking all sad like that I was going to have to find her ex-boyfriends and ruin their lives one by one, "I really like fucking you, and I think we should do more of that."

She stopped looking sad. "Well, good. Because I've been thinking about *why* it's so different with you. Do you know what it is?"

"Yes." I nodded firmly. "It's my magic dick."

She snorted. "It's a very nice dick, but no. If it were actually magic, it would have made me come, and it didn't."

I reeled back against the booth, clutching my chest like she had shot me there. "Goddamn, Hannah. You can't just *say* things like that."

She pushed up her glasses with a little frown and blinked at me. "Why not? You already knew it was true."

"Duchess, truth has no place in a civilized world."

She squinted at me like she was trying to decide

whether to take me seriously. "If you really thought that, you wouldn't have made me touch myself in front of you."

I grinned. "Touché."

She gave me that perplexed look again. "I think it's this, right here. This is why sex is different with you. It's because we're friends. That's why it's easy."

That knocked me back a bit. "Friends?" I repeated. I wasn't sure how I felt about that. Had I ever been friends with a woman? Essie. And James. But they were both paired up with my brothers, so maybe they didn't count. Not that I had anything against being friends with a woman. It just hadn't happened before.

She nodded. "We're friends. That's why we can talk like this, and why talking like this doesn't end in disaster." She pulled off a bit of crust and popped it into her mouth. "I was never friends first with anyone I dated. A classmate would ask me out, or a co-worker, or what have you. We'd go out on a couple dates, decide to be exclusive, and then we'd have sex. My therapist told me to be honest, and I tried that, I really did, but talking about sex only ever made things worse. Because it meant I couldn't fake it anymore."

I nodded slowly. "I could see how that would happen, if he's an insecure dillweed."

She blinked like she hadn't considered that. "I didn't know how to reassure them, I guess. My inability to orgasm became this whole *thing*. They took it personally. Or they'd get mad, like I was doing it on purpose, or I was being unfair to them somehow. Sex became a fight, or a chore. They resented me. They always resented me for ruining it."

"Insecure dillweeds," I said again, and I meant it.

"Maybe." She fiddled with the edge of her plate. "But I was the common denominator, and that made me feel... broken. Hopeless. I tried a one-night stand once, just to see if I could break the pattern. Maybe I could orgasm if it wasn't all so *fraught*. If the stakes weren't so high, and I never had to see him again."

"Did it work?" I asked, even though I suspected I knew the answer.

"No, of course not." She grimaced. "Since then, through talking to other women and reading a lot, I've come to realize that the female orgasm is elusive during one-night stands. Which makes sense. Alcohol is often involved, and men tend to do better when they actually know the woman's body."

I paused, considering that. I'd had a *lot* of one-night stands.

She suddenly seemed to remember that. "I'm sure you're the exception," she said diplomatically.

I laughed. "Obviously." But I wondered. Hell, there had been a few times when I'd been too drunk to finish myself.

She frowned down at her sandwich. But when she looked up at me again, she wasn't frowning. "But *you* don't resent me. And I think that's because we're friends. It makes hard conversations easier. I actually *like* you, and I think you like me, too."

Was that what friendship was? Liking someone? I

could handle that. Hell, I liked everyone. It felt a little different with Hannah, though. A little *more*, somehow. Maybe it was all the talking. That was new. There had to be a word for that, when you wanted to listen to every last thought in their head, but you also wanted to do unspeakable things to their ankles.

A conundrum, that's what it was.

"I like you, Hannah," I said. "I like you a hell of a lot."

"Good," she said briskly. "Because I think you could be my breakthrough."

"What do you mean?"

"I mean..." She clasped her hands together, squared her shoulders, and looked me dead in the eyeballs. "I want you to teach me how to orgasm with a man."

12

HANNAH

I had the feeling I was witnessing an event that had never happened before: Charming, glib, rodeo star Zack Hale stunned speechless. I didn't mind. I'd had a whole night to think this through, so the least I could do was give him a few minutes. I calmly ate my grilled cheese sandwich, now lukewarm and a little rubbery, and waited for his brain to remember how to make words.

It took a moment, but he got there.

"I beg your fucking pardon?" he demanded.

I swallowed my food. "I think it's the *intimacy* of sex I have a problem with. I have trouble staying in my body when someone else is…you know…*also* in my body. It feels like a threat. But with you, it's…I don't know. Not as bad."

He gave me a slow, stunned blink. "*Not as bad?*"

I nodded. "Because we're friends. But more importantly, I think it could get better. With everyone else, it only got worse. I think I could get used to you."

"Get used to me...being inside you, you mean?" His eyebrows went up and his eyes did that crinkly thing they did when he was amused. "If you don't quit sweet-talking me, duchess, I'm going to fall in love with you."

He was teasing me. I knew that. What I didn't know was whether his teasing meant he was trying to let me down easy. Maybe he didn't want to teach me how to orgasm with him. That hadn't occurred to me last night, with the words *Heaven, Hannah. You feel like heaven* ringing in my ears.

"I know it seems ridiculous, but I really think it could work," I said. "The first time, I didn't think I could do it with you in the room, watching me. But I did. And the next time, at your cabin..." I bit my lip, remembering. "It was easier."

When I peeked up at him, I found him watching me intently.

"What if it doesn't get easier?" he asked. "What if you don't get there with me?"

I *had* actually considered that last night. In all honesty, it was a pretty likely scenario. "Don't worry about that."

"Duchess, you just asked me to teach you how to orgasm. I kind of *have* to worry about it. I don't like to fail."

I huffed. "You can't possibly fail."

"Why's that?"

I crossed my arms over my chest and refused to meet his gaze. "I don't want to tell you. It will only feed this whole delusion you have about your magic dick."

"Well, now you have to tell me. I'm a broken man, Hannah. My delusions are all I have left."

He was doing that thing again, where he told the truth but made it sound like a joke. It made my chest hurt when he did that. It also made it impossible for me to do anything but give him what he wanted.

I glared at him. "You can't fail because even if it doesn't work, it's still the best sex I ever had."

He leaned forward, cupping his ear like he hadn't heard me. "Come again?"

My glare was withering. "Let's not get ahead of ourselves, shall we? See if you can make me come once before we worry about coming again."

He burst out laughing. "Damn, duchess. Only you would proposition a man and insult him in the same breath."

"So will you do it or not?" I asked.

"Will I have lots and lots of sex with the world's most exasperating and beautiful librarian, with a goal to make you come as often as possible, but even if it doesn't work out, provide you with the best sex of your life, courtesy of my magic dick?" He stroked his chin thoughtfully. "Yes, I believe I can oblige you, duchess."

I rolled my eyes. "Thank you."

"You know, that would look great embroidered on a pillow, if you're ever in the mood to *really* thank me for my services." He held up his hands as if holding an imaginary pillow between them. "Zack Hale's magic dick gave me the best sex of my life."

"I'm already regretting this."

Under the table, his legs captured mine. His gaze turned heated. "No, you're not."

There was a promise in that look, of all the things he would do to me. I wanted those things. "No, I'm not," I agreed.

He released my leg and leaned back, smiling. "You know, you looked so serious when I walked in here. I really thought you were going to give me bad news about Hurricane Red."

"Hurricane Red!" My eyes widened as I remembered. "I *do* have news. Not bad news," I added hastily when his face paled. Literally paled. Zack might honestly be the most sentimental man of my acquaintance. "Good news. Jeremiah found him. There's an auction three hours west of here on Saturday. Four hundred and thirty-seven horses, most of them quarter horses from ranches and rodeos. Hurricane Red is number three hundred sixty-eight."

13

HANNAH

After meeting Zack for lunch, I was back on solid footing. I had a *plan*. A pretty list of bullet points to give structure to this nebulous mess inside me that giddily kicked its feet every time Zack was in eyesight.

Step 1: Have lots of sex with Zack.

Step 2: Have orgasm(s) with Zack.

Step 3: Be normal.

Step 4: Live happily ever after.

And because Zack didn't strike me as the kind to make his own list, I made one for him:

Step 1: Rescue Hurricane Red

Step 2: …

Step 3: Live happily ever after.

Obviously, Step 2 needed some work. I suspected it would take more than saving Hurricane Red from slaughter to get Zack his happily ever after. What, I didn't know. Maybe he was perfectly happy already. But when I thought about the look on his face when he said he hadn't planned on surviving the rodeo, I doubted it. The man was in crisis, even if he didn't know it.

Hopefully, saving Hurricane Red would be the first step to get him out of it.

"I brought snacks," I said as I tossed my bag on the floor of Zack's truck, settled my travel mug of tea in the cupholder, and climbed into the passenger seat. He shut the door behind me and limped around the hood to the driver's side. My brow furrowed as he carefully eased behind the wheel. "Are you all right?"

He put the truck in reverse and buckled himself in with one hand while he steered us down my driveway with the other. Dang it, why was that hot? He was just so *competent*.

"I'm fine," he said. "I get a little stiff in the mornings, that's all."

I took a good look at him—or tried to, anyway. With the brim of his ball cap pulled low, it was hard to see his face. But even in the shadows, I could see the purple half-moons under his eyes and his signature half-smirk, half-smile was nowhere to be seen. Even looking like he hadn't slept in a week, he was still handsome as ever.

"Rough night?" I asked.

"All my nights are rough, duchess." His smirk came out of hiding briefly.

I pushed up my glasses. "Is that an innuendo or a fact?" I asked sternly, despite the fact that his smirk made me want to crawl into his lap and purr like Evie.

He chuckled softly. "Both."

"Oh." I stared straight ahead. I refused to ask him what he meant by that. He could spend his nights however he wanted. We weren't dating. We were...having intercourse for instructional purposes. He had never promised to be exclusive, and it hadn't even occurred to me to ask. "Well, I hope you stayed safe," I said stiffly.

There was a long pause during which I refused to look at him for fear he would see right through me to the petty jealousy inside.

Then he laughed again. "I was alone last night, which you know damn well, Hannah Bell, because you weren't with me." He said it like there was no other option, like it was me or no one. I didn't know what to make of that. "Nights are rough because everything hurts and itches too much to fall asleep, but sleep is what I need most to heal. And even if I take a painkiller, my brain won't shut up anyway. What snacks did you bring?"

I wanted to know more about the things that kept him up at night, but he clearly wanted the conversation to be over. "Egg white muffins." I dug into my bag and pulled out the container. I had noticed he liked to stick to healthy food, and I doubted we'd find much of that on the road. "I baked them this morning, so they're still warm. Did you eat breakfast?"

"Just coffee."

I popped off the top and offered him the open container. He grabbed one, wolfed it down in two bites, and then grabbed another.

"Thanks," he said. "These are great."

"I also brought red vines. But those are more of an afternoon snack for the way back."

My e-reader and latest embroidery project was also in the bag, just in case Zack wasn't in the mood for conversation or we ran out of things to say. It turned out to be unnecessary. Sometimes we talked, sometimes we were quiet, but it never felt awkward.

I had never been to an auction before, but it was about what I expected. There were two long barns lined with stalls much smaller than what I'd seen at Lodestar Ranch. The horses looked fairly well cared for, from what I could tell, which gave me hope that Hurricane Red hadn't been mistreated. I had the auction catalog with me, but it didn't tell me where he was being held.

"He's number three hundred sixty-eight," I reminded Zack as we walked down the aisle of the first barn. I frowned. There were a lot of stalls here, but not *that* many. "The stalls are numbered in order, but there can't be more than seventy here."

"We won't find him in the barns, Hannah," Zack said quietly. He took my hand and walked faster. "These are the saddle stock, the horses sold for riding. He'll be in one of the pens. That's where they keep the horses sold by the pound."

I flinched. *By the pound.* I felt sick. "Oh."

He glanced down at me, then pulled me to a stop. "They're usually in good condition. No open sores, decent weight to them. Unhealthy horses don't sell well, not even for dog food. But we're leaving here with only one horse, so if it's too much for you knowing where the others are going, you can wait by the truck. I'll text you when I have him."

I adjusted my glasses and squared my shoulders. "It's not too much for me, Zack. There's suffering in this world and pretending it doesn't exist won't change that. If the most we can do is acknowledge it and save one horse, then all right. Today that will be enough."

He studied me for a moment, then nodded. "All right, then, Hannah Bell. Let's go do the bare minimum."

I stared up at this man who had said yes to helping me with the rodeo when no one else would, who had thrown himself into getting dressed in sixty seconds like it was an Olympic event, who refused to let me fake a single thing, who had said *every horse, every ride.*

"Zack Hale, you've never done the bare minimum in your entire life," I declared.

He blinked down at me in surprise, and then his lips crooked in that half-smile, half-smirk that made me simultaneously want to smack him and kiss him. "Then maybe it's time to start."

I couldn't help but laugh as he took hold of my hand again, but my laughter faded as we came to the large, metal-railed pens full of stock horses.

"There must be a hundred horses here," I said quietly. A hundred horses bound for slaughter.

"Must be." He frowned as he surveyed the pens. "There should be more. The catalog lists over four hundred horses for sale, and less than a hundred of those are saddle stock. This can't be the rest of them."

"Maybe some were sold already," I suggested.

"The slaughter-bound horses normally don't get auctioned off until early afternoon," Zack said distractedly as he looked around. "The transporters prefer to load them up in the evening and drive all night. People don't like to see trucks of horses being transported like chickens or pigs. Better to do it in the dark."

I nodded. All animals deserved humane treatment, but Americans felt a special kind of way about horses. It was part of our lore. That was why horses couldn't be slaughtered in the United States. They had to be taken to Canada or Mexico.

"I hate that," I said.

He looked at me questioningly.

"I hate that we didn't solve the problem, we just put it where we don't have to look at it anymore," I explained.

He wrapped one arm around my shoulders and rolled me against his body. "I know, Hannah." He pressed his lips against my forehead. "I hate it, too."

We searched through the people milling about until we found a man who seemed to be in charge.

"Who are you looking for?" he asked.

"Three hundred sixty-eight." I pointed to his description in the catalog. "This one."

The man shook his head. "That lot has been sold already. The driver loaded them up an hour ago."

14

ZACK

"**F**uck!" I roared. "Fuck!"

Hot rage clawed underneath my skin. My vision turned hazy at the edges, the animals and people blurring together like a kaleidoscope. I wanted to rip it all apart with my bare hands. The people, the animals, the auction, the world. Myself, most of all.

I kicked at the ground, sending a cloud of dust and gravel into the air. People shouted; I didn't care. I did it again. I threw my hat on the ground, and then I kicked that, too.

There was a light touch on my shoulder and then Hannah's soft voice cut through the storm. "Zack."

"What?" I shouted, rounding on her, my fists clenched.

"Come with me."

She didn't give me a chance to say no before wrapping my elbow in her small hand and tugging me along with her. I could have shaken her off, but even furious as I was, there wasn't a single part of me that didn't want her touch, so instead I followed her like a dog on a leash.

Hurricane Red was gone. Loaded up on some single deck trailer crammed full of other horses, most of which he probably hated, because Red hated most horses. Terrified and pissed as hell. Whether he was heading to Canada or Mexico, he was in for at least a solid twenty-four hours of misery. He wouldn't be allowed off to stretch his legs or piss. He wouldn't be given any food or water, because what was the point? He would be dead soon, anyway.

It would have been kinder for me to put a bullet between his eyes than put him through the slaughterhouse pipeline.

"Give me your keys, Zack." Hannah held out her hand, palm up.

Somehow we had made it out of the auction grounds and to the parking lot without me being aware of it.

I dug the keys out of my pocket and tossed them to her, not trusting myself to put them into her hands. She fumbled them and huffed a little as she scooped them off the ground, then opened the driver's side door.

How was I supposed to go home without Hurricane Red?

I kicked the tire, and when that wasn't enough, I slammed my hand against the truck bed. "Fuck!"

She nudged and prodded me until I was seated inside and then shut the door. I gripped the steering wheel with both hands and then thumped my forehead down between them.

"I don't think I should drive yet," I muttered. "I need a minute."

She didn't answer, but I took her silence for agreement.

Shit. I tried to breathe. My heart was pounding like I had just taken an eight-second bronc ride.

It wasn't like I hadn't known about the dark side of rodeo. There was abuse, both of people and of animals. I knew washed-up animals sometimes ended up in slaughterhouses in Mexico and Canada. I hated it, but I didn't love rodeo less because of it, as crazy as that might sound. There wasn't a damn thing in this world that didn't have a dark side, and you couldn't let all that darkness push out the bright spots. What would be the point of living?

I could live with knowing rodeo wasn't perfect and doing my best to make it better where I could.

But knowing that Hurricane Red's last hours on this earth would be miserable, followed by a hellish death, and that it was my fault? I didn't know how to live with that.

Fucking hell.

"All right," I said. "Give me the keys."

My words were met with more silence.

I pushed off the steering wheel and stared at the empty passenger seat.

Hannah was gone.

I groaned and thumped my head against the seat rest, wishing I could knock some damned sense into myself. Of course Hannah was gone. She had witnessed a full-grown man have a meltdown. I felt sick when I remembered how I had kicked the dirt. How I had raised my voice at her with my hands in fists. Shit, had I scared her?

I bolted from the truck, my phone pressed to my ear. She didn't pick up. Fuck, fuck, fuck. There was no sign of her in the parking lot, so I started for the auction pens.

"Hey."

I whirled and found her behind me, cheeks flushed, breathing heavily. My knees damn near buckled with relief. Slowly I lowered the phone from my ear. "Hannah."

"Were you calling me?" she asked. "I figured that was you. I could feel my phone buzzing in my bag, but my hands were full." She waved two white paper bags. "Are you—"

She didn't get another word out. I wrapped my arms around her waist and hauled her against me. "I'm sorry, Hannah. I'm so sorry." I buried my face in the crook of her neck.

"For what?"

"For being a damn fool. For scaring you. I wouldn't have hurt you, I promise. But I'm sorry if it seemed like I might."

"I know. You didn't scare me, Zack." She had her arms around me, returning the hug as best she could with the bags in her hands. "You said you needed a minute, so I gave you a minute."

Oh. Right. I had said that.

I still didn't want to let go of her, though.

"What's in the bags?" I asked, pulling back, but keeping my hands on her hips.

"Lunch. Chicken strips and fries was the best I could do, but I'm starving and we've got a long drive ahead of us."

Three hours wasn't what I considered long, but I wasn't going to argue with her just because fried foods scared the shit out of me now. Anyway, I'd made her feel bad enough for one day. "Chicken strips and fries are my favorite." I grabbed the blanket I kept behind the seats. "You want to eat in the back?"

"Sure." She held up her arms. "Help me up?"

I boosted her into the truck bed and climbed in afterward with the blanket. I spread it out over the dust and dirt that had built up, since washing my truck was never high on my list of priorities, and we settled in for a picnic.

"How's your leg?" she asked, watching me try to get comfortable.

"Nothing worth complaining about." Because if I complained every time my leg or some other body part hurt, I'd never have time to do anything else.

"How do you think it would feel after a fourteen-hour road trip?"

I paused, considering her. "Why do I get the feeling you have a reason for asking me that?"

"Because I do." She pushed up her glasses. "I asked around. Hurricane Red and the others that were bought for slaughter are being transported by Reliable Trucking. They're headed to Canada, not Mexico."

I closed my eyes. I wasn't sure I wanted to know this. The details didn't change anything. Canada or Mexico, Hurricane Red was still going to die.

"So, anyway," Hannah continued. "If they're going to Canada from here, then Calgary is the most likely slaughterhouse, which means that they'll unload the horses at Shelby, Montana, where there's a feedlot and horse assembly center."

"What the hell is a horse assembly center—no, you know what? Never mind." My appetite gone, I pulled the brim of my hat down over my eyes. "Why are you telling me all this?"

"Because Shelby is fourteen hours from here."

I tilted my head up just enough to squint at her from under my hat. "Hannah."

"No, listen." She popped a fry into her mouth, wiped her fingers on a napkin, and pulled out her phone. "I had some time to kill while I was in line for our food, and I took notes. It's a fifteen-hour drive, but if you're hauling horses in a long trailer, it probably takes longer because you're driving slower. RT left here with Hurricane Red less than an hour ago. There are laws about how many hours truckers can work, and how long they can drive. A workday is no more than fourteen hours, and they can only spend eleven of those hours driving, and that's only if the driver has had a full ten-hour rest before he starts working."

Jesus. "How did you learn all this?"

Her spine snapped straight like I had offended her. "I am a *librarian*, Zack. Finding information is what I *do*."

Why was that so fucking hot? I grinned at her. "Damn, duchess. I'm impressed."

"Good," she said tartly. "You should be."

"I am," I assured her. "But I don't see why trucking laws matter to Hurricane Red. He's headed to a slaughterhouse in Canada, and even if the driver gets to stop for a ten-hour rest, the horses don't get unloaded until they reach their final destination."

"That's awful. You would think animal welfare laws would prevent that, even for animals sent to slaughter. Cruelty is cruelty." She frowned. "But my point is that it's only fourteen hours over two days, and there's no way RT can get there before us, because his work day started a few hours before he got on the road with the horses, and he can't drive more than eleven hours, anyway. When he gets to the horse assembly center, we'll be there waiting, and we can just buy Hurricane Red back or something."

What the hell was she telling me right now? She couldn't mean—

"It's not too late to save him." She leaned forward and grabbed my hand. "We can do this."

I stared down at our hands. "It's fourteen hours there and back. That's nearly thirty hours. Four days of driving eight-hour shifts, at least. There could be accidents and delays that make the drive longer. You really want to do this?"

"I already asked someone to cover my Monday and

Tuesday shifts at the library, and Essie said she'd feed my cats. And, look." She showed me her phone screen. "I've got our route mapped out. We'll go right by Yellowstone National Park, so even though it's a long drive, at least it will be beautiful."

Goddamn, this woman. She'd planned all this while I was throwing a tantrum? I'd shown her all my big, messy feelings and she hadn't run away screaming. She'd done *this*.

I swallowed hard. "Why? I mean, you don't have to do this. I could bring you home first."

"That would add at least another three hours to the drive," she argued. "Anyway, you're going to want to take breaks. We'll get there much faster if we take turns driving. I know you could do it alone, but why would you want to?"

I don't want to. Why would I want to spend fourteen hours alone with my thoughts when I could have Hannah with me instead?

She nudged my boot with her own. "We're friends, remember? Isn't this what friends do?"

I smiled wryly. "I have lots of friends. I'm not sure any of them would volunteer to drop everything and drive to Canada to save a horse."

"Well, then, you've never had a friend like me before," she said. *Ain't that the truth.* "But today's your lucky day, because you do now."

She kept using that word. *Friend.* I laughed, even though I still wasn't sure how I felt about it.

"Come on, Zack." She tugged at my hand. "Let's go get your horse."

15

HANNAH

JAMES:

The quarantine stall is all ready for Hurricane Red. He'll have a small paddock to himself, too.

JANIE:

I'm already a registered volunteer at the library, so I offered to help out with the after-school programs while you're gone. We've got you covered.

ESSIE:

All 5(!) cats are alive and accounted for. Brax is cuddling the little one and it's so ridiculously cute I've decided to let him put a baby in me.

CHLOE

You know, as long as you're out there saving one horse, you might as well ride a cowboy and save a few more.

The plan was to get in as many hours today as we could tolerate, eight hours being the minimum, and having a shorter drive tomorrow. Missing Hurricane Red by a mere half-hour had made Zack furious and determined to not let it happen again. Zack took the first shift. We'd switch when we needed gas.

We hadn't been on the highway for more than fifteen minutes when my brother called. Dang it. I swallowed a groan. I should have called him already. "Do you mind if I answer it? Jeremiah gets worried if I don't pick up." Worried was an understatement.

"Nah, go ahead."

My phone was plugged into the dashboard so we could use the map, so I hit accept on the screen and before I could get a single word out, Jeremiah's voice boomed through the speakers.

"Where are you headed, Hannah?"

I rolled my eyes. "Hello to you, too, Jay."

He sighed heavily and I had the feeling he was raking his hand through his hair and pulling on it. He tended to do that a lot in our conversations. "Hello, Hannah. Where are you headed?"

"Well...remember how I told you I'd be taking a road trip today to pick up that horse I told you about? It turns out, our road trip is going to take a little longer than I thought."

"What happened?"

"He was gone when we got here. People say Reliable Trucking is taking him to Canada."

For a moment, Jeremiah didn't say anything, but I could hear him typing. Then he said, "Got him. He just left the weigh station on the border of Utah. You going after him?"

I glanced at Zack, who was looking back at me with raised eyebrows. "Yeah, we're going after him."

"I'll see what I can hear on the CB radio, but my guess is he's headed to Shelby, Montana."

"That's what I figured, too," I said. "We should make it there tomorrow, early afternoon."

There was another pause. "We meaning yourself and Mr. Zachary William Hale?" He said it pleasantly enough, but there was no mistaking the underlying threat. I cringed. I had never told Jeremiah Zack's full name. I hadn't known it myself.

Apparently Zack heard it, too, because his eyes narrowed on my phone. "That's right. Hannah's with me." His voice was every bit as pleasant as Jeremiah's, and every bit as dangerous.

I rolled my eyes so hard they nearly fell out the back of my head. *Men.* Honestly.

"You're taking U.S. 191?" Jeremiah asked, like he hadn't heard him.

"Yes," I sighed, because he already knew that. "One

ninety-one to I-15 North. It will take us through Utah and Idaho, then up into Montana. Fourteen hours, if everything goes all right."

There was more typing. "Take MT-3 back to Aspen Springs. It's the same mileage, give or take twenty. You'll go through Wyoming. Stop at Mercy River, spend the night here at the ranch. I'll see you then."

He disconnected before I could agree...or argue.

I sighed and looked at Zack. "Do you mind? My brother's place is in Wyoming. Mercy River Ranch."

"I don't have a problem with that. If you want to stop and visit your brother, that's what we'll do."

I chewed my lip. "I do want to see my brother. But he's...protective."

Zack's mouth quirked. "So I gathered. When did he run the background check on me?"

"Argh." I covered my face with my hands and groaned into them. I should have known Jeremiah would look into Zack when I told him he was helping me with rodeo. "Probably when I asked him to help us find Hurricane Red. I'm sorry. I should have warned you. He has a tendency to run checks on anyone I spend a lot of time with."

He pondered that for a moment, then shrugged. "I'm not proud of everything I've done, but I've got nothing to hide."

I stared out the window. "He has a tracker on my phone. That's why he called. He expected me to be heading east back to Aspen Springs, but instead I was going north."

"He might be taking his big brother duties a little too far. Then again, if I was responsible for something precious, I might take it too far, too," Zack said.

Heat suffused my entire body. He thought I was precious? Or maybe he didn't mean *me*. He meant sisters. Family. That made more sense.

"You can turn off the tracker, you know," he said.

"If I turned it off, he'd find another way." I shrugged. "It doesn't really bother me. I'm used to it. Sometimes I even like it. It makes me feel safe. And he's never crossed a line of telling me where I can and can't go, even when he doesn't like it."

"He's the one who came and got you? From...the compound?"

I nodded. "Honestly, I don't think he's ever recovered from that. He hadn't thought they'd marry me off so young. He was almost fifteen when he was sent away, and I was only seven. He managed to get me a letter a couple years after that, when I was twelve, telling me where he'd settled and how to reach him if I needed anything. But it never occurred to me to leave until they told me I had to marry. Most women didn't marry until they were seventeen or eighteen."

Zack's jaw clenched so tight a muscle popped. "That's still too young. Teenagers have no business getting married and having babies. Why did they marry you at fourteen?"

I pulled my embroidery out of my bag. My hands shook slightly as I took up my needle and pushed it through the resisting linen. "My uncle told me I was tempting other boys into sin. I was too pretty, he said. My hair attracted too much attention. I needed a husband to keep me from leading other boys to hell."

The silence was deafening. I chanced a look at him and found him glaring out the windshield, both hands on the steering wheel with a white-knuckled grip.

"Hannah," he said at last. "That's bullshit. You know that's bullshit, right?"

"I know." I stabbed another stitch. "Or at least I try to. Some days are harder than others."

FIVE HOURS INTO OUR DRIVE, we stopped for provisions at a small town in northern Utah just shy of the Idaho border. It had dawned on us that we were embarking on a four-or-five-day trip with nothing but the clothes on our backs and the snacks in my purse. Zack kept an overnight bag in his truck with an extra pair of clothes and a toothbrush, but I had nothing. At the very least, I would need clean underwear and a toothbrush.

We pulled up to a store that would have everything we needed. I told him I'd meet him at the register so we could both find our personal items without the other looking over our shoulder. I was already feeling scraped raw from the events and conversations of the day, and we still had to make it through the night together. It was too much. I had never been alone for more than ten minutes growing up. After I left the compound, Jeremiah gave me plenty of space while he worked, and I often found myself alone for hours at a time. I grew to relish the time to myself.

Right now, I needed a moment without Zack's outsized presence taking up all the oxygen in my brain.

I started in the beauty aisle and grabbed a travel set of a toothbrush and toothpaste, travel-sized bottles of hair products and body wash, and deodorant. Even though it was stupid, I threw a disposable razor in the basket, too. No one was going to see my unshaved legs, but then again, that was true almost every night of the week. I shaved because I liked the feeling of smooth skin, not because a man was going to touch me.

And then it suddenly occurred to me that in all probability, a man *was* going to touch me, actually.

Zack.

I had never gone on vacation with a boyfriend or spent a weekend away. I had never even spent two nights in a row with him. That was my choice; I liked my personal space, and towards the end of those relationships, I tended to need even more of it.

And now I was going to spend three nights in a row with a man who was *not* my boyfriend but probably did expect sex since I had very deliberately propositioned him. What was the protocol here? Would we share a hotel room? Was I supposed to buy condoms? What about sexy underwear?

I stared at the rows of condoms. I couldn't possibly be expected to handle that. There were too many variations.

"Hannah, what are you doing?" Zack asked behind me.

I didn't turn around, just kept staring at those darn condoms. "Having a nervous breakdown, obviously."

"Obviously." The inside of his bicep grazed my cheek as he reached over my shoulder and grabbed a box. "Size large. The regular size tends to break for me. Can't have mini Zacks and Hannahs running around, can we?"

My brain short circuited. I had seen his baby pictures. I knew exactly how cute little Zacks would be. "Um...no?"

His soft laugh gusted against the crown of my head. He dropped the box in his own basket and turned me around to face him. "What's got you nervous, duchess?"

I frowned at my basket. "I don't know the rules. In most romantic relationships, going away for the weekend is a big step. But you and I...this isn't that kind of relationship, and we're not going away together on *purpose*. It's for a horse. So, what are the rules? Do we share a room? Do we..." My gaze fell on the condoms in his basket. "Well, I guess you already answered that question."

"Hannah, listen to me." He tilted my chin up with his index finger. "There's only one rule. You say yes when you want to say yes, and no when you want to say no. That's it. As for sharing a room, I'm in favor of the option that keeps your body as close to mine as possible, but if you want a door between us, then I'll accept that without much fuss."

I flushed, thinking about long hours with our bodies close together. "It would be cheaper to share a room."

"Don't worry about that. You're not paying for a damn thing on this trip, Hannah, and I don't want to hear any arguments about that. Now, what else do you need? We should get back on the road."

I peered into his basket. "You're done already?"

"I've got a t-shirt, some underwear, a razor, and condoms. I'm good to go."

"I haven't gotten clothes yet," I admitted. I'd been too busy freaking out over the condoms, which was ridiculous. I'd never bought condoms before, but I'd always insisted on using them, so it wasn't like it was anything new to me. There was no reason to treat this trip as anything but what it was. It didn't have to *mean* something just because we were sharing a hotel room and having sex.

"Then let's go do that." He nudged my shoulders in the direction of women's clothing.

With a sigh, I turned my attention to the arduous process of finding something to wear. Everything here was so far out of my comfort zone. Jeans, short skirts, tops meant to entice rather than hide. The winter sweaters had been banished, and it was all summer clothes now.

I tossed a five-pack of black cotton underwear and a six-pack of socks into my basket and then scooped up two pairs of jeans in different sizes to see what would fit.

"I'm going to try these on," I said, holding up the jeans. "Can you watch my basket?"

With a nod, he took my basket from me, and I disappeared into the dressing room. Both pairs fit well enough. The smaller size clung to my thighs and butt. The larger size didn't cling so much, but the waist was loose enough that they rode lower on my hips. I tried to imagine myself walking around, wearing one or the other, and realized I wasn't going to feel comfortable in either, so I eenie-meenie-minie-mo'ed it and left the loser behind in the dressing room.

Zack was waiting for me, but he wasn't waiting alone. A woman was with him, looking up at him with surprised delight like she had discovered the Hope Diamond in the clearance bin. He smiled down at her, no doubt noticing the ample cleavage being served up by her low-cut tank top. I couldn't blame her for serving and I couldn't blame him for looking. Her breasts were fabulous, and, unlike me, she seemed to be perfectly comfortable in her own skin.

Feeling bad about myself—and feeling bad about feeling bad, because I thought I'd made peace with all this a long time ago—I pretended I didn't see them and turned toward the t-shirts. Two should be enough. How dirty could I really get sitting in a truck all day?

"Hannah." Zack's voice boomed across the women's section. "Over here."

Rats. Now I was going to have to stand next to her. Like my self-esteem hadn't suffered enough already.

Heaving a sigh, I added a plain black t-shirt and a plain pink t-shirt to the jeans, then turned to face my doom. The woman watched me approach with a perplexed expression.

"This is the woman you're shopping with?" she asked.

"That's right," Zack confirmed, his eyes crinkling as he looped an arm around my waist and pulled me into his side. "Toss your stuff in, duchess. Let's get this show on the road."

The woman eyed me head to toe, her bafflement only increasing, then gave a small shake of her head. "Lucky."

Zack squeezed my hip. "Don't I know it," he said, like he had *no idea* she meant *I* was the lucky one. He tipped the brim of his hat to her. "Thanks for your help."

Oh, I just *bet* she was helpful. Not that I blamed her.

I saw her take one last lingering, wistful look at him as he steered me toward the registers. I didn't blame her for that, either.

16

ZACK

"I can't leave you alone for five minutes," Hannah said sourly as we left the store with our supplies.

I smirked. She sure was cute when she was jealous. And jealous was exactly what she was, even though she'd deny it with her dying breath. I hadn't done it on purpose, but I wasn't above enjoying the results. "Can I help it if women like to talk to me?"

"No," she sighed. "You can't. You're a rake."

I took that in stride. Hannah was always speaking metaphorically, and I only ever understood half of it. "I am not a rake. If I'm any kind of tool, it's a plow."

"No, I mean—" She broke off with a laugh as she got the joke. I grinned, pleased with myself. "Like in a historical romance novel. A rake is a man who is popular with women and sleeps around. You're a rake and I'm a wallflower. Wallflowers are invisible."

Now I knew what she was talking about, thanks to the

books I'd perused on her shelf. I took her bag and slid it with mine in the narrow space behind our seats in the truck. "Good."

She wrinkled her nose. "Good?"

"Yeah. Good." I leaned one arm on the passenger door and waved her inside. "Don't you want to be the wall-flower? She's smart. Funny. Kind. And in the end, she tames the rake and lives happily ever after as a duchess." I narrowed my eyes at the back of her head. "Because all those rakes are also dukes, I've noticed."

She froze halfway into the truck. Slowly she stepped back down and turned to face me. Her eyes were round with surprise. "You read my books."

"Skimmed them," I corrected. Then I grinned. "Except for the good parts. I took my time with those."

Her cheeks flushed as she caught my meaning.

I caged her in, my arms braced against the truck on either side of her. "I see you, Hannah. I've always seen you, no matter who else is in the room. Why do you think I call you duchess?"

She gaped at me, speechless, her blue eyes wide. Her glasses slid down her nose. When she made no move to rectify that, I indulged myself and did it for her. She blinked.

I circled her waist with my hands and lifted her into the truck. "Up you go, honey."

By the time I had buckled myself behind the wheel, she'd recovered her powers of speech and promptly used them to hurt my feelings.

"I've changed my mind," she said, prim and proper as you please. "You *are* a plow."

WE MADE it through Idaho and a good chunk of Montana before we decided to call it quits for the night in Butte. Letting her park the truck with the horse trailer attached at the hotel was a harrowing experience, but as she killed the engine, she rewarded me for my patience.

"One room," she said.

Thank god. I would have kept my word and not raised a fuss if she wanted separate rooms, but I would have been pretty sulky about it. "Yes, ma'am."

Our room was nice enough. Nothing fancy, but it was clean and the hum of the air conditioner drowned out the street noise outside. After a quick shower—taken separately—we were both refreshed and wide awake.

"Want to get a drink to unwind?" I suggested. We had grabbed fast food for dinner two hours ago, but tired as I was from our long drive, my brain wasn't ready to shut off yet. "There's a country-western bar next door to the hotel. That might be fun."

"All right. I'll go change." Still wrapped in her towel, she grabbed the plastic bag with her new stuff and disappeared into the bathroom.

I chuckled under my breath. Her modesty was pointless. The shape of her naked body was already imprinted on my brain.

I pulled on fresh underwear, my old jeans, new socks, and the new gray henley I had bought. It took Hannah a little longer, but when she finally emerged from the bathroom, I damn near swallowed my tongue.

Good fucking god.

Her new jeans hung low enough on her waist that I could see the tiniest crest of her hip bones. Her pink tee-shirt was fitted and cropped. Between the hem of her tee-shirt and the waistband of her jeans was a solid two inches of creamy pale skin that made my mouth water. Her damp hair was down in a braid instead of her usual bun.

"I didn't know it was a crop top." She pulled at the hem, but it didn't do her any good. "Maybe I should wear my sweater."

I didn't know how I felt about that, mostly because I couldn't get a read on how *she* felt about that. I dragged my eyes up from her tempting belly. "Wear whatever makes you comfortable."

She frowned, looking down at herself. "I want to be comfortable in *this*."

"Well, what's wrong with it? You look great. If you're worried about being cold, bring your sweater."

She pulled at her shirt again. When that didn't work, she tugged up her jeans, which slid right back down again. She huffed in annoyance. "What if someone says something?"

My eyebrows went up. "What's someone going to say?"

"I don't know." She pulled her braid over her shoulder and fiddled with the end of it, like she could hide herself behind it. "Something."

The look on her face made my chest feel spiky. Because once upon a time, someone *had* said something to her. Her own fucking uncle. He had made her feel like shit, like it was her fault if a boy didn't keep his hands to himself or got a boner in church, and I sure as hell wasn't going to let something like that happen again.

"Duchess, you can walk into that bar in nothing but your underwear and a smile, if that's what makes you happy. Wear whatever you want." I wrapped her braid around my fist and used it to tug her head back, forcing her to look at me. "I'm your wild cowboy, remember? I know how to brawl."

HANNAH

There was live music playing when we entered the bar, a country tune that we had heard on the radio five times at least. I sang the words under my breath, and then I caught Zack doing the same thing.

We both laughed and then he said, "Booth or bar?"

I looked around. Half the room was tables and booths. The other half was open space for dancing. Stretching between the two was the bar, encircled by red-cushioned bar stools.

"Booth," I said.

No one would notice me or my crop top there. I wouldn't get to people watch, though. If I had been in my regular clothes, I would have chosen the bar. Someone might have looked at me funny, or asked if I was Amish, but I never cared about that.

So why did I care now?

They were still living rent-free inside my head. Their

rules, their beliefs, their morals. I didn't agree with any of it, but here I was, letting them dictate my choices all these years later.

"Bar," I said.

We claimed two stools next to each other. A man on my left gave me a friendly smile and I returned it politely before turning away.

"Two tequila shots," Zack told the bartender, then bumped his shoulder against mine. "For courage."

"I've never done a shot," I admitted as the bartender placed the clear liquid in front of me. Not for any particular reason. It just never came up. I studied too much to party in college, and when I went to bars or dinners with friends, no one ever did shots.

"The idea is to get it down in one swallow, but if you can't manage it, just drink it like you would anything else." He tossed his back to demonstrate. It looked smooth and easy and...sexual in a way I couldn't quite put my finger on. But then, everything Zack did looked sexual. The man was made for sin.

"All right." I eyed the shot glass. It really wasn't all that much. "I can do that."

I brought it to my lips, paused, then tilted my head back and opened my mouth. It took two swallows, and lord, did it burn, but when I slammed my glass down on the bar, I looked up to see Zack grinning at me.

"How'd that feel?" he asked.

I considered. "Warm," I said.

He laughed. His phone buzzed in his pocket and he

pulled it out, frowned at the screen, and looked at me. "It's my dad. Are you okay here for a minute if I take it outside? I'll keep it short."

"I'm okay," I assured him.

He squeezed my shoulder and disappeared into the throng.

"You and your boyfriend from out of town?" the man next to me asked.

"He's not my boyfriend," I said automatically, like that was the important part, and dodged the question of where we were from.

I loved eavesdropping on conversations and imagining the lives of strangers but actually talking to people I didn't know made me nervous. Another residual gift from my childhood. It had been drilled into us that strangers were very bad things. Living with Jeremiah hadn't dispelled me of that notion.

But Zack would be back any second. How much trouble could I really get into simply by being nice?

"It's my first time in Montana," I offered. "You have a beautiful state."

He grinned. "Thank you kindly." He told me his name and I promptly forgot it. "I see you tapping your foot there. How about a dance?"

I looked to where people were laughing and stomping in rows. How was it they all knew the moves? Did they learn through osmosis or something? "I don't know this one."

"That doesn't matter. It's easy. You'll catch on quick."

He signaled the bartender. "Two shots of tequila." The bartender poured the shots, and he lifted his to his lips. "I don't know if this will help you learn the steps, but it will make it more fun."

The tequila burned less this time.

He helped me off my barstool and plopped his cowboy hat on my head. "Let's go make a cowgirl out of you, sugar."

"Oh, I don't fucking think so," Zack said pleasantly, coming up behind me.

"He means a dance," I explained, smiling up at him. He looked back down at me and his lips quirked. My stomach felt warm. "I'm not actually going to ride a horse."

The man smirked. "Not a horse, no."

"Again," Zack said, "I don't fucking think so." He took the hat from my head and handed it over. "I'll thank you to keep your hat to yourself. And anything else you plan on leaving here with."

The man held up his hands. "Hey, man, she said you weren't together. I wasn't trying to make a move on your girl."

Zack tugged on my braid to get my attention. "You didn't tell him we're together?"

"Semantics." I looked up at him, feeling fuzzy. Was he mad? No, his eyes were doing that crinkly thing at me. "It's a different kind of together. I think there's been a misunderstanding."

"Is that so?" Zack's delicious mouth hooked up. "Then let me clarify things for you."

He grabbed my wrist and moved toward my midsection in a way that had me instinctively blocking him. My eyes widened as I realized what he meant to do. "You wouldn't," I sputtered.

I backed up a step and he followed. "Duchess, you're about to find out that when it comes to you, there's not much I wouldn't do."

And with that he dropped his shoulder to my belly and hauled me off my feet in a fireman's hold. I squealed and smacked his back as he strode out of the bar with me.

"What in the world do you think you're doing?" I demanded when he set me back on my feet on the sidewalk.

"Making a point." He gripped my chin with his thumb and forefinger. "I don't share, Hannah. Do you understand?"

My eyes darted back and forth as I searched his face, then I pulled free of his grip with a little shake of my head. "No, I do *not* understand, actually. You share all the time."

"The hell I do." He paused and his brow furrowed. "Wait, do you mean threesomes? I've done that, yeah."

Of course he had. I huffed and rolled my eyes. "No, I do not mean threesomes. I mean, you sleep with lots of women, and I think it's safe to assume they are not only sleeping with you, too. It's just sex, like what we're doing."

He laughed. "There's no comparison, duchess. Those other women? It was a one-time thing. Sometimes twice, but only by accident. They were past tense the second we put our clothes back on. So, no, it wasn't sharing when we both moved on to someone else the next night. It's different with us. You and I are still happening, and whether our clothes are on or off has nothing to do with it."

What was he saying? That this relationship *wasn't* only sex?

"Zack…" I trailed off and my mouth opened and shut a few times without saying anything. I blinked rapidly. "Are you saying you *are* my boyfriend?"

Uncertainty flickered across his expression, mirroring my own. Did I even want him to be my boyfriend? Wouldn't that ruin *everything*?

He leaned in. "You can call it whatever you want as long as you understand that I'm the only one in your bed." He took my hand. "Now, let's go, duchess. It's time for your first lesson."

18

ZACK

The second the elevator doors closed, I backed her against the metal wall and slammed my mouth to hers. Her head fell back on a gasp and I took full advantage, sliding my tongue against hers.

"Zack." She said my name like a plea and pressed her hips to mine.

I took that as an invitation and slid my thigh between her legs and shoved her up against the metal wall of the elevator. She swiveled her hips, grinding her pussy down on my thigh.

"What a terrible time to not be wearing a skirt," she muttered, right before grabbing fistfuls of shirt and dragging me in for another kiss.

I laughed against her mouth, my shoulders shaking. "I take back everything I've ever said about how you dress. I love your skirts."

The elevator dinged and a woman got on. I cupped the back of Hannah's head and tucked her out of view against my chest. "Ma'am," I said politely.

Her eyebrows went up, but then the elevator lurched and she lurched with it. "Oh," she said with obvious surprise. "I thought we were going down."

"I'm about to," I promised. Hannah made a muffled squeak into my shirt and I grinned.

The next floor was ours and I hauled a mortified Hannah out of there, still grinning at my joke.

I barely got us into our room before she launched herself at me.

She liked this, going fast. It was like she was trying to outrun her demons. Get to the finish line before they could stop her. But I had the feeling it wouldn't work any better this time than it had in the past, and if I let her try, we would end up in the same place as before, with her getting herself off. Which would be fine, if I thought for even a second that was what she wanted.

But it wasn't.

Running from her demons hadn't ever worked. She needed to turn and face them head on. We needed to try something different. And that meant slowing down.

So even though it was the last thing I wanted to do, I eased out of her embrace and took a step back.

"Do you want a glass of water?" I asked.

She stared at me with glazed eyes, her glasses askew, her hair mussed from me tangling my fingers in her braid.

Not pulling her back into my arms was the hardest thing I'd ever done. "Water?" she echoed.

I grabbed the two disposable cups from the tray next to the coffee maker and ripped off the plastic, then headed into the bathroom to fill them up at the sink. "Yeah, honey. Water. Gotta stay hydrated."

"Hydrated?" she repeated. It gave me deep satisfaction to know I had kissed her senseless.

She was standing right where I left her. She hadn't even righted her glasses. I handed her one of the cups with a smirk. "You're going to need it."

I downed the full cup in three long gulps. Hannah took a small sip from hers and then set it aside. She fixed her glasses. Her hands dove for my belt buckle, and I barely managed to shackle her wrists before she got it undone.

"No, darlin'." I pulled her in closer and brought her hands behind her back. "My pants need to stay on for now." Otherwise, I didn't have a prayer of slowing us down.

"How inconvenient."

My laugh ended on a groan as she dragged her lips up my throat and sucked at the pulse point beneath my jaw. I was such a sucker for neck kisses.

"What, exactly," she murmured between kisses, "are you planning to teach me? I promise I'll learn a lot faster with your jeans off."

I looped her arms around my neck. "Maybe, but this lesson is for both of us. My brain doesn't move as fast as yours, so we're going to be slow and thorough about this until I've learned every"—I kissed her right cheek—"inch"

—I kissed her left cheek—"of your body"—I finished with a peck on her nose.

She pulled her head back to glare at me. "Don't you try that *gee, shucks, I'm just a dumb cowboy* routine with me, Zack Hale. I know you're not dumb. You're just..." Her nose scrunched as she tried to figure out my game plan.

"I'm just what?" I goaded. "Making up reasons to spend all night worshipping your body? Damn right I am."

"We don't have all night. We have to sleep so we can drive tomorrow," she said, ever practical even when horny, and honestly, that only turned me on even more. It was just so *Hannah.*

"I'll take the first shift," I told her. "You can sleep while I drive."

I could tell from her mulish expression she was about to argue some nonsense about me needing more rest than her and insist on taking the first shift herself, so I pulled my shirt off over my head. The distraction worked like and charm and the only thing that came out of her mouth was a happy sigh. Her hands went to my abdomen like they were pulled there by six magnets attached to my muscles.

The hours I spent working out had always been less about vanity and more about keeping my body strong enough for the brutal rides I asked it to endure and then the healing and recovering from said rides, but damn. *Damn.* The way Hannah looked at me, like I was the answer to her every prayer, I would happily double my time at the gym and never complain.

"You've been driving me crazy all night in this outfit," I

muttered, tugging her t-shirt off. "I'm not used to seeing this much skin from you. It scrambled my brain. I have Hannah overload." I unhooked her bra and tossed it aside like it had personally offended me.

"*Zack*," she gasped as I circled her nipple with my tongue, then sucked it into my mouth.

I scooped her up and deposited her on the bed. "How am I supposed to behave in public when you're out here with bare arms?" I kissed my way down her arm, from her shoulder to her wrist, making her laugh breathlessly. "And your belly? Christ, darlin'." I kissed and sucked along the waistband of her jeans. "But you know what? I missed your ankles." I flicked open the fly.

"My...my ankles?" she stuttered, like maybe I had scrambled her brain as much as she had scrambled mine.

I tugged her jeans down her legs, tossed them aside, and knelt at her feet. "Your ankles. Wearing those skirts of yours, you have a tendency to flash me a little ankle now and then. Gets me hard every time."

She snorted. "You're ridiculous."

"I'm not ridiculous, Hannah. I'm fucking obsessed with you. There's not a single part of your body I don't want to explore. That little curl behind your ear, when you wear your hair up? I want to wrap it around my finger. That dimple above your elbow? I want to kiss it. Your pussy? I dream of tasting it. But your ankles, Hannah." I caught her foot with one hand and lifted it to my shoulder. "I spend so much time fantasizing about your ankles that even the devil thinks there's something wrong with me."

I traced the arch of her foot with my thumb, using enough pressure to make it feel good instead of ticklish, and circled her ankle bone. Then I followed that same path with my tongue. And then—because I had always been fascinated by the strong, delicate curve of her Achilles up to her calf, I bit her there.

"Zack!" She was up on her elbows, mouth agape as she stared down at me.

I kissed the top of her foot. "What?"

"I…" She rolled her lip between her teeth.

My eyebrows went up. "I don't think I've ever seen you flustered before."

"Yes, well, no one has ever bitten my foot before. So."

"Well, hold on to your tits, darlin', because I'm about to get the other one."

Hannah giggled and flopped back on the bed. I reached for her other foot and cupped the arch in my palm. She had one arm draped over her eyes, like she couldn't bear to watch what I was doing to her, but I could see her smile peeking out by her bicep while I lavished her right ankle with the same care and attention I had given the left.

She was relaxed. Happy. And judging from the way she whimpered when I bit her Achilles, still very much turned on. There was no fear right now. No desperation to get through it before her demons caught up with her.

It hit me suddenly, that maybe all this time she had been trying to get out of her head when what she really needed was to get in it and *stay* in it. It was my job to keep her focus centered on me and her. Nothing else existed here. I'd be damned if I would cede even an inch of that space to anything or any*one* else.

I kissed my way up the pale slope of her calf, did things to her knees that made her legs shake, and then sucked at the silky skin of her inner thigh. I left a mark there accidentally, but I didn't regret it. No one would see it, but I would know.

I pushed her thighs wide and her breath stuttered. Christ, her pussy...I thought I had it bad for her ankles, but that was nothing compared to what her pussy did to me. So fucking plump and pretty that my mouth watered. I wanted to do things that made no sense. Squeeze and bite and...

I lost my damn mind and bit my way down her labia, not hard enough to cause damage but sharp enough to make her gasp.

"Zack!" she yelped.

"Too much?" I nipped her again and she bucked. "Sorry, I don't know what...You know when something is so cute and sweet you want to squeeze the ever-fucking life out of it? Like a kitten or a puppy."

She blinked down at me. "You...you have cute aggression for my pussy?"

"Don't be so surprised. Have you seen your pussy?"

"No. I can't say that I have."

"Well, you should. Because it's..." I rubbed my thumb over the fading red marks left from my teeth and groaned. "God, I want..." I bit my lip, wishing I was biting *her*.

"More," she said. "Do it again."

I did it again, going up her other side in a line of love bites while she made sounds that made me push my hips against the mattress for relief.

But I didn't stop there. I lightly scraped my teeth over her clit and then licked it gently to ease the ache. She rocked her hips against my mouth, her hands twisted in the bedsheets, her belly tight with sudden tension. She wasn't close to coming yet, but she was at that point where she thought *maybe* she could, if she sprinted.

But I wasn't going to let her do that. I wasn't going to let her fail again.

I pulled back. "Hannah."

"Hm?" Her hips lifted in agitation, searching in vain for my mouth.

"What do you think about when you touch yourself?"

She lifted her head. "I...what?"

"What do you think about when you touch yourself?" I repeated. "Like when I left you alone for ten seconds and you got yourself off. What did you think about? Body parts? Celebrities?"

She stared at me like I had sprouted a second head. "You want to have this conversation *now*?"

I raised my eyebrows, waiting.

She swallowed. "Nothing. I...my mind goes blank. I don't imagine anyone or pretend anything. I just feel."

I considered that. "Well, then, I'm going to give you something to think about."

I licked from her entrance to her clit, sucked gently,

then licked down again to her entrance. Back up again, licking, sucking, swirling. Her hips caught the rhythm and followed it. She made incoherent sounds of desperate pleasure, and when she dug her nails into my forearms, I eased back.

"No—what—why—" she sputtered, panting. "Why do you keep stopping?"

I laughed darkly and lazily traced her clit with my finger. "Hannah Bell, are you telling me you've never been edged before?"

She let out a frustrated growl. "That depends. Is it edging when you're never allowed to fall off?"

"That doesn't sound like a good time to me." I blew gently on her clit.

"I don't care. Please, Zack," she begged. "Don't stop. I don't care if I stay on that edge forever. It feels so good."

I lowered my head. Fuck if I was going to leave her there, on the edge. Not this time.

I spread her open with both thumbs, baring every single bit of her to my hungry mouth, and sucked hard at her clit. Her hips canted in invitation and my tongue delved inside her entrance. I wrapped my arms around her thighs and hauled her closer to my mouth and drank from her like a holy chalice.

Suddenly everything flipped. I was the desperate one, desperate and aching, chasing a pleasure just out of reach. I was drunk on the scent of her arousal. The pleading sounds she made. The taste of her like honey on my tongue.

"Wait—oh, god, wait—" she sobbed, and I would have tried, but she gripped my skull with both hands and kept me on her and it was too late for both of us. I couldn't wait—

Oh, fuck, I couldn't wait—

Wetness flooded my mouth as her inner muscles clenched like a drumbeat. *Boom, boom, boom.* With each squeeze of her pussy around my tongue, my hips pushed harder against the mattress until I soaked my jeans the way she soaked my tongue.

I still didn't stop, not until she curled away from me and weakly pushed my head away from her sensitized body. I crawled up her flushed body, panting, and pressed a kiss to her damp forehead.

"You," she said, her voice thick and stunned. "*You.*"

"You," I said, every bit as stunned.

She didn't move a muscle, just laid there, completely boneless, watching through half-shut eyes as I took off my jeans and used a dry part of my boxers to clean myself off. By the time I tossed my clothes aside and got us both under the covers, she was fast asleep.

Hannah slept on her side facing me, our bodies interlocked like Tetris pieces. My arm around her neck, her cheek pressed to my chest, my hand on her hip, her leg draped over my thigh.

She snored a little.
Her hair tickled my chin.
My skin itched.
My leg ached.
My arm fell asleep.
I didn't move.

19

HANNAH

It would be a shame to let such a beautiful hard-on go to waste.

The morning sun peeked through the cheap hotel curtains that didn't quite stretch across the full window. I had awoken first to find that I had kicked off the blanket in favor of wrapping my limbs around Zack's warm body and using it for my personal space heater. Zack wasn't up yet, but his dick certainly was.

His beautiful, beautiful dick.

The jury was still out on whether it was magic, but as far as his tongue was concerned, I had my answer.

My god, the things that man had done to me with his tongue.

I shivered, remembering, and my stomach turned warm and melty. Before Zack, I had never gotten off with anything but my own fingers or a toy, and even then a man had never been in the same room with me.

But he had done it...with his tongue, of all things. I hadn't thought that was possible. Oral had always been a thing for me. I enjoyed the feel of it, but not the pressure. All that attention focused solely on my pussy with the expectation of a reward that I *wanted* to provide but couldn't quite seem to manage.

And wow, did men ever take that personally.

Like I was *ungrateful*.

So, I had been a little nervous when Zack settled between my thighs like he intended to be there for awhile. But he didn't seem at all concerned about how long it would take, or if I'd even get there at all. Like he was perfectly content to spend hours kissing me there and talking his Zack nonsense. It hadn't felt like pressure. Only pleasure.

Cute aggression. For my *pussy*. What on *earth*.

I shook my head, smiling, and then continued to peruse Zack's naked body in a way that would have been rude if he'd been awake—although I doubted very much that he would have minded. If there was one thing Zack Hale was *not*, it was shy about nudity, particularly his own. I loved that about him. It wasn't even a sexual thing for him. He was simply comfortable in his own skin.

Of course, his body was magnificent, scars and all, so that probably helped. My eyes lingered over the angry, fresh scar that swooped under his rib, the one from his spleen removal. That had altered the course of his life, something he still seemed to be struggling to come to grips with. I had noticed his aversion to unhealthy foods and tried to accommodate that as much as I could on this road trip, but with limited fast-food options, it wasn't easy.

But that seemed to be his personal hangup, although a common one among people who were recently spleen-less. From everything I'd read on the internet—I'd done an extensive search after he'd first told me at the rodeo—living without a spleen didn't mean the end of everything. It was a good idea to avoid dangerous activities like bronc riding, but it didn't have to change every factor of your life.

I made a mental note to talk to Chloe later to see if there were any mental health resources that could help him—without betraying his confidence, of course.

That could wait until we got back to Aspen Springs. Right now, I had a very beautiful, very hard dick to take care of.

I mean, my god, it was just so *lovely*. Thick and long, with a fat, dark pink head. I wanted to lick that vein pulsing along the underside of his length. So I did. I crouched between his legs and licked his lovely, lovely dick root to crown. I liked that so much that I did it again.

He whimpered, stirring, one hand going to my head as he murmured something unintelligible. It occurred to me that this could go badly. He might say another woman's name. It wasn't like he didn't have a couple dozen to choose from. He might—

"Hannah, baby. What are you doing?" his sleep-rough voice cut through my doubts.

"I think it's pretty obvious what I'm doing." A bead of pre-cum formed at the tip and I lapped it up.

Zack groaned. "God, your mouth feels so good. Do we have time?"

"We have time." This wasn't going to take long. Not to brag, but blowjobs happened to be a particular skill of mine. It turned out that being really good with my mouth was great for distracting men from the real issue. They were so busy with their own orgasms that they forgot all about mine.

But that's not what I was doing now. And it wasn't payment for last night, either. I just liked him, a lot. I wanted to make Zack feel good. Really, really good.

I slipped my lips over the silky-smooth crown of his cock and flicked my tongue over the frenulum. God, he was thick. I took the first pass slowly, enjoying every ridge and vein of cock, making it only halfway before I had to pause. I slid up again, dragging my tongue along the underside of his cock as I went, making him groan.

"Fuck, duchess, you're so pretty with my cock in your mouth," he muttered. He propped his arms behind his head to better enjoy the view.

With my eyes locked on his, I sucked gently on his crown. His hips bucked, pushing his dick deeper into my mouth. I took him in, and this time I got further down his shaft before he hit the back of my throat and I gagged like an amateur. But he liked that, too, and moaned in response.

My hand made up the difference I couldn't stuff into my mouth, and I set a steady rhythm that made his dick thicken even more.

"Yes, Hannah, just like that, oh, fuck—" he hissed between his teeth. "I'm gonna come, don't—"

He tried to push me off, but I ignored his warning and kept going. With a shout he thrust up and shot hot bursts of cum into my mouth. I swallowed every last drop then slowly slid him from my mouth and dropped a kiss on his crown.

I followed that with a kiss on his cheek. "Get dressed, Zack. We have a horse to save."

TRUE TO HIS WORD, Zack took the first shift driving—over my protests—but I didn't use the time to sleep. Even when I was tired, I didn't like wasting a long drive on sleeping. I loved road trips because it gave me a glimpse, however brief, of a place I would never truly visit.

"You're not sleeping," Zack accused.

"I'm fine. I slept really well last night."

His chin dipped to consider me, and then he pulled his gaze back to the road. "Did you?" He sounded smug.

I supposed that was fair. I had slept like the dead for a solid six hours, thanks to his magic tongue. I still didn't entirely understand it. I had given myself plenty of orgasms over the years. Not a single one of them had been like *that*. So...intense. It made me wonder if I was actually gaslighting myself. It was like someone spending their whole life living in Alaska, believing they knew what heat felt like, then suddenly moving to Arizona in the middle of summer.

"How did you sleep?" I asked, because I knew rest didn't come easily for him.

"No worse than usual."

I decided not to take that personally. Instead, I took it as a challenge. Everyone should get to experience the deep, restful sleep that came from a fully satisfied body and, by god, I was going to make that happen for him, one way or another.

He turned on the radio and spun the dial until he found something that wasn't static. A country station, of course. That was about all there was out here. Country, classic rock, and conservative talk shows.

That same song we had already heard a million times yesterday came on again. I hummed along and watched rural Montana go by out the window. White-peaked mountains hugged the distant horizon. Mostly it was just wide-open fields with the occasional cow, but every now and then we would drive through a cluster of small houses, some in various stages of dilapidation and some as pretty as a postcard.

Regardless, I had questions. I always had questions.

"Where do you think they work?" I pondered out loud.

"Who? The people who live here?" Zack peered out my window, then out his. He shrugged. "The ranches, mostly. Gas stations, hospitals, schools. There's probably a dollar store around here somewhere, too. And we're close to a few different national forests and parks that might employ a lot of them."

"A national park. That might be a fun place to work."

"Sure," Zack agreed. "Except for all the people."

I looked at him in surprise. "But you like people."

"I like entertaining them. Cleaning up after them? Not so much."

I laughed. I had done my fair share of cleaning up after people in the library. It wasn't always a great experience.

We passed a woman sweeping her front porch like she was teaching it a lesson. "She has oatmeal every day for breakfast," I said. It was a compliment. "Also, her husband is a jerk." That was self-explanatory.

Zack snorted. "Maybe he ate the last of the oatmeal yesterday and forgot to put it on the grocery list."

I shook my head. "No. Margaret would never live so close to the edge like that. She's got a full month's worth of oatmeal in the pantry. I bet he forgot their anniversary."

"Oh, her name is Margaret, is it?" Zack kept his eyes on the road, but I could see the smile lines crinkle. "All right, then. But Jimmy didn't forget their anniversary. He used her favorite spatula to unclog the toilet, and now she can't look at it the same way anymore."

"No!" I squealed, laughing. "Why would he *do* that?"

"He swears it's clean now," Zack said, completely straight faced. "But she says it's tainted. And it still smells like shit."

"Ew! No!" I covered my mouth with my hands, still laughing so hard my eyes stung.

"It's her special spatula, the one she uses to mix up the batter for cakes and waffles."

"*Zack*," I wheezed.

We were long past Margaret and Jimmy's house now, but eventually we passed another row of houses, and we made up stories for them, too. I had always been like this —or, at least, I had been like this ever since I'd left the compound and realized that people led all sorts of lives that I had never considered. I wasn't all that interested in the big adventures or the shattering catastrophes; it was the mundane parts that fascinated me the most because that's what life was, really. Ordinary moments strung together like pearls on a string, and it was only looking back, after time had polished them up a bit, that you could see how richly they gleamed.

It was funny, having an ordinary moment of my own, imagining the ordinary moments of people I would never see or probably even think of again.

But with Zack it felt extraordinary.

As PLANNED, we arrived at the horse processing center before Reliable Trucking. That was the last thing that went right.

"What do you mean, he's not for sale?" Zack demanded.

Mr. Biller, the manager of the operation, didn't look

like he cared for Zack's tone. "Exactly what I said. None of these horses are for sale. They've all been bought and paid for, every last one of them. The horses will be branded for slaughter, and once they get through processing, they'll be taken to the border station and into Canada."

Zack's eyes narrowed. "Well, that's too damn bad, because—"

"Thank you for your time, sir. Zack, let's go." I grabbed his arm, prepared to use force if necessary to get him out of there. I knew a losing argument when I saw one. We needed a new plan, and that would be hard to pull of if Zack was sitting in a jail cell for assault.

Fortunately, he didn't fight me. He stormed behind me, looking mad enough to set the building on fire.

"This mother fucker," he muttered. "I'm going to call the slaughter company in Alberta. Tell them I'll pay double what he's worth on the food market."

"All right." I turned in a circle, taking in our surroundings, as Zack stepped away to make the call.

There were probably close to a thousand horses here. They were in much worse shape than the horses we had seen at the auction yesterday. Thin, with a listless look to them. There were no stables, stalls, or lean-tos. Just metal pens and haybales stacked all around. Not a whole lot of people, either. The horses were left to themselves. Anyone could walk right up and pet one.

Or take one.

"Fuck!" Zack slapped his phone on his thigh. "No one is answering."

A truck pulled up with more horses. I lifted my hand to my forehead to shield my eyes from the sharp sunlight and squinted at the emblem on the driver's door. It wasn't Reliable Trucking.

Zack went back to trying to call the slaughter company. I kept watching. A plant employee meandered over to help unload the horses. The back of the truck was lined up with what looked like an old shipping container, which opened up into the horse pen. The horses ran out of the truck, through the shipping container, and into the pen. The employee threw in some hay and disappeared.

Interesting.

"Zack," I said.

"They're still not picking up. What the fuck? Who is in charge of this shit show?" Zack ranted. His shoulders slumped as his anger faded to hopelessness. "I really thought we would win. I thought we would save him."

"We haven't lost yet. I have an idea." I tapped my chin. "WWEPD?"

"WWEPD?" Zack repeated. "What does that mean?"

A smile spread across my face.

"WWEPD. What would Essie Price do?"

20

ZACK

It turned out that stealing a horse from a slaughter processing plant was ridiculously easy.

No one paid any attention to us as I entered the horse pen. Hurricane Red was the only one who kicked up any fuss. Having just been released from a long twenty-four hours spent cooped up in a loud, smelly, bumpy truck, he had absolutely no interest in going back through that shipping container. I had a feeling he knew another truck was waiting for him on the other side and he wanted no part of that. Hurricane Red had always been too smart for his own good.

With him acting out, tossing his head high to keep it out of my reach, it took me a while to slip the halter over his nose and ears. But I finally managed it and brought his face close to mine so we were eyeball to eyeball. "I'm trying to save your hide. Show a little gratitude, would you?"

Hurricane Red snorted, and swear to god, it sounded

like a curse word. I'd found myself on his back three times and I remembered each one. The first time had been a winning ride for me. The second time, he'd bucked me off in a heartbreaking 7.3 seconds. And the last one...well, let's call that a draw.

I knew he remembered that last ride, too. That's why he was here, in this fucking feedlot waiting for someone to brand him with an S for slaughter. He was here because he remembered our last ride so well that he refused to go out there again.

So, yeah, I knew he remembered that ride. But I didn't think he remembered *me*. But maybe there was something that felt familiar to him, something good that made him willing to take a chance on me, because his nostrils flared and he lowered his head.

Maybe he trusted me. Or maybe he took note of the horse laying down on its side, preternaturally still, in the adjacent pen. Maybe he caught the scent of death.

Whatever it was, he let me lead him back through the shipping container and practically jogged into the horse trailer attached to my truck.

Hannah was behind the wheel, engine running, and the second I was in the passenger seat, she hit the gas without waiting for me to buckle up.

"You make a damn fine getaway driver," I said as I got myself situated.

"I didn't want anyone to try to stop us. I would have had to run them over." Her eyes darted up to the rearview mirror, her shoulders bunched around her ears, checking to see if anyone was following us.

I chuckled. "Run them over?"

Her lips flattened into a grim line. "Run. Them. Over."

And that's when I realized she had seen the dead horse, too.

HANNAH PLUGGED her phone into the dashboard and typed in Jeremiah's address. I winced when the directions popped up on the screen. Mercy River Ranch was a seven-hour drive from here. Of course, Aspen Springs was still fourteen hours away, barring traffic and accidents, so Hurricane Red was in for another long road trip, whether he liked it or not. It was better than slaughter.

Kind of hard to explain that to a horse, though.

The map told us we'd pull into Mercy River sometime early evening. Hannah called her brother to let him know. He pretended like it was brand-new information, even though we all knew he was tracking her through her phone. Still, he sounded really excited to see her, so I'd refrain from forming an opinion until I'd actually met the guy.

With Hannah driving, I pushed my seat as far back as I could to stretch my tight muscles and took the opportunity to get some work done on the charity rodeo. Everything was coming together. Brax had emailed me copies of the various permits we needed last night, and now I pulled them up on my phone and spent some time looking over them to make sure I understood what they all meant. I *didn't* actually understand most of it, but Brax had included very thorough notes, so that helped.

"Permits are in order," I told Hannah, still scrolling through the information on my phone. "I also just got the contract for the porta potties, too. I forwarded it to my dad." I made a note to follow up on that later. Paperwork wasn't Dad's friend.

"That's great. Thank you."

She gave me a quick smile before gluing her gaze to the windshield again. Hannah wasn't one-hundred-percent comfortable driving my truck with the trailer attached, I had noticed on our drive out to Shelby, and she was even less so now that there was a real live horse in that trailer. But she hadn't complained once, and I knew that if I offered to drive the whole way, she would refuse.

Maybe I should have felt guilty about that, because it was my fucking broken body that made her so determined to do her share, after all. But I didn't. Not even a little bit. She was doing perfectly fine. Being scared didn't make her incompetent, and I wasn't one bit worried that she would get us to Mercy River Ranch safely and all in one piece. Even if it meant white-knuckling the steering wheel the whole way there.

But that was the thing about her, I realized.

Driving this trailer. Wearing clothes she had grown up believing were sinful. Wrangling a wild cowboy into sex lessons. Hell, I couldn't imagine the amount of courage it had taken for her to run away from the sick bastard who had married her, leave her family behind, and start a new life in a world that must have seemed like something out of science fiction to her.

Hannah Bell was damn good at doing the thing that scared her.

And more than anything, I wanted to be the man standing next to her while she did them. Protecting her if necessary, but mostly I just wanted to support her.

"Did I tell you the high school equestrian drill team agreed to perform?" Hannah asked. When I shook my head, she continued, "I meant to, but forgot with the whole Hurricane Red debacle. I talked to their coach Friday. It's all worked out. They'll do a show at four, right before the closing ceremonies."

"Great. I'll add it to the schedule." Since we were keeping things small and only working with one arena, none of the events could overlap. We also needed time between each event to clean the ring, if necessary, and get set up. "Which reminds me, I reached out to some rodeo buddies about entering the roping competition. Their names will draw a bigger crowd. They said they'd be happy to come."

"That's great!" She was so excited she took one hand off the steering wheel to slap against her thigh like she was giving me a one-handed round of applause. I laughed. "Thank you again for doing this. To be honest, I thought it was a long shot when I walked into the Painted Cat that night. I mean, you don't even use the library. I was prepared to bribe and beg, but you didn't make me do any of that. I don't know why you said yes, but I'm so glad you did. I don't know how I would have gotten this done without you."

I shrugged even as I internally basked in her praise. "It's a rodeo. Of course I said yes."

I said yes to most everything people asked of me. Crappy ranch chores, favors small and large, a ride home. So asking me to help with a rodeo...I missed rodeo something fierce, and it was hard as hell watching cowboys ride out a bucking bronc, knowing that would never be me again. But I didn't love it less for that ache. Of course I said yes.

The truth was, just about anyone could have asked me to help put on a rodeo, and I would have said yes.

The other truth was that Hannah Bell could have asked me to stand on my head, fully nude, and sing all the lyrics to *The Cowboy in Me* in the middle of Aspen Springs, and I would have done it.

THE MAP DID NOT LIE. We turned off the highway onto a long gravel drive shortly after dusk. But Hannah did not relax. If anything, she got more nervous.

"I feel obligated to warn you. Jeremiah is..." She

chewed her lip. "Well, he's a big old teddy bear, really." She paused. "A grizzly teddy bear."

I smirked. "I'm not concerned, duchess."

She gave me a dubious look that clearly stated, *you should be.*

"All right." I chuckled. "Tell me about him, then."

"Well, we grew up the same way. At the compound. He was banished at fourteen. The elders said he had sinned, and he could come back when he had repented. But they didn't even tell him what sin he had committed. They just dropped him on the outskirts of a town two hours away and *left* him there to fend for himself." Her voice pitched high with indignation. "He wasn't the only one, either. There were so many boys they sent away. Every year, they banished a handful more."

My forehead wrinkled. "Why would they do that?" It didn't make a whole lot of sense to me. In a rural community like that, with heavily dictated male and female roles, wouldn't they need able male bodies for farming?

"I've thought about it a lot since I left. You know, they never sent away girls. And I think...that's it. All the men had multiple wives. At least three, but sometimes even more. But the birthrate doesn't change across history unless you do something to *make* it change. It's always a pretty close fifty-fifty split of male and female babies. There weren't enough women to go around, not when men expected to have three of them apiece."

I felt sick. Fucking hell. "How did he survive?"

"The town where they dropped him...It's common

enough that there are now community organizations there to set up Lost Boys—that's what they call them, the kids who were banished—with foster families and group homes. He joined the army at seventeen."

"And now he's at Mercy River?"

She nodded. "He went in on the land with some of his squadron when the land was still cheap. It was their retirement plan. The cattle operation came with the land, but it wasn't enough to make a living from. So, they kept that going, but it's also a guest ranch. Not really one of those dude ranches set up for families. More like…recuperation."

"Like a resort or a spa?"

She laughed. "I dare you to say that to his face." Her nose scrunched. "On second thought, please don't. I'm growing rather fond of *your* face and I don't think it will fare well."

"That so? In that case, darlin', I'll do my best to take care of it for you."

Her mouth pursed like she was going to say something sharp and sarcastic, but we pulled up to the ranch house, where a man was leaning against a porch pillar, and instead she said, "There he is."

There he was, all right. A grizzly bear of a man, with a shotgun in one hand.

21

HANNAH

"You made it." Jeremiah stretched his arm out to keep the shotgun safely away from me, his finger nowhere near the trigger, and wrapped me in a one-armed hug.

"What's the gun for, Jay?" I asked. "Put it down."

"Wasn't sure if I was going to need it." His gaze shifted to Zack just long enough to make a point before he set it down. "Mateo saw a grizzly. I wanted to make sure it didn't come for the herd or the horses. Fired a few shots to scare it off."

"You get grizzlies this far from Yellowstone?" Zack asked.

"Not usually, but we're starting to see an uptick. Mostly we have black bears in this part of Wyoming. Like what you have in Colorado, but bigger."

I ignored their dick-measuring competition in favor of more important things. "Mateo is here?" I asked excitedly.

He hadn't left the army yet, and our visits to Mercy River rarely overlapped, but I always loved seeing him.

Like I had summoned him with his name, the door opened and there he was. He grinned, all dimples and white teeth that gleamed against his brown skin.

"She's here!" he hollered over his shoulder before crossing the threshold and hauling off my feet in a big hug.

A second later there was a stampede of tier-one operators and Mateo's hug became a group project.

I laughed as they jostled me around. "Put me down so I can introduce you to Zack."

Immediately, they formed a line with their backs to me, facing Zack like a high-stakes game of Red Rover. I rolled my eyes and elbowed my way through them to stand next to Zack.

"This is Zack Hale." The wall of scowls was not for the faint of heart, so I added, "Zack is helping me with the charity rodeo for the library. Zack, this is Liam Cole, Sebastian—Seb—Ashcroft, Mateo Alvarez, and Holly Delaney." As I pointed to each one in turn, they shook Zack's hand. He didn't flinch, but I noticed he flexed his hand, stretching out the muscles, after Holly was done with him. "And, of course, my brother, Jeremiah. But we call him Jay."

"My friends call me Jay." He eyed Zack doubtfully. "You can call me Jeremiah."

I narrowed my eyes, but Zack remained unfazed.

"Sure thing." That easy, charming grin of his was firmly in place. "Where can I put my horse? He's been around a thousand other horses from all over the place, so if you have something isolated, that would be best."

Jeremiah jerked his head at Liam, who stepped forward.

"We've got the quarantine stall ready for him, but he'd probably prefer the pasture for the night to stretch his legs. I'll take you there," Liam offered.

Zack squeezed my bicep—Jeremiah's gaze zeroed in on the contact—and followed Liam down the steps. The second they were out of ear shot, I whirled on my big brother. "Seriously, Jay?" I lowered my voice in imitation of Jeremiah's deep growl. "*You can call me Jeremiah.* What was that?"

He shrugged. "He needed to know."

"Know what?" I demanded.

"That you have friends."

I blinked.

"Highly trained friends with a very particular set of skills," Seb put in.

"Don't quote that movie at me. Zack isn't going to sell me into sex slavery," I said, but I was oddly touched.

"Well, he's not *now*," Mateo deadpanned. "You're welcome."

I shook my head. "Zack is a good guy. And I think you're going to like him most of all, Mateo. You're like two peas in a pod."

Holly snorted. "That's not the ringing endorsement you think it is."

Mateo smirked at her. "Yeah? Because that's not—"

"You're wearing jeans," Jeremiah cut in. I had the feeling he wasn't just now realizing it, but had been waiting for the moment to say it. "That's different. Is this Zack's doing?"

"Not Zack. Necessity. We went straight from the auction to the feedlot in Shelby, and I didn't have anything with me."

I knew Jeremiah didn't care what I wore. He hadn't fussed when I asked for new, modern clothes when I left the compound, and he hadn't fussed when I stopped wearing those clothes in favor of my old prairie-style dresses. Eventually I had outgrown those clothes and settled into what I wore now: long skirts paired with long-sleeved sweaters. Jeremiah hadn't said a word about any of that. He was fine with all that.

What he *wasn't* fine with was a man telling me what to wear.

Life outside the compound had been...an adjustment. I had been raised to believe that a man's word was the final authority, regardless of who that man was. Jeremiah had been raised the same way, but he'd been out for years at that point, and several women had already knocked some sense into him.

But for the first year I lived with him, he didn't realize that I acquiesced so easily—to him, to my boyfriend, to male teachers, to random men on the street—not because I wanted to, but because I didn't know how *not* to. And when he finally saw the pattern, whew. Was that ever a hard reckoning for both of us.

I pulled anxiously at the hem of my cropped t-shirt. I *wasn't* wearing this for Zack, but I had to admit, I liked seeing his reaction when I put it on. What did that mean? I didn't want to fall into old, unhealthy patterns. I had spent years brainwashed into believing that my body was entirely created to be of service to men. Their whims, their lust, their needs. I was to bring them pleasure, feed their bellies, bear their children. I was not entitled to my own body.

And even though I knew Zack didn't feel that way about it, I wondered if part of me still did. If maybe the misogynistic call was coming from inside the house.

"You look great," Holly said, sending Jeremiah a stern look. "And if you want to throw your dirty clothes in with mine, I'll do a load tonight."

Holly was two years younger than me, but she had clucked over me like a mother hen from our very first meeting. Well, no, not a mother hen. More like a Canada goose. Either way, it was maternal. Murderous, but maternal.

"Thank you," I said. But I was still feeling off kilter.

Jeremiah was watching me keenly, but whatever he was thinking, he kept to himself. "Come inside for dinner."

22

ZACK

By the time we were finally ready for bed, my body felt like it had been run over by an eighteen-wheeler. It was the lack of physical activity that had stiffened me up. Twenty-four hours of driving plus a night on a hotel bed that seemed personally offended by my presence had not helped. My body required gentle, steady movement and lots of stretching to keep it in workable order. I had done my best to stretch, but movement had been impossible in the confines of the truck.

Hannah had showered first, and then I had followed, letting the hot water pound my muscles into some semblance of submission. Of course, that same hot water also left my scars tight and angry. There was no winning.

She was on the bed, wearing pajamas I assumed she borrowed from Holly, when I emerged from the bathroom with a towel wrapped around my waist. She rolled up onto her knees and adjusted her glasses when she saw me.

"I want to try something," she said.

My dick perked up. I was fucking exhausted, but it was the kind of exhausted that made sleep harder, not easier. My body was twitchy from lack of exercise and my skin itched something fierce. Still, tired and sore as I was, there wasn't a chance in hell I would say no to whatever it was Hannah was offering.

I dropped the towel. "Anything you want, duchess."

Her gaze briefly snagged on my abs but then she was all business. "Great." She swung her legs off the bed and pushed to get up. "Don't move." She darted into the bathroom and came back with a fresh towel, which she spread horizontally on the bed.

I looked at the towel. "Is this...so you don't have to sleep in the wet spot?"

"Ew, Zack. No." She wrinkled her nose. "It's for you. So we don't get oil all over the sheets because oil stains are almost impossible to get out." She patted the towel. "Lie here, face down."

I arched a brow at her, but did as she told me, biting back a groan as I settled onto the bed. I didn't want her to know how badly I was hurting. I heard her rummaging through her purse for something, and when I craned my neck to look, I saw her pull out a bottle of some kind of oil.

Interesting.

"I bought this at the convenience store while you were pumping gas. It's arnica oil. It's supposed to be great for muscle soreness and healing scars." She pumped a teaspoon amount into her palm, rubbed her hands together, and held them to her nose for a sniff. "Not bad. It smells like a mowed lawn."

This was starting to sound less like a sexy massage and more like physical therapy.

I eyed her as she came to the edge of the bed, where my head was cradled on my arms. "You don't have to do this."

She blew a raspberry. "I don't *have* to rub my hands all over your incredible muscles? Gee, thanks. I was really dreading it."

I sighed. "This is going to hurt, isn't it?"

"If you're a good boy, I'll make it worth your while."

My dick twitched at her promise. "I'll be so good."

"I have a theory about you." She placed her oiled hands on my shoulders, then leaned forward, her hips over my head, leaning her weight into her hands as she slowly pushed them down either side of my spine.

Holy mother of god.

"Wasshat," I muttered because forming coherent words was suddenly beyond me.

She laughed softly as her hands continued to work magic on my stiff muscles. "I bet you showed up to every single physical therapy appointment you had and put in the work. You built your strength back. You worked on your flexibility. You did everything they told you to do... except this. And I bet they *did* tell you to get regular massages to heal your muscles and break up the scar tissue, but you didn't do that. Because suffering to get stronger is one thing, but laying still and letting someone make you feel good is something else entirely. It wasn't tough enough for you. It felt like weakness."

"You dunno me," I mumbled, but I suspected I was wrong about that. She did know me.

And she wasn't wrong.

I had shown up to every physical therapy session and done the exercises they told me to do. Not once did I phone it in. I pushed myself as hard as they let me. But I had never followed up on those massages they told me to get. It seemed like such a wussy thing to do.

She worked my back and shoulders thoroughly, her touch gentle and careful when she got to my lower back, where I'd fractured my spine. "I'm not going to go too deep here, even though I can feel how stiff you are. I'm not trained, and I don't want to mess you up worse. Promise me you'll go see a licensed massage therapist when we get back to Aspen Springs."

There wasn't a massage therapist in Aspen Springs. I'd have to drive an hour to the physical therapy clinic, but I said yes anyway. I would have said yes to anything right then.

I had to bite my fist when she joined me on the bed and got to work on my hamstring and calf muscles. That fucking *hurt*. But when she was finally done, it felt like for once, there weren't rocks under my skin.

"All right. Turn over." She slapped me gently on the butt.

I rolled after hesitating a moment, because I knew what she'd see when I did. She took in my hard dick with an arched brow and then reached for the bottle of oil, pumped it twice, and then got to work on my chest.

"Now, *this* is probably going to hurt," she admitted. She dug into the muscles right below my collar bone.

It did hurt. "Take off your shirt. It will distract me from the pain."

She huffed an exasperated sigh, but paused the torture long enough to whip her shirt off over her head. I watched her tits as she did awful, wonderful things to my pecs, the front of my shoulders, and my biceps. It wasn't so bad with that for my view, and even though the massage hurt, it was a *good* pain. A healing pain.

"This might feel a little odd," she said as she moved to my scars. Her touch was light as she rubbed the puckered skin. "You really need to keep the scars hydrated. Scars tighten the skin, and you want it to be flexible to keep your mobility."

Then she was back between my legs, where she had better access to my thighs. I groaned as she kneaded my tight quads. And then, with one last, lingering stroke, she was done. She rocked back on her heels and regarded my dick, which was still at full mast.

But it was the only thing that was hard right then. My muscles were so relaxed I wasn't sure I could move. I had melted into the mattress.

"You were *such* a good boy," she murmured. "I promised. And I want to. *I* want to."

She said that last part with a ferocity that I didn't understand, but before I could try to decipher it, she leaned forward and pressed a kiss to my leaking slit and that effectively put a stop to all brain activity. I whimpered and she parted her lips over the crown and sucked me into her mouth.

It didn't take long. The woman was a genius with her mouth, and my body was primed and ready to go. With one hand gently kneading my balls, her lips and tongue worked my cock. I came in her mouth and she swallowed every drop.

"Sleep," she whispered, kissing my forehead.

And for once, I did.

23

ZACK

"The rules of the game are simple," Liam said. "Get from Pole A to Pole Z before anyone else, with more points than anyone else. Each wicket is five points. Hitting another player's ball is ten points. Reaching Pole Z before anyone else is twenty points. Making someone bleed is fifty points."

"Hence the name of the game?" I asked, watching Mateo set up the wickets and poles while Liam explained. They told me it was blood ball, but it looked an awful lot like croquet.

Seb snorted. "No. We call it blood ball because Holly said the four of us playing any game involving wooden mallets and balls, someone was going to bleed. She was right. So we figured we might as well award points for something that was going to happen anyway."

I glanced at Holly, who stared back at me with a little

smirk. I had the feeling she was plotting exactly which part of me would be the first to bleed.

"Don't look her in the eyes, man," Mateo muttered, shaking his head. "It's a trap."

That only served to pull her attention to him instead of me. His shit-eating grin made me wonder if maybe that was the whole point.

We had decided to stay an extra night at Mercy River Ranch and leave first thing tomorrow morning. It was more for Hurricane Red's sake than ours, but I had to admit I was in no hurry to end this adventure Hannah and I found ourselves on. For the first time in months, I hadn't thought about that fucking cliff. It was a relief. And even though I knew it was still there, waiting for me, it felt like there was a forest standing between us here. This road trip was a pause on real life. Here, I had a purpose.

And right now, with Hurricane Red finally getting the rest he deserved, my purpose was blood ball. I felt good about it. After Hannah's attentions to every aching muscle and itchy scar last night, I had slept like a baby. Even better, I had woken up actually feeling good. I couldn't remember the last time that had happened.

Hannah had opted out of blood ball, preferring to enjoy the spring weather with a mug of hot tea and a book. But I noticed her spot on the porch swing gave her the perfect viewpoint of our shenanigans.

"A few logistics," Liam continued. "No carrying a weapon of any sort—"

"Except the mallet," Mateo broke in.

"No weapons except the mallet," Liam agreed. "We don't take turns. You just get your ball through the wickets and try to keep other players from doing the same. The game ends when the first player knocks his—"

"*Her*," Holly said.

"His or her ball into Pole Z. We stop the game and look at the video to determine who won. Winner is the player with the most points, even if they never made it to Pole Z." Liam pointed across the field, to where a camera was set up on a tripod. "There's the camera. Don't knock it over. It's an automatic last place for fucking with the evidence, and you get latrine duty. Got it?"

I nodded. "Got it."

"I saw the news articles on your injury. It looked brutal." Jeremiah eyed me. Even odds on whether he was concerned for my health or checking for weaknesses to use to his advantage. "You sure you want to do this?"

"Bronc riding wasn't my only rodeo event. I also wrestled steers. I think I can hold my own." Even before the words left my lips, I had the feeling I was going to live to regret them.

Not that I was scared, exactly. It was just that the lack of tattoos that gave me pause, that was all. I had spent time with plenty of people who served in the military, and every last one of them had tattoos. Except for Jack Price, Essie's twin brother. But Jack Price was a tier one operator with a team that wasn't allowed to have tattoos.

Maybe it was just a coincidence. Maybe it meant nothing at all.

But I suspected it meant exactly what I thought it meant.

Jeremiah, Liam, Seb, Mateo, and Holly exchanged glances and in that glance, something was decided. I hoped it wasn't my death.

Liam rubbed his hands together. "This should be fun."

I grinned. "Absolutely, it will be."

Ten minutes later, I found myself flat on my back, the breath knocked clean out of me. Five blurry faces peered down at me.

"Dude, you killed him," Seb said in a hushed tone.

"I did not!" Holly protested, shoving his shoulder.

"Didn't I tell you not to look her in the eyes?" Mateo demanded.

"What's going on?" Hannah called from the porch swing. I heard it squeak as she pushed to her feet.

In an instant I was scrambling to my feet because fuck the blurry vision and burning lungs, I wasn't about to let Hannah see me brought low like this. Dizziness nearly knocked me down again, but Jeremiah offered a hand to steady me.

"Easy," he said quietly.

I would have knocked him off me, but then I'd probably fall injure myself falling back down again, and how would I fuck his sister tonight if I threw out my back?

"Everything is fine!" I hollered. "Stay there. I'm good." I smirked at Holly. "Not even bleeding, so no points for you."

She looked almost bored as her gaze drifted over my grass-stained body. "Check your elbow."

I raised my bent elbow to verify and saw a streak of red. "Dammit."

"Better luck next time, cowboy." She swung her mallet over her shoulder and sauntered off.

Liam turned to face me. "Can I give you a few pointers?"

I nodded. "Sure."

"Blood ball is a combination of chess, rugby, and croquet. From how you've played so far, you get the rugby and croquet parts. You're not bad with a mallet. Your aim is pretty good. You've even managed to get in a few tackles, although I'm gonna be honest here, I think it was because they didn't see you as a real threat. Still, you're doing pretty good."

"Thanks," I said cautiously.

"But you're missing the strategy aspect. It's not enough to make someone fall, you have to make them fall on a rock. Aim for something sharp. You know what I mean? You want to make them bleed and get those fifty points."

"Jesus Christ," I muttered.

"Strategy." Liam clapped me on the shoulder. "That's the part you're missing."

And despite my best efforts, I kept right on missing it for the rest of the game. I managed to get in a few decent tackles, but when the points were tallied, I was dead last.

"You held on to the end, and that was more than any of

us expected of you," Mateo said as he headed for the house. "Good game."

Holly shook her head. "You almost had me. You just didn't want to hurt a woman."

I snorted. "I wasn't even close."

"Because you weren't trying." She paused, looking up at the porch. "Hannah's waiting for you."

"Yeah." I moved faster and broke into a jog.

"Hey," Hannah greeted me. She cupped my sweaty, filthy face in her palms and looked me over. "You survived."

Holly, Mateo, Seb, and Liam smirked at us as they filed into the house. I ignored them and wrapped my arms around Hannah's waist with a smug grin. "Of course I did. No chance in hell I wasn't coming back to you, duchess."

Jeremiah was not smirking when he passed us, but he definitely felt some kind of way about seeing his sister's hands on me. Hannah didn't seem to notice. She was too busy checking me for damage. "Is your back okay? It looked like Holly took you down hard."

Yeah, I was going to feel that tomorrow. Hell, I was already feeling it now. "I'm fine. Really."

I was about to suggest she take me to our room so she could see my bruises without my clothes getting in the way, but Jeremiah returned with two beers.

He nudged his sister's arm, and she pulled free from me. "I picked up a box of books last week at the used book store in town. Why don't you get them settled into the library?"

Her eyes lit up. Damn. No wonder Jeremiah had won blood ball. Strategy sure as fuck wasn't the part *he* was missing.

"Is that okay?" she asked me hesitantly. "Do you mind?"

Like I was going to stand between her and anything that made her happy. I'd face a whole pack of demented, possessive brothers before I did that.

"I don't mind." I pecked her cheek and squeezed her arm. "I'll come find you in a minute, okay?"

Hannah's smile was like the sun coming up. It brightened everything in its path.

Totally worth it.

THE BEER HISSED like a sigh of relief as I popped the top open. I eased into one of the cedar Adirondack chairs that faced the fields and mountains and tried not to moan.

Jeremiah had taken a few hard hits himself, but he didn't slouch or relax into the chair. Like Hannah, he seemed to believe the straighter the spine, the closer to heaven.

"You did better than we thought you would." There was grudging respect in his tone as he tipped his beer back for a swallow.

"I lost," I pointed out.

"Yeah. But we thought you would quit."

I grunted. Tapping out of the game with Hannah's eyes on me? Not an option. She didn't care about shit like that, but I did. It didn't matter that I knew down to my bones that I did not have a snowball's chance in hell against an elite special forces team, I would go down fighting.

"So," Jeremiah said, real casual like.

"So," I said cautiously.

"What's going on with you and my sister?"

My eyebrows went up. "That's none of your business."

"The fuck it's not." His tone remained pleasant despite his words. He reminded me of a rattlesnake giving a friendly warning with a shake of his tail before the strike.

The last thing I wanted to do was get into it with Hannah's big brother, but this man was sorely in need of some boundaries, and I was going to lay them out for him.

I leaned forward. "You track her phone. She allows it, so it's not my place to put a stop to it. But the relationship between her and me, that's no one's business but our own. She's your sister, and I'll grant you that her past earns you the right to enquire after her health and well-being. But you need to be asking Hannah those questions, not me. I don't speak for her."

He considered me with a tilt of his head. "You ever cross a line I don't like, that makes it my business."

"If I ever cross a line *Hannah* doesn't like, she'll decide whether to make it your business," I corrected.

He wanted to fight me on it. I could see his annoyance in the tick of his jaw. But then he shook his head. "Yeah. I can live with that."

"Good." I meant it. Hannah thought the world of her big brother, and trying to come between them was a losing proposition.

He studied me, tapping his finger against his beer can. "Holly thinks you're good for her. She likes you."

I shifted, wincing as a bruise on my hip made contact with the hard wood of the chair. Fully half the hits I had taken out there came courtesy of Holly. "What makes you think that?"

He ducked his head behind his beer can, but I still caught a fleeting glimpse of his smirk. "You're alive, aren't you?"

I supposed he had a point. Blood ball was the perfect opportunity to make a death look like an accident, and there was no doubt in my mind that Holly could accomplish it.

"Seems Hannah told you about Nevada?" Jeremiah asked slowly, like he was feeling me out before showing his hand. "About our family and her...husband?"

Husband. My jaw clenched so hard my teeth clacked. "You mean the middle-aged asshole who thought it was fine and dandy to marry a child?"

Jeremiah snorted. "Yeah, she told you."

She had hit the highlights, but there was a lot she had left unsaid. Not like she was purposefully keeping things from me. Judging from the conversations we *had* had on the subject, I suspected she simply hated talking about it. That was fair. I wasn't going to make her relive it just to satisfy my curiosity.

Except it wasn't just curiosity. I cared about her, dammit. I wanted to understand. She had asked for my help, and the more facts I had, the better I could do that. Right now, I didn't have all the facts.

And I had a lot of questions.

"She told me," I said. "But I still don't understand. How did they get away with it? Fourteen years old. It was fucking illegal what they did to her."

Jeremiah looked to the mountains and blew out a harsh breath. "Yeah, it was illegal, but she didn't know that. She didn't know there was a town an hour from there that had police and teachers and social workers who could help her. We were born and raised completely outside the system. No birth certificates, no social security numbers, nothing. Someone has to report it for the authorities to do anything. There were rumors, sure. But they can't just walk into your home and check for child brides based on a rumor."

I shook my head incredulously. "And your parents fucking allowed it? They just let some old ass dude take their little girl as his fucking *wife*?"

"He was a high-ranking elder of the community." Jeremiah followed the rim of his beer can with his middle finger in slow, methodical circles. "He was a predator, in the kind of community that allows predators to flourish. Child-rearing was the responsibility of the older kids and the lower-ranked wives. It was rare for adults and children to interact, but he was connected to her family, so he was just always around. Hannah was probably only eight or nine when she started minding his children in addition to her own younger siblings. His status in the community... his connection to her family...They allowed it. I allowed it." He rolled his shoulders like he still carried the weight of that choice. The guilt.

Logically, I knew that Jeremiah had been only a kid himself at the time and didn't deserve that weight. But a small, mean part of me was glad he suffered from it. Because Hannah suffered, too, and I fucking hated that.

"Through his connection to her family, he had always been around since she was a baby. He was like a father figure to her. Looking back, of course it was odd that he gave her so much attention. Maybe our parents thought it was a good thing for her, that he'd find her a good husband when the time came. I guess I thought that, too. When I was sent away, he promised to protect her." Jeremiah's voice went tight with fury. "Instead he fucking married her."

"But fourteen..." I still couldn't wrap my mind around it. "She was still a kid. Why didn't your parents tell him to wait?"

He snorted. "Oh, he fed them some lines about keeping her soul pure. She was too pretty, he said. Her beauty tempted boys off the path of righteousness and straight into damnation."

Ice slid down my spine. "That's what her uncle said, too."

For a moment Jeremiah stared at me, his eyebrows knit together in a frown. "Yeah, he was her uncle."

I stared back, refusing to comprehend his meaning. Because what he was saying was that—

"The fuck?" I shot to my feet. "They married her off to her fucking *uncle*?"

"Uncle by marriage," Jeremiah clarified, like that made it better.

Which, okay, it did, actually because at least we weren't talking about literal incest. But that was like saying *oh, my arm is on fire, but at least my legs are okay.* Yeah, sure, it was better, but you were still on fucking *fire.*

"Our aunt—our mother's sister—was his second wife. He took Hannah as his fourth."

Fury still pounding in my veins, I looked down at him. "You keep saying *was* like this is all in the past. He *was* her uncle. Your aunt *was* his second wife. But he can still go to prison for it."

"Well, no. He can't go to prison. I keep saying *was* because he's dead."

"How did that happen?" Not that I cared about his life being cut short, but damn. What was I supposed to do with all this helpless rage if I couldn't drag him into a jail cell with my own two hands?

Jeremiah's gaze flicked away. "He made a choice."

Suicide? My eyes narrowed. Had Jeremiah helped him make that choice? I wasn't going to ask. It wouldn't matter if I did; Jeremiah wouldn't tell me if he had.

"Does Hannah know?" I asked.

"Hannah knows."

I nodded.

Fuck. *Fuck.*

Because now I understood.

She had grown up thinking her uncle was a family member. She loved him. She trusted him. And he had done *that.* Betrayed her childhood devotion to him. The person who was supposed to protect her and keep her safe had stolen her innocence.

How the hell was she ever supposed to feel safe again?

24

HANNAH

I had no idea how long Zack had been standing there before I noticed him, but it was long enough for that genial mask he always wore to slip from his face. When I spun away from the bookshelf with a book in my hands and found him watching me with dark intensity, I startled us both.

"Zack! Geez, you scared me."

He blinked a few times, then sauntered closer with is familiar easy grin. "Sorry about that. Having a good time, duchess?"

"Very much so." I hugged the book to my chest as I looked around the cozy library. It was my favorite spot on the ranch.

Zack looked around, too. "Jeremiah built this for you?"

"Not exactly. Mercy River Ranch didn't start taking guests until after I left for college. Before that, this room was empty. Then they renovated the ranch to make this the main lodge, a place where guests could come and hang out when they didn't want to be alone in their cabins or out hiking, hunting, or fishing. At first, the only thing in here was one bookshelf, a chair, and a pool table. After a while, Jay noticed that even guests who claimed they didn't like to read would eventually find their way to the library and curl up with a book. So, he started frequenting the used bookstore in town, getting a little something of everything."

"There must be a thousand books here," Zack noted.

I nodded. "He's been at it a couple years now. He built all these shelves, too. The ladder was my idea. I told him if he was going to build a library, it needed to rival Belle's in *Beauty and the Beast*."

"So you could live out your Disney princess fantasy?" The warmth in his tone, the way he smiled...he wasn't making fun of me. He said it like this was something he liked about me.

"Exactly."

His large hands spanned my waist as he picked me up and set me down on the ladder with a laugh. "All right, duchess. Let's take you to your favorite book."

I did not even try to stop the wide grin that spread across my face. I did, however, manage to check the girlish sigh that would have informed him my underwear had melted clean off my body.

"Left three shelves, sir, if you please," I commanded.

"As you wish, duchess."

He kicked up the brake, set one foot on the lowest

rung, bracketed me with his arms, and pushed off, sending us rolling across the bookshelves. And I—

I squealed with delight. I did. I couldn't help it.

"This one." I pulled a slim novella from the shelf. "I have a lot of favorites depending on my mood and what I read recently but this one…This is my *favorite* favorite."

He glanced at the cover. "Are all your favorites romance?"

"I read fairly widely, but yes. My favorites are romance." I pushed up my glasses and braced for his response. I was used to people making fun of romance books. I'd heard it all. Mommy porn. Unrealistic. And the one that made me want to set things on fire: *a harmless break from real literature.*

"Why?" he asked, like he actually wanted to know.

My gaze dropped to the book in my hand. To the woman in her yellow ballgown on the cover. "Because *she* wins. Do you know how rare that is in books? In life? Women don't win. But they do in romance books. She might have to overcome terrible things. She might even *do* terrible things. And still, she wins. She doesn't have to die so a man can fulfill his hero's journey. She doesn't have to be punished for enjoying sex or stepping outside of the box society built for her to prove some morality point. In romance books, she doesn't have to be perfect to be worthy of love. In the end, she wins. No matter what." I traced the folds and swirls of her ballgown with my finger. "It gives me hope."

I lift my gaze to his face and found him watching me

intently. With me on the ladder and him now on the floor, we're the same height and I can look him straight in the eye. "It's funny how people say the most important thing in life is love. Loving your family, your friends...that's the best thing you can do. No one ever looked back on their life from their deathbed and thought, *gee, should have spent less effort there.* But the second a woman writes a book about it, it's suddenly silly and meaningless."

"It's not silly." His voice was rough. He touched my hand while I touched her dress. "It's not silly at all."

"Not all romance books have sex in them, but I think sex is part of the reason they're not taken seriously. Women aren't supposed to enjoy sex the way men do. But I think...I think sex like that...mind-blowing sex with someone who cares for you...I think that's part of winning."

He took the book from me. For a long moment, he said nothing while he stared down at it with an inscrutable expression. Then he set it aside—in the wrong place, but I fixed that—and looked at me.

"I want you to win, Hannah. You deserve the world. Everything you ever wanted. I want you to fucking *win.*"

I didn't have a chance to ask what he meant by that because Zack leaned in and kissed me hard enough to send my head whipping back against the wooden ladder rung, but his hand got there first, cupping the curve of my skull with gentle tenderness.

"Mmph," I said eloquently into his mouth.

He chuckled in response and it was so perfect that I

wanted to laugh, too, because *this*. A wild cowboy kissing me senseless in a library? This was a fantasy I had never known to dream of.

His lips opened against mine and his tongue nudged into my mouth. I curled mine against his, loving the familiar taste of him. I let myself sink deeper into the kiss with a happy sigh and slid my hands to his shoulders, gripping the hard muscles there.

"Hannah," he murmured as his hands skimmed the curves of my body down to my thighs. "You're wearing a skirt again."

"I keep a few things here so I don't have to pack as much for visits. All of our clothes are in the washing machine. Except for what you're wearing."

"No more jeans for you." He pushed his thigh between my legs and we both groaned. "Ever."

My heart was pounding through my entire body, so hard I could feel it at my throat, my wrists, heck, even the soles of my feet. He kissed me again, his tongue dancing with mine, and I ran my hands down his torso and then ducked under the hem. For a moment I lost focus of what our mouths were doing as I traced every scar, counted every muscle. He laughed into my mouth and then pulled back, breaking the kiss to whip his shirt off over his head.

"Someone might walk in here at any second," I protested, even as my eyes ate him up. It didn't matter how many times I saw this man naked, I would never get tired of looking at him.

"Don't move," he instructed. He left me there on the

ladder while he locked the door. "There," he said, coming back to me. "Happy?"

"Yes," I said. *So happy.*

"Good." Then he dragged up handfuls of my skirt and pushed his hand between my thighs. I gasped as his fingers brushed over my damp underwear. "Already wet," he rasped approvingly. He pushed his hand into my underwear and found my clit instantly.

God, it felt so good. My legs had gone shaky, so I wiggled my butt onto the closest rung and kissed him everywhere I could reach, his jaw, his neck, his lips, while I fumbled with his belt buckle, all the while his slick, clever fingers played my clit like it was a song he knew by heart. Finally, I got his jeans open and slid my fingers over the silky head of his cock. With a growl, he kissed me again, hard.

I wrapped my hand around the shaft and squeezed. He groaned into my mouth, and I squeezed again, loving the way he filled my hand. The heavy length of him. He pushed his dick into my fist, and I took the hint and stroked him up and down. When he leaked precum, I rubbed it over the crown and down the shaft.

He broke the kiss on a gasp. "Fuck. Oh, fuck. Hannah." He ducked his head, pressing his forehead to mine. "I don't have condoms on me."

"Are you...Can we..." I swallowed. "I was tested at my annual checkup. I'm safe and on the pill."

He stopped breathing.

"Zack?" I asked.

"Need a second to pull myself together, duchess." A beat passed, and then another. He let out a shaky breath. "I'm tested and safe, too."

"Inside me," I said. "*Now.*" I widened my legs.

One heartbeat, and his dick nudged at my entrance. Another heartbeat, and he was fully inside me.

I exhaled hard and turned my head. *Just feel. That's all.*

And then his fingers gripped my chin and forcibly turned my face back to his. My eyes blinked open and I looked straight into his fierce blue gaze.

"Eyes on me, Hannah. Only me. There's no room in this pussy for anyone else, do you understand? I don't share. Your demons can't have you here. You're *mine.*" He didn't pull back, just thrust forward enough that our hips came flush with a little slap.

I stared at him, my mouth falling open.

And then he shifted ever so slightly and his pubic bone brushed my clit in the most exquisite, *tortuous* way. I made a sound, a soft, desperate sound. He did it again, watching me, a look of ruthless concentration on his face, and I made that sound again.

"There?" he asked, his voice low and husky.

I could only nod, my eyelids fluttering closed again.

"Don't close your eyes, Hannah." Desperation tinged his voice, like he was hanging on by a thread. "Stay with me."

I opened my eyes and looked at him. Our bodies still flush together, he did it again, that short, shallow thrust that hits somewhere so deep I swore it found my soul. I wrapped my legs around his hips and dug my heels in. Again and again he did it, his arm wrapped tightly around my waist, holding me to him as he pushed even deeper inside me.

I kept my eyes open and it was Zack.

Zack's breath mingling with my moans.

Zack's sweat dropping onto my bare arms.

Zack's cock touching those places deep inside.

Only Zack.

And I was safe.

Then I couldn't keep my eyes open any longer, oh god, I couldn't do anything but feel and hold on. I came on an explosion, sobbing and shouting, pulse after pulse of pleasure rocketing through me. I heard another shout, hoarse and deep.

Zack. It was Zack.

I opened my eyes. My glasses were fogged up, but for the first time, I felt like I was finally seeing clearly.

And what I saw was Zack.

25

ZACK

ADAM:

Where the fuck are you? Why aren't you home yet?

BRAX:

Yeah, get your ass back here. Some of us are sick of covering your ranch chores while you relax on vacation.

ZACK:

We'll be there by dinner.

BRAX:

Good. I'll save you some chores.

ADAM:

Did you get Hurricane Red?

ZACK:

Yeah. We Essie Price'd that shit.

BRAX:

...

ADAM:

...

BRAX:

Oh, hell. You stole a horse, didn't you.

I woke up sore but rested. Hannah had spoiled me last night, after we left the library and retreated to our room. She had patched up the cut on my elbow and my knee and then given me another coconut-oil massage. She had also suggested I look up my insurance benefits and see if they covered massage for injury recovery. I told her I would, but I had the feeling it wouldn't work as well as her hands. A trained masseuse might be more technically skilled, but Hannah was...Hannah.

I turned my head to the side and found Hannah looking back at me, a speculative light in her pretty blue eyes.

"Hey," she said.

"Hey," I returned.

She smiled.

I smiled.

"Let's see if I can still do it," she suggested.

"Do what?" I asked.

"Come on your dick."

"Well, I'm not going to say no to *that*."

I wrapped an arm around her naked body and hauled her, laughing, on top of me. I took her with me as I scootched backward until I was half reclining against the headboard, with her straddling my abdomen.

She slapped her hands on my pecs and leaned forward to kiss me, bumping her nose against mine in the process. She laughed. "My depth perception isn't great without my glasses," she said against my mouth. I felt her lips tilt up in a smile. "Also, your dick is poking me in the butt." She was still smiling when she pulled back.

I cocked my head, studying her. She was different this morning. Normally, Hannah was reserved. Not shy. I wouldn't call her shy. But she was…brisk. Matter-of-fact. I had no complaints about any of that. She was who she was, and I *liked* who she was. A whole hell of a lot, in fact.

But this morning, she was as warm and bright as the sunshine peeking through the curtains. She seemed lighter, somehow. Like some trouble had eased away.

She pushed up on her knees and lifted her hips, then reached for my cock, gave it a squeeze, and brought it to her entrance.

I put a stop to that immediately. "Oh, no, you don't. You're not ready for me yet."

She scowled. "Shouldn't I be the judge of that?"

I flicked both my thumbs over her nipples.

"All right," she said. "Foreplay it is."

I grinned. "Great idea."

I tweaked her nipples, gently at first and then harder. She squirmed against me and…yeah, she was damp. But I wanted her *soaked*. Soaked and begging. Last night wasn't a fluke, but I wasn't going to leave it to chance and risk disappointing her today.

I slid my hands over her soft, sleep-warm skin and pressed against her spine, guiding her breasts to my mouth. I captured one nipple and swirled my tongue around it, sucking gently. She gasped and dug her nails into my neck.

When I released her nipple with a wet popping sound, she dove for my mouth, cupping my cheeks in both hands. The kiss caught me by surprise. The fervor of it. The sweetness. For a moment I lost myself in it, completely forgetting that I'd had other plans for her body when she waylaid me with her mouth. All I want is for her to kiss me like this, forever.

Forever.

The thought shook me up so much that I literally *shook*.

She pulled back and looked at me, still cupping my face. Her lips started to form words, but I didn't give her the chance to get them out. I lurched forward, sitting fully upright, and kissed her again. With her mouth occupied, I maneuvered my hand between us until I found her clit. She groaned into my mouth.

She got even wetter with me rubbing her clit, but it still wasn't enough. I slid a finger into her entrance, the heel of my hand still pressed firmly against her clit. She broke the kiss with a gasp as I slowly pumped into her. When I added a second finger, her hips started rocking back and forth, riding my hand.

"That's it, duchess," I growled in her ear. "Take it."

"Please," she gasped. "More, please."

There it was. She was soaked and begging.

I slid my fingers out of her. "Put me inside you."

Bracing one hand on my shoulder, she lifted up on her knees and found my cock with her other hand, guiding it to her entrance. Her eyelashes fluttered and her lips parted as she slowly sank down on my cock, inch by inch. My cock pulsed inside her and I gripped her hips hard.

"Jesus fucking Christ, Hannah, I nearly came just watching you sit on my cock like that."

"Hmm." There was a sweet little half-smile on her mouth that made me want to bite her. She moved her hips slowly...experimentally. Finding what felt good. "You're so *big*. It takes me a second to get used to it."

I groaned. "I'm glad you like it."

"I didn't say I liked it." She circled her hips again, still so fucking slowly I was going to lose my goddamn mind, and stroked my jaw. "I *love* it."

My chest felt like it might crack open. I wanted to do the dumbest shit. Laugh. Cry. Make her tell me every other part she loved. Maybe if she loved enough parts, it would add up to the whole of me.

Fucking terrifying that I wanted that.

I grabbed a handful of her fantastic ass and squeezed. "Duchess," I growled. "*Ride.*"

She smirked. And then she rode. Hard.

She tilted her hips, pitching forward slightly, seeking pressure.

"You need more?" I asked.

"Only a little," she whispered.

I brushed her clit with my thumb and she whimpered. I pressed a little harder, my eyes searching her face.

"There," she gasped. "Oh, god, *there.*"

Her words made me want to push harder, drive deeper, move faster, but I held on and didn't change a goddamn thing. Her eyelashes fluttered again. She managed to force them fully open, bright and blue and boring straight into mine.

"*Zack.*"

She said my name like it was everything and then her eyes slammed shut and she came on a cry, squeezing my cock with her pussy and making me lose my goddamn mind. I grabbed her hips and thrust into her, again and again, with brutal, desperate thrusts. And then I was there, coming harder than I've ever fucking come in my life. I bit down on her shoulder as I spilled into her.

She collapsed on me and I nuzzled against her. There's a red spot on her shoulder where I put my teeth. I kissed it and she sighed like she was letting something go.

"I wasn't sure it would happen," she said. "I thought it might have been the library."

"The library?"

"Yeah. It's a fantasy. Lots of romance books have a library sex scene. It's a whole thing."

I had noticed that, actually. But it hadn't been on my

mind last night. The only thing I had been thinking of was telling her demons to fuck all the way off. I knew it wasn't really a cure. Maybe her demons would fade with time, or maybe she'd be fighting them the rest of her life. But at least she had taken something back.

"It wasn't the library," I growled into her neck. "It was my magic dick and you know it."

She laughed. "Maybe. To be fair, magic dicks are another theme in romance books. Magic dicks that lull you into a false sense of security right before the third-act breakup hits." She paused. "I guess we couldn't break up anyway, since this is just sex for instructional purposes."

It was like she had poured a bucket of ice over my head. "I thought you said I was your boyfriend now," I teased, smirking like her words hadn't opened up a black hole in my chest.

"No, I asked you if you were my boyfriend, and you said I could call it what I want to. I haven't decided what that is yet. It seems presumptuous to hand you a title you don't want."

"I want it." The words practically tripped over themselves in their haste to get out of my mouth. "I want it, Hannah Bell."

Her eyes searched my face, her forehead creased in a puzzled frown, like it was only just now dawning on her that I was completely serious. Then a slow smile spread across her face. "All right, then. You can have it."

"Good. I'll take it." I kissed her smiling mouth, then pulled away and gave her hair a gentle tug. "But when this third-act breakup hits, I need you to remember something."

Her eyebrows went up. "What's that?"

I leaned forward. "I'm not going to just take you back after some basic apology. I want a grovel. A big, messy, public grovel."

She rolled her eyes. "You're ridiculous. The man is supposed to grovel in romance books, not the woman. Readers love a groveling man."

"What can I say, I'm a feminist. And if anyone is capable of breaking a heart, it's you, duchess." She opened her mouth but I kissed her. "I'll try to find it in my heart to forgive you," I said against her lips. "A blowjob will probably help."

She laughed.

And then she kissed me back.

HANNAH

ESSIE:

Cats are all still alive, although I can't guarantee that Brax won't try to smuggle one home in his pocket.

JANIE:

Story time at after care went pretty well. I think we're going to make it a regular thing. All the kids missed you!

JAMES:

Quarantine stall is ready for Hurricane Red. And Blaine is back from college for the summer. Tell Zack Blaine is hoping Zack will let him work with Red.

CHLOE:

Exactly how many horses did you save, Hannah?

HANNAH:

A lot of horses, Chloe. A LOT.

I took my coffee to the porch, where I knew Jeremiah would be waiting for me. It was our tradition to have coffee together on the last day of my visit. This visit was different, in that it was unplanned, short, and included Zack, but I figured the traditional would hold true. And I was right, because Jeremiah was already there in an Adirondack chair, a steaming mug of coffee cradled between his palms.

"Hey." I took the chair next to him and brought my knees up to my chest for warmth. Mornings never stopped being chilly here. We were too far north, and too high in elevation. But I didn't mind it. That was what warm sweaters and hot coffee were for.

"You're coming back for Christmas, right? Because this doesn't count as a real visit." The words were gruff, but I knew that was because he missed me.

"I'll be back," I promised. Even with the days I had just taken to rescue Hurricane Red, I had plenty more vacation time. The library had a generous leave policy, but because we were so short staffed I tended not to use it, except for one week to visit Jeremiah every Christmas.

"Anytime you want to move home, you know you can. I hear the Fremont County Library is hiring."

"Fremont is a full hour from here, at least."

"I'm just saying."

I shook my head and sipped my coffee. I wasn't going to trade my twenty-minute walk for an hour drive, each way. Even more than that, Aspen Springs was home now. I had built a life there that brought me deep satisfaction and joy. I truly loved it. The town, the people, my friends.

Zack, a voice sighed dreamily in my brain.

But that was just the orgasms talking. I had worked too hard to build myself into an independent woman who didn't need a man for salvation to start making decisions about where I wanted to live based on his location. I was a whole, worthwhile person all on my own, and I intended to stay that way.

As though he could see in which direction my thoughts turned, Jeremiah raised an eyebrow. "He's all right."

"Who?" I said like I didn't know.

"That cowboy who follows you around, looking at you like you summon the sun every morning."

I scoffed. "He does not."

"You look at him kind of the same way." He studied me for a moment. "This one is different. Those other boys you dated, they weren't right for you." In case I hadn't already been aware of his opinion of them, he put the slightest emphasis on *boys* to drive his point home.

I rolled my eyes. "They were fine."

On paper, they were perfect for me. Academically minded, somewhat timid in mannerisms, generically courteous and kind.

"Fine." He shook his head. "That's what you said about

them at the time, too. They were all fine. The truth is they bored you. You liked them because you thought you were *supposed* to like them. They were good for you. Like broccoli."

All right, that analogy was a little more apt than I'd like. Maybe I had been a little bored. Certainly, not a single one of them would ever had a race against the clock to get dressed. And despite all of them being bookish, none of them would have imagined Jimmy using his wife's favorite spatula as a toilet plunger, either.

It was the same thing I had realized a month ago. I *liked* Zack. I liked him in a way that went beyond mere compatibility on paper. We had nothing in common but were somehow in perfect sync.

But I still felt obligated to point out, "There's nothing wrong with broccoli. It's healthy."

"Sure," Jeremiah allowed. "But too much of it gives you gas."

I made a face. "Jay! That is disgusting."

He smirked and took a sip of coffee, his gaze moving to the distant mountains. "You deserve more than broccoli, Hannah," he said gruffly. "That's all I'm saying. You deserve chocolate."

THAT SAME SONG was on the radio again. It had followed us from Colorado, to Utah, to Montana, to Wyoming, and now it was playing again as we crossed the border into Colorado. We had come full circle. I had the feeling five years from now—ten years, twenty years—if I randomly heard this song, it would bring me right back here, to this road trip. To Zack.

Five days. It felt like a lifetime, and now it was ending in the blink of an eye.

I had taken the first shift driving, and now Zack was behind the wheel for the final stretch. I was feeling restless. We were so close to home, comparatively, but we still had a couple hours to go. I read a chapter on my e-book, and then, since this stretch of highway was smooth and straight, I took out my embroidery. But after a while, even that failed to keep my focus.

What I really wanted to do was talk to Zack about something that had been eating at the back of my brain ever since he took me to the rodeo. I had the feeling neither of us was going to enjoy this conversation, but I couldn't ignore the shadows I saw in him. Anyway, what better time to talk about it than now, during a long drive where no one could interrupt us and he couldn't run away from me?

"I've been thinking." I turned down the volume so he could hear me. "When you make that appointment to see a massage therapist, maybe you could also make an appointment for a mental health therapist."

His hands tensed on the steering wheel, and then slowly he flexed them and laughed under his breath. "You saying I'm crazy, duchess? I guess I know a few people who would agree with that assessment."

That laugh didn't fool me for a second. *Lord, grant me patience to deal with stupid patriarchal ideals of manhood.* "I don't think you're crazy, Zack," I said, with all the patience of a saint, if I did say so myself. "At least, I don't think you're crazier than any other man who thinks a good time is riding a nine-hundred-pound animal whose sole mission in life is to buck you off."

He smirked. "Don't knock it until you try it, darlin'."

"I will not be trying that."

"Oh, I don't know. I think you ride pretty well." The look he gave me was heated with meaning. "But suit your-self." He turned the radio back up.

Oh, absolutely not. He was not going to charm me out of having a difficult conversation. I cared about him too much for that.

I turned it back down and he narrowed his eyes at me.

"I saw a therapist when I left the compound," I said. "Social services insisted on it when Jeremiah filed for guardianship of me with the court."

"Yeah, Hannah. You grew up in a cult and were forced to marry your uncle at fourteen fucking years old. I should fucking well hope they sent you to a therapist."

"Then you understand that therapy can be helpful." Pushing further, I added, "Jeremiah saw a therapist regu-larly a few years back." This was also more to adequately deal with my issues than his, but I didn't volunteer that information. Jeremiah and his whole team would greatly benefit from therapy, but unfortunately they were suffering from the same nonsensical, patriarchal ideals of manhood that Zack was.

"It's not the same thing. I had a physical accident. It's a dangerous rodeo sport, so it's not like I could claim it was unexpected. I didn't lose a limb. I lost a career that I wasn't going to be able to do much longer anyway, because eventually your body is just too old and too broken. So, really, what does it matter?"

What does it matter?

I twisted in my seat so I could fully face him, even though the only thing I could see was his profile, since his eyes remained forward to the road. "You said you never expected to make it out alive. That you didn't *want* to make it out alive. But here you are, alive. That accident changed everything for you. That's why it matters."

His jaw tensed. "I'm not going to kill myself."

I reeled back, stunned. "I didn't think…" My mouth opened and shut like a fish gasping for water. "Do you think about killing yourself?" I whispered.

"Everyone thinks about it sometimes."

"A lot of people think about it," I said slowly. "But I don't think that's an argument against seeing a therapist. I think that's an argument for an increase in mental health services."

Zack snorted. "What's a therapist gonna tell me, duchess? That I should be grateful I'm not dead? That there are plenty of other ways to be happy? To stop feeling sorry for myself? I already know all that. I'm trying. I should be grateful that I can still ride a horse at all, and I know there are many people who aren't as lucky as I am. I always have a place at Lodestar. What does it matter if I can't get excited about a lifetime of the same ranch chores every damn day? It's an honest living." He blew out an angry breath. "Why can't I just be fucking grateful? Why does it have to feel so…bad?"

I stared at him, baffled. He sounded so…guilty. But he had nothing to feel guilty about. These feelings weren't *wrong*. They were painful, but they were perfectly valid.

"Mom would have given anything for even one more boring day at the ranch," he said quietly. "Just an ordinary day with her family and the horses, a day where she felt good enough to be outside with the sunshine on her face." The lines of his throat bobbed in a swallow. "I owe it to her not to be a little bitch about my own problems. I don't even *have* any fucking problems."

Self-loathing coated his words and made my chest feel tight.

"I didn't know her, but I doubt she would be disappointed in you for being sad," I said carefully. "You lost something you loved and you're grieving. And not that long ago, you lost a *person* you loved, and you're still grieving that, too. That's…that's a lot of grief, Zack. There's no shame in getting help to manage it."

"You don't understand. This is who I need to be for my family. The happy-go-lucky clown who could make them laugh when they were feeling down. And we felt down a *lot* when Mom was sick."

"You weren't the clown, Zack. You were the linchpin. You held them together because you *could*. But that doesn't mean you don't ever need help yourself."

"Maybe," he said, but it was clear he didn't believe it.

I sighed. "Would it be okay if I talk to Chloe and ask her for a recommendation? She probably knows someone you can talk to."

Zack grunted. "No, I'll ask her myself."

I had the feeling he was putting me off. "Promise me."

He grunted again. I tapped his thigh, and he glanced at me. "Promise me," I insisted.

He sighed. "I promise."

As if to prove to me how fine he was, and how little he needed help, he kept up a stream of entertaining nonsense for the rest of the ride home.

27

ZACK

ZACK:

What are you wearing right now?

HANNAH:

It's 11 p.m. What do you think I'm wearing?

ZACK:

I need you to describe it. Every detail.

HANNAH:

It's a light blue nightgown with a ruffled hem that hits right above my ankles. There are three pearl buttons down the chest.

ZACK:

You've got it buttoned up to the very top, don't you.

HANNAH:

I get cold.

It should have been a shitty morning. I woke up exhausted. I never slept well, but last night had been the worst night I'd had in a long time. Even after I'd fucked my own hand, imagining flicking open the buttons on Hannah's prim nightgown one by one, I'd laid awake for hours missing her.

Dropping her off at her bungalow and then continuing on to Lodestar Ranch without her had felt all kinds of wrong. I should have been sick of her company and eager for a night on my own to decompress, but no. Every two seconds I had looked around like I expected her to magically appear at my elbow, and when she failed to do that, it felt like everything was off kilter.

I'd had half a mind to drive out to Aspen Springs and crawl into bed with her, but that was dumb. She had to be at the library early today, and ranch chores started at dawn. I would have only had two or three hours in her bed before I'd have to be up and driving back to Lodestar.

The crazy thing was, I thought it was totally worth it. The only thing that stopped me was worrying about disrupting Hannah's sleep.

So, yeah. It should have been a shitty morning.

But it wasn't.

I didn't wake up refreshed, but I woke up eager. Hurricane Red was here, and his health and wellbeing were now my responsibility. I needed to see how he had done overnight and if the last week on the road had upset his stomach. I needed to get a vet out here pronto to check him for any communicable diseases and his overall health.

I moved slowly, my body letting me know exactly how much it was missing Hannah's massages. It annoyed me a little how stark the difference was. She was right; I should have been scheduling regular rubdowns once my bones were healed enough. I would try to find some time to do something about it, even if Hannah's hands were the only ones I truly wanted on me.

By the time I got to Hurricane Red's quarantine pasture, the sun was low in the sky. Dew still clung to the grass and birds were calling good morning to each other. Adam was at the fence with Blaine, who had been working at Lodestar since he was sixteen. Now that he was in college, he was only with us for the summer.

I joined them at the fence. "Good to see you again, Blaine. How's school going for you?"

Blaine rubbed a hand over his short black curls, then grinned. "Straight A's."

"Two more years, and then you'll be heading to veterinary school?"

"That's the plan."

I nodded. Blaine's dad was the only local veterinarian Aspen Springs had left, and I knew he was looking forward to his son joining him. The Gunnel family had been in Colorado almost as long as the Hales. They had come through here as freed slaves turned cowboys, moving cattle from Texas up to the north after the Civil War, and ended up sticking around, some settling here in Aspen Springs, and others going to Five Points in Denver.

"Speaking of plans," Adam said. "What's yours for Hurricane Red?"

I leaned forward, folding my forearms along the top rail of the fence. "Don't really have one, I guess. I hadn't thought much beyond getting him here."

"Makes an expensive lawn ornament, doesn't he?"

I smirked. "Didn't pay a dime for him, actually."

"Care and feeding isn't free, you know," Adam pointed out. "He's, what? Five, six years old? Probably has a good twenty years left of eating hay and getting vet checks."

My shoulders tensed. "So take it out of my pay."

"We're not going to do that, Zack. He's your horse. Of course you can keep him here." But he sounded grouchy about it.

"Real magnanimous of you," I said drily.

"You could sell him, is what I'm saying."

"Right," I scoffed. "Because that worked out so well for him the first time. Nothing's changed. He's still a young gelding who will buck off any rider in about eight seconds. The only buyer we're going to find will be sending him straight back to Canada."

"Maybe that's not such a bad thing," he muttered.

My head spun in his direction. Adam might be a grumpy son-of-a-bitch, but he was a big softy when it came to horses. "What the fuck?"

"I hate his stupid face, that's all."

"What did that horse ever do to you?" I demanded.

Adam glowered at Hurricane Red, who was nibbling clover and minding his own damn business. "Well, he stomped my baby brother, for one thing."

Well, shit.

I blinked.

My big brother was holding a grudge against a horse for hurting me. That was so fucking sweet I was afraid I might actually blush.

I tipped my hat and smirked. "I knew you loved me."

Adam grunted.

I grabbed him in a hug and lifted him off his feet —I remembered to lift with my legs, but I was still going to regret that later—making him holler. Blaine snorted a laugh and I heard him snap a picture with his phone.

"Get off me, you idiot!" Adam growled.

Grinning, I released him.

"Fucking dumbass," Adam muttered, shaking himself out. But I caught the barest glimmer of a smile beneath the brim of his hat.

Blaine turned the conversation back to Hurricane Red. "Have you considered breaking him?"

"I already broke him. That's how he ended up in the slaughter pipeline. He's refused to go back in the chute since our accident."

Adam and Blaine exchanged a look and then Blaine turned to me, his dark eyes assessing. "I meant, have you considered trying to train him under saddle? He probably wouldn't be reliable as a show horse or for cattle work, but with a strong rider, he could be a decent pleasure mount."

I scratched my jaw. "The thing is, he's already trained. He's spent the last few years being rewarded for bucking riders off. Now you want to convince him to let a rider stay put and tell him what to do and where to go? It's unlikely."

"But we could try," Blaine pressed. "No one thought Belle could be ridden either, and James turned her into a world champion. Improbable does not mean impossible."

"So you're a philosopher now?" I grinned at him, but in the back of my head, the wheels were starting to turn. Slowly, but determinedly. What if we *could*? "They teach you that at your fancy university?"

"Nah, got it from my mom," Blaine said. "I used to say *I can't* a lot, when what I really meant was it seemed hard. She hated that."

Adam slowly rubbed his hands together, his head bowed. "Moms are always saying shit like that."

I swallowed past the sudden lump in my throat, knowing what he was thinking. Our own mom hadn't been much for *I can't*, either. Jenny Hale did not raise her boys to be helpless in the face of adversity.

"I suppose it doesn't make much sense to retire a six-year-old horse that's perfectly sound," I mused. "It couldn't hurt to ask James what she thinks. She's got a reputation for handling problem horses."

Adam tensed. "James isn't riding that fucker."

"Sure," I drawled. "I'll let her know you said so."

Adam growled. He knew as well as I did that if we decided to try to retrain Hurricane Red, James wasn't going to be able to resist working with him herself, and no amount of worried fiancés was going to stop her no matter how much he grumped. But he also knew what she was capable of, and getting dusted was part of the job. There was always a risk when animals were involved.

"It would make good summer project for me," Blaine said. "Between the three of us, I think Hurricane Red has as good a shot as any. James is the best there is. I've trained a few myself. And you..." He shrugged.

"Need a new hobby?" I suggested.

"I was going to say, you've got nothing better to do, so you might as well fix what you broke, but sure."

I stared at him with my mouth agape. "Damn, kid. You got vicious." I pulled of my hat, smacked him on the shoulder with the brim, then plopped it back on.

He grinned. "Just calling it like I see it."

I looked at Hurricane Red and let out a piercing whistle. Hurricane Red lifted his head, his ears pricked forward. His nostrils flared and I wondered again if he recognized my scent, and what it meant to him if he did. Was I merely the dumbass who got himself tangled in Red's legs? Or was I something else, too? Something good.

I let out another whistle and he ambled over. When he reached the fence, I pulled out the apple I had halved for him. He lipped it up with a soft nicker.

Beside me, Adam growled again. "Goddammit, you're going to do it, aren't you? You're going to get right back on the horse that stomped you." He shook his head in disbelief.

I caught Hurricane Red by the halter and brought his face to mine so I could rub his nose. "Yeah. That's exactly what I'm going to do."

I was finally getting back on the fucking horse.

28

HANNAH

It was strange being back in Aspen Springs after our whirlwind road trip. Everything was exactly how I had left it. Nothing had changed. My cats, Jo's, the library—everything was the same way it had always been.

I was the one who was different. And it was all Zack's fault.

It hadn't even been a full forty-eight hours since he'd dropped me off at my house and went on to Lodestar Ranch with Hurricane Red, but I missed him. It was *ridiculous*.

I walked to the library, and I thought about Zack.

I stopped in at Jo's for a cup of tea, and I thought about Zack.

I showed a patron how to create an account and print out tax forms, and I thought about Zack.

I didn't eat my lunch. I just sat there staring at it, because I was thinking of Zack.

We texted throughout the day. Random little things, like how I daydreamed of murdering our ancient printer like they had in *Office Space* or how much I had missed the group of kids who showed up after school every day, even though they seemed more feral than ever because the weather had turned warm, and they could see summer break on the horizon. Zack told me about how annoying Adam and Brax were, and how proud he was of Blaine, and that Hurricane Red was settling in well at the ranch.

I shouldn't have had *time* to miss him, what with how busy I was and the texts that came through every hour. But his texts never told me the important things.

Like if he was wearing that stupid belt buckle of his.

Or if someone told a joke that made his eyes crinkle in that special Zack way.

If he had found something healthy for lunch.

Those were the things I wanted to know.

There had to be something wrong with me. Surely it wasn't normal, being this obsessed over a man. It was embarrassing. I was mooning over him like one of those buckle bunnies, except it was even worse. At least they treated it like a game: bang as many rodeo champions as possible, get bragging rights. I just wanted the one rodeo champion, and I didn't care about his winning record at all. I only wanted *him*.

It was like I had gone on a five-day Zack bender, and now I was suffering withdrawal.

In the back of my mind, there was a niggling worry. We

both had busy lives and jobs that required early starts, but Zack's never really let up. I couldn't expect him to spend the night with me in Aspen Springs and then get up at three in the morning to drive the hour back to Lodestar Ranch. Would weekends be the only time we could spend together? How could I possibly go five days in a row without seeing him?

God, I was pathetic.

"Your mom is a silly goose, Annabelle." I pushed to my feet, empty soup bowl in hand, and moved to the sink to clean up from dinner. "I'm sorry."

Annabelle winked her green eyes at me. She didn't say anything. She didn't have to. I knew she agreed.

My phone buzzed on the table. I dropped the bowl into the sink with a clatter and sprang for it, much to the disapproval of Annabelle. She jumped out of my way with a yowl of displeasure.

ZACK:

I miss you.

HANNAH:

Do you have plans for Friday night? I know ranch chores don't stop for the weekend, but I could come out to Lodestar, if that's okay.

ZACK:

That's cute.

HANNAH:

What is?

ZACK:

That you think I'm waiting until Friday to
see you. Open your door.

With a sharp squeal of excitement, I rushed to the door and pulled it open. "Zack! What are you—"

It was as far as I got before his mouth crashed down on mine. He wrapped his arms around my waist and leaned back, taking me off the floor, and walked us inside. He kicked the door shut behind him while I returned his kiss like he had just come back from war.

Ridiculous.

I didn't care.

"Hey, you," I said breathlessly as he set me back down on my feet.

His lips hooked up. "Hey."

We stood there, smiling goofy smiles at each other. He straightened my glasses, and my smile became exponentially more goofy, if that was possible.

Then he dropped to his knees. "Have I told you how much I love your skirts? Here, hold this." He scooped up handfuls of fabric and deposited them in my arms. "God, I'm so fucking hungry," he muttered as he dragged my underwear down my legs. "Step out, duchess. I have you." He squeezed my hips.

My arms full of my dress, I wobbled slightly as I lifted one foot, then the other, to kick my underwear aside. "We can go to the bedroom."

"I'm not waiting another second to eat you, Hannah.

Evie, *no*. Shoo." He gently pushed the little cat away from my ankles and I bit back a grin.

He lifted one of my legs and slung it over his shoulder, then cupped my bottom and brought me to his mouth. When he buried his face there, we both groaned.

For once, I didn't think about coming. I was too busy thinking about *him*. The way he smelled like summer. The sounds he made as he devoured me. I didn't think about coming as he dragged his tongue down my lips. I didn't think about coming as he found my clit and sucked. I didn't think about coming as he pushed one finger inside me, then another.

So when an orgasm came barreling down on me like a freight train, it caught me by surprise. I rocked my hips against his mouth, dropped my skirt in favor of grabbing Zack by his hair, and hung on for dear life.

My legs shook as he lapped up every last drop. Slowly he pushed to his feet.

"That was so good, duchess. Here, taste." He kissed me and I tasted myself on his tongue, sweet and tangy. "All right, *now* we can go to the bedroom."

He scooped me into his arms and I laughed. "Are you giving me a ride, cowboy?" Good thing, because I wasn't sure my knees would get me there. They had turned to goo from Zack's wicked tongue.

He smirked. "Damn right I am. But first I'll carry you to bed."

I buried my face against his neck, giggling.

He set me down next to the bed and tugged off his

boots. I pulled off my sweater, the camisole underneath, and unhooked my bra. He took off his shirt and I shimmied out of my skirt. I stood there, naked, and watched while he used one hand to remove his belt in the sexiest way possible. His cock tented his boxers, but then he pushed them down along with his jeans and I got the real thing. I bit my lip as another bolt of lust shot through me.

He knew what he did to me. I could see it in the glint in his eyes, the smirk of his lips, when he picked me up again, this time depositing me on the bed. He hovered over my body, spreading my thighs wide, lining us up. His cock bumped against my entrance, and I whimpered.

"I want to go slow," he rasped as he eased inside.

"All right," I whispered back.

He slid out and pushed in again, a little further. My hips canted and I rolled my lips together to keep from begging for more. Again he slid out, again he pushed in further, edging deeper inside me inch by inch.

"You feel like fucking *heaven*, Hannah," he said, and then slid all the way home.

"Oh, goodness," I breathed.

His shoulders shook with laughter. "That's it, duchess. Talk dirty to me."

I pushed my glasses up my nose and fixed my severest librarian glare on him. "Be a good boy and give me a reason."

He froze. Then, with a low growl, he pulled out and rolled off me. I lifted my head, confused, and he grabbed me by the ankles and pulled me across the mattress toward him.

"Hey!" I yelped. "What are you—"

But he had me at the edge of the bed now and wasted no time in tossing my legs over his shoulders. He sank into me, and I gasped.

"Oh, god, Zack. You're so deep inside me I can feel you *everywhere*." My eyes practically rolled in my head as I arched my back, impaling myself even further on his dick.

"Yes," he hissed through his teeth, his gaze riveted to my face. "Tell me what you want."

"Touch me. Please touch me."

"You beg so pretty, duchess." He squeezed my ankle, then stroked his large hand down my leg until he reached where we were joined. "Is this what you want?"

"Yes. Please, yes." My hips rocked off the bed, seeking more. He gave it to me, pinching my clit between two fingers. "I'm going to come," I said, the wonder of it in my voice. "Oh, my god, I'm going to come."

And then I did, exploding with pleasure as every muscle in my body contracted at once. His thrusts grew harder and more erratic and then he came, too, turning his head and biting my ankle as he pushed himself as deep into my body as he could go.

My legs trembled as I slowly unhooked them from his shoulders. He maneuvered us both under the covers, nudging me backward with his torso until my head met the pillow. Then he rolled us so he was on his back, and I collapsed over him like a ragdoll.

"Are you staying the night?" I mumbled.

"I'm staying." He stroked my hair.

"Your dick is still inside me."

"I know, duchess. Go to sleep."

IT WAS STILL DARK when I awoke. I blinked sleepily, my eyes adjusting to the lack of light, and tried to figure out what had woken me. My body was still draped over Zack's chest. I could feel the steady rhythm of his breath as his abdomen rose and fell beneath me. My hips were cramping a little from straddling his hips. I wiggled carefully, trying not to wake him. That's when I realized his dick was still inside me.

And now it was hard.

Oh, my *goodness*.

I wiggled again and felt him twitch inside me. I shoved my face into the pillow to muffle my groan. And then I did it again.

"Hannah." His sleep-rough laughter rumbled against my cheek. "What are you up to, duchess?"

"*You're* the one who's up, Zack," I returned pertly.

He scraped his teeth against my shoulder. "Is that so?"

I rocked my hips to prove it. "Yes, that's so."

"Your pussy is still full of my cum, and you want a second round of it? Is that what you want?" His fingertips trailed down my spine, then dug into the globes of my butt.

I groaned, rocking harder. "Yes, that's what I want."

"Good. Then that's what I'm going to give you."

He thrust upward, hard and rough, again and again. His hands pinned me in place. All I could do was surrender as he fucked me senseless. I rarely had reason to use that word, but that was what this was. Fucking. There was no other word to possibly describe it.

And I loved every second of it.

I came crying his name, and that made his thrusts turn harder. Wilder. And just when I thought he might truly split me apart, he came, too. His body went rigid as he pulsed inside me.

We lay there for a moment longer, breathing heavily, and then I rolled off to use the bathroom. I didn't want to look back on this gorgeous moment and think, *yep, that was it. That was what gave me the worst UTI of my life.*

When I came back, he was right where I left him, his eyes half shut, his mouth half smiling. I crawled back under the covers and rested my cheek on his chest, my body still warm and glowing from what had just happened.

It had been so *easy*.

"I think I'm actually getting used to you being inside me," I marveled.

Zack barked a laugh. "You're a fast learner, duchess."

I lifted my phone from the nightstand and took in the time, then sighed and put it down again. "It's time for you to head back to Lodestar, although you could squeeze in a shower if you hurry."

He nuzzled my hair. "I wish I could take you with me. I'm not ready to let go yet."

I laughed and snuggled closer. "I know it's going to be hard, figuring out how to see each other with me here in Aspen Springs and you at Lodestar. I'm open to ideas."

"Well, you could marry me."

29

HANNAH

"Marry you?" I squeaked. I pushed from his arms and frantically scrambled out of the bed. "That's ridiculous. I can't marry you."

He eyed me from his position against the headboard, his expression wary. "Calm down, duchess. It just slipped out, that's all. It's not a real proposal. Come back to bed."

"Thank goodness." I pressed my hand to my chest, where my heart still thumped like I had run a marathon—or, since I had never run more than five steps in my life, a single mile. "You scared me."

"I *scared* you?"

"Yes, Zack. Of course you scared me. We barely know each other."

I reached for my glasses on the bedside table and put them on just in time to see him recoil from shock. I pretended not to notice. I should get dressed, shouldn't I? I needed to be at the library soon.

"What do you mean, we don't know each other?" he demanded.

"It's been what, a month? A month isn't enough time to decide you want to *marry* someone," I said impatiently. It was ridiculous that I had to explain such an elementary fact to him. I marched to my dresser and pulled open the top drawer with shaking hands.

"A month might be enough time for some people," he said from the bed. "Kinda like how five cats isn't too many."

I sniffed. What nonsense. I wasn't going to dignify that with a response. I wiggled into a pair of clean underwear and a clean enough bra.

"It's been a hell of a month, hasn't it?" The bed creaked as he shifted.

"Where is that sweater?" I muttered, rifling through the middle drawer. It was here somewhere. I had worn it to the rodeo, but I had washed it before we went to the horse auction.

"Hannah, for fuck's sake, will you stop getting dressed for a minute and talk to me?"

I froze, but I didn't turn around. I felt weak and shaky, like I hadn't eaten in days. "I have to get ready for work."

"I'll drive you. You won't be late."

Suddenly, I felt his heat on my back and every muscle in my body tensed in response.

"You're hurting my feelings, duchess." His soft laugh gusted against my temple. "Tell me you know this month has been worth a whole lifetime."

And that laugh…that's how I knew he wasn't joking. He was completely serious. "It's a *month*, Zack," I said crisply.

He turned me by my shoulders to face him. His eyes searched mine. "Don't give me that bullshit. You know me. I know you. Not just names and facts, but the real things. The things that matter. I know your heart and soul, and you know mine. And I…" His mouth worked like he was trying to find the words. "I love you, Hannah Bell."

I could barely hear his words over the sudden ringing in my ears. A metallic taste flooded my mouth like I had sucked on a roll of pennies.

I pushed at his chest. "You don't love me, Zack." I didn't recognize my own laugh. It sounded like a panicked hyena. "You just think you do because of all the sex. Orgasms pump your body full of hormones like dopamine and oxytocin. It makes you think you're feeling something you're not. That's all it is. Euphoria. Like being on drugs."

"I admit there's a strong possibility I'm addicted to your body." One corner of his mouth flicked up in amusement. "But that's not what this is. You think I don't know the difference between sex and love? No offense, duchess, but I've had lots more orgasms than you. Thousands of them, by myself and with others. And not once did an orgasm make me think I was in love."

My knees were melting. I gripped his forearms because if I didn't, I would keel over.

"I'm in love with you, Hannah," he said again, quietly this time. "It's all right if you need a minute. You don't have to say it back."

But he didn't sound like he believed that it was all right.

Because it wasn't all right.

Nothing was all right.

Danger, screamed my brain. *Danger*.

I wrenched from his arms and strode to my closet. Why was I still *naked*? I yanked a skirt from the hanger and pulled it on, nearly falling over as I tried to balance on one leg. But Zack was suddenly there, his hand on my elbow, holding me upright.

He said nothing as I pulled on a blouse and cardigan. He made no move to get dressed himself, as though being naked at a time like this was a perfectly acceptable proposition instead of absolute agony. I pulled in air through my nose, let it out through my mouth, and kept repeating that process while I brushed my hair and wrapped it into a bun. His gaze burned on me the whole time.

I clasped my hands together and turned to face him. "This isn't going to work."

"Don't—" He reached for me and when I flinched, he dropped his hands to his sides, clenching them into fists. He swallowed. "You don't need to decide anything right now. You need to eat something and take a minute. You'll feel better. You don't really have to marry me. We'll just keep doing what we've been doing, and it will all work out."

"No." I shook my head. "This isn't going to work. This isn't what I want. I don't like...I hate feeling this way. I hate it." With every word, the panic receded a little more, until I was left with nothing but numbness.

"Are you seriously doing this right now? You're breaking up with me? I don't understand."

I couldn't seem to stop shaking my head, like if I did it long enough, thoroughly enough, I could shake loose all these terrible thoughts and send them careening into the ether.

"Please don't do this, Hannah," he said softly.

"You'll see that I'm right. It's just sex, Zack. It's not love."

His brows lowered, and this time when he lifted his hand to me, I didn't move. "Just sex?" He swiped a thumb under my eye. "Then why are you crying, Hannah?"

"I'm not—" My hand went to my cheek and came away damp. I stared at my fingers, confused.

He pressed his lips to my forehead, and his face felt wet, too. "All right. It's all right. You are loved, Hannah. This love is safe. And if the only way I can prove it to you is to let you go, then all right. I'll do that."

I didn't stop him from pulling away, from getting dressed, from walking out the door.

The tears kept falling.

But I didn't feel a single one.

ZACK

ADAM:

You planning on leaving your cabin today or nah?

BRAX:

Don't make us come get you.

ADAM:

We know where you live, you know.

ZACK:

Fuck all the way off. I don't need a babysitter.

ADAM:

Suit yourself.

Brax?

BRAX:

Meet you there in 5.

Heartbreak was bullshit and I wasn't going to put up with it.

No, I was going to stay right here and become one with my old, cracked-leather sofa until it passed. Which, if I followed the usual trajectory of Hale men, should be any year now.

Brothers being brothers, they couldn't even give me that.

At first I figured if I ignored the pounding on my door, they would go away, but that just pissed them off and made them louder. I pushed off the couch powered by a surge of righteous fury and wrenched open the door.

"What?" I demanded.

"That's what we want to know," Adam said as they shouldered past me into the cabin.

Brax crossed his arms like a principal facing down an unruly child. "What the fuck are you wearing?"

I stood tall and proud in my pink bunny slippers, black boxer briefs, and the cardigan Hannah left in my truck draped over my bare shoulders like a shawl. It was a tossup whether the unrelenting scent of her was my hell or salvation.

"It's my house. I wear what I want. If you don't want to look at it, you know where the door is."

"You've been holed up in here for two days. What's going on?" Adam asked.

"Two days? Dad fell down a whiskey bottle for a year when Mom died." I jabbed my finger at Adam. "You were in a decade-long bad mood when your first wife left you." I spun to Brax. "And you spent years following Essie around like a playground bully until you finally tricked her into marrying you."

"That was *your* idea," Brax reminded me.

"I had just finished two rounds of surgery and was high as a kite on pain meds. My point is, so what if I've been rotting on my couch for two days? I'm well within the grace period of Hale men acting like fucking disasters over women."

"Wait...wait." Adam braced a palm against the wall like he was about to keel over. "Are you saying this is about a *girl*?"

Brax let out a disbelieving guffaw. "No. It can't be. The only girl trouble Zack has is remembering all their names."

I split a baleful glare between then and sank back onto the couch, my butt finding the indentation that was slowly becoming permanent. "You know, I'm getting real tired of people telling me what I feel or don't feel."

You don't love me, Zack. You only think you do because of all the sex.

Hannah's words still echoed in my brain. Bullshit. Complete bullshit. I knew I loved Hannah the way I knew my blood ran in the soil of these Colorado plains. It was a goddamn *fact*.

Still, she had sounded so sure. And that made me question things. Not my feelings; I knew where I stood. But maybe where I stood was a long way from where Hannah stood. Maybe for her, what we had was nothing more than sexual chemistry.

And then I remembered her tears.

My girl felt something for me, and it terrified her.

I couldn't even blame her for that. The way I felt about her...shit. It scared me, too. And I hadn't even been forced to marry a family member at fourteen years old.

So, yeah. Love was fucking terrifying.

I dropped Hannah's sweater over my face to black out the world, especially my two annoying brothers who didn't seem to understand the conversation was over.

"It can't be a girl." Adam sounded like he was trying to convince himself it was true. "The only woman he's spent time with since the accident is that librarian. Hannah."

"Hannah?" Brax echoed. There was the heavy thump of his boots against the wood floor and then the sweater was unceremoniously yanked off my head. "What did you do to her, Zack?"

Nothing except teach her how to orgasm with a man and fall in love with her. "Nothing," I grunted. I lunged for the sweater.

Brax held it out of reach and glowered down at me. "Then why did she look like hell today when she came to my office to sign rodeo paperwork?"

"She looked like hell?" My gut twisted. Was I happy that there was the slimmest possibility that Hannah was as miserable as I was? Of course not. But I wasn't unhappy about it, either.

"Dammit, Zack," Adam snapped. "She's friends with James and Essie. You can't just—" He scrubbed a hand over his scruffy jaw. "She's a librarian, for fuck's sake. She's not one of your buckle bunnies who wants a quick fuck and won't care if you never call her again. She's nice."

Rage boiled over.

"Don't you fucking tell me what she is. I know her, okay? I know she cares so much about libraries because she believes income should not be a barrier to knowledge. I know she calls her cat a slut and doesn't mean it as an insult. I know she likes to make up stories about strangers and she loves that women win in romance books and if a friend needs help, she'll drop everything to drive across the fucking country to rescue a horse. And for the record, she's *not* nice, but she is kind."

I stood to face my slack-jawed brothers and stepped toward Brax. "Now give me that fucking sweater or I'll rearrange your insides so bad it will make what Hurricane Red did to me look like nothing."

Silently, Brax handed me her sweater and I immediately wrapped it around my shoulders and breathed in Hannah's scent.

"Holy shit," Adam said. "Holy shit, you're in love with her."

"It doesn't matter if I am," I muttered, turning my back

to them both. "She doesn't feel the same way." She didn't think she did, anyway. And even if that was just the fear talking, she deserved to have me take her at her word. She had done the same for me, over and over—until now, anyway.

You could marry me.

If I could have gone back in time and duct taped my mouth shut, I would have. Not because it wasn't true. I hadn't meant to say it, but I meant every fucking word of it. But she wasn't ready to hear it.

"So what are you going to do about it?" Adam asked. "You can't stay in here forever. It's only been two days and it's already starting to smell stale in here."

"Don't forget what the doctors said," Brax put in. "Lying around in bed all day is only going to make every-thing hurt worse."

"I'm not lying in bed. I'm rotting on the couch."

But he wasn't wrong. Everything hurt. It was just that none of those aches and pains in my muscles could hold a candle to the ache in my chest.

If Hannah were here, she would have been on me to make that appointment with a massage therapist. And then she'd remind me about the *other* promise I made her.

Fuck.

I'd *promised.*

I heaved to my feet with a groan.

She had broken my heart, but I'd be damned if I would break a promise to her.

HANNAH

Stab. Pull. Stab. Pull. Stab. Pull.

There was something almost hypnotic about embroidery. The satisfying *ping* as the needle breached the drum-tight linen. Tugging the thread taut. Doing it over and over again. A single stitch added only a drop of color, but a thousand of them created something beautiful. I didn't have to think or feel. My brain could be quiet. My heart could be numb. It didn't matter. The design I created with needle and thread would still be beautiful in the end.

Stab. Pull. Stab. Pull. Stab. Pull.

"Hannah."

Blinking at the sound of James's concerned voice, I looked up and found my friends watching me. It was time for our weekly sewing club.

"Oh, you're all here." I pushed to my feet and then real

ized Janie had someone with her. "Who's this? Does she want to embroider with us?"

"I'm babysitting for my parents. This is Maya." Janie's hand dropped to the girl's shoulder. "Hannah can get you an embroidery project, or you can color or read a book."

She must be Janie's little sister. They looked exactly alike, with wavy red hair, brown eyes, and a sprinkle of freckles across their noses. Maya held up her coloring book. "I'm going to color."

"Okay." Janie watched Maya grab a floor pillow and take it to the far corner, where she proceeded to dump out a large plastic bag of crayons. Janie heaved a sigh full of rueful affection, plopped into a chair, and pulled out her embroidery project. "I'm not sure I want her to have access to something sharp and pointy anyway, so I brought activities to keep her busy."

"Good," Essie said. "Because the conversation we're about to have is not fit for innocent ears."

"What conversation is that?" James asked.

Essie smirked. "The one where Hannah tells us how many horses she saved riding Cowboy Zack."

Hearing Zack's name spoken out loud instead of being an endless echo inside my head caused me to push the needle too far and jab my own finger with it. "Shoot," I muttered.

A small bead of blood swelled at the tip of my index finger like a shiny red balloon. I stared at it, remembering the small smear of blood Zack had kissed onto my wrist.

He had looked at me like he never wanted to look away. The room turned blurry, and I hastily pushed to my feet.

"I'm going to clean this up in the bathroom," I said, making a beeline for the door.

Chloe stood. "I'll come with you."

She followed me from the room and through the library stacks to the bathroom. By the time I bumped the door open with my hip, I had pulled myself together enough to say, "I'm fine. I'm just going to wash my hands and use a paper towel to stop the bleeding."

That didn't stop her from coming in with me. "Sure. But I wanted to talk to you about something." She hesitated. "Zack."

I ignored the little zing in my belly and concentrated on washing my hands. Apparently that was just something that happened now. Every time I heard his name, my body jerked to attention. How inconvenient.

"All right," I said. "What is it?"

"He found me at Jo's yesterday. He said he made you a promise, and he needed to keep it." Chloe's eyes met mine in the mirror. "I just thought you should know."

"Oh." I dried my hands on a paper towel while my brain raced. I looked down at my finger. The bleeding had stopped. "Did you...Were you able to help him? Is there someone who—"

"I think you need to ask Zack that. I'm not his therapist, but I don't feel comfortable giving you that kind of information without his consent."

"Right. Of course." Swallowing the lump in my throat, I pushed out of the bathroom with Chloe on my heels.

"Hannah—" Her gaze snagged on something behind me and her eyes narrowed to emerald slits. "No. Absolutely fucking *not*. Get the hell out of here, Steven."

Stunned by the animosity in her tone, I whipped my head to see who she was talking to. The tall man wearing a tan Stetson looked vaguely familiar, but then again, most cowboys around here did.

The man scowled. "This isn't the coffee shop, Chloe. You can't kick me out just because you don't like me."

"Well, good news, dipshit. Because I don't have to. James is here. How about I give Adam a call and let him know you're in her vicinity?"

His scowl deepened. "I'm here for a book, not for her. I had no idea she was here. I'm not stalking her."

Chloe arched a brow. "Cool. I'll just let you explain that to Adam's fist."

Suddenly I realized who he was. Steven MacAllister. His employment at Lodestar Ranch had been cut short when he'd purposefully spooked a horse James was riding. James had ended up with a couple of bruised ribs, and Steven had ended up with a broken nose, courtesy of Adam.

"Jesus, Chloe. It was an accident. Why do you hate me so much? You don't even know me."

"I know you." Her mouth twisted like she tasted something nasty as her eyes traveled from his dusty cowboy boots, up his Wrangler's, and landed on his face. "You're the guy who always comes in second and gets mad about it, because no one deserves first place more than you. If someone doesn't laugh at your joke, it's because they don't have a sense of humor. Someone gets promoted over you, they must have cheated. A woman turns you down, she's a bitch. The world never gives you everything you're owed, and your list of grievances is *long*. It's not fair, right? All of that should be yours. Because you're *such a nice guy*." She leaned in. "But guess what? No one owes you shit, and you're trash."

My gaze bounced anxiously between them. The rage arcing from their eyes was hot enough to start a wildfire.

"Listen," I said, because if I didn't say *something*, there was a good chance I'd be emptying my bank account for Chloe's bail tonight, "the library is open to the public, and you, Steven, are the public. But I don't think it's in anyone's best interest for you to be here right now. If you tell me the name of the book, I can put it on hold for you and you can pick it up tomorrow."

"That won't be necessary. I'm leaving." He dragged his gaze from Chloe's long enough to give me a brief nod. "Ma'am."

With a last glare at Chloe, he turned toward the door —right as James, with Essie on her heels, came around the corner. James stopped so fast that Essie bumped right into her, her chin colliding with the crown of James's head.

"James," Steven rumbled. "I just—" He froze when her eyes widened. I couldn't see his face, but his shoulders hitched up before lowering again. He cleared his throat. "I was just leaving."

None of us said a word as he strode out of the library.

"What was Steven doing here?" James asked.

"Looking for a book, apparently." Chloe snorted. "Like he can read."

"Chloe," I chided softly. Not that I harbored any good will toward the man, but it made me uncomfortable to poke fun at a person's lack of intelligence. Maybe because so much of it had to do with parenting and being lucky with good teachers. Morals and manners, on the other hand, were fair game. I turned to James. "He wasn't here to talk to you, don't worry."

"I was surprised to see him, that's all. I'm not worried about Steven. I'm worried about *you*, Hannah." She touched my arm gently. "What's going on?"

"It's because I said that thing about Zack, isn't it?" Essie asked, her eyebrows pushed together in a worried frown. "Brax asked me if I knew anything, which I obviously took to mean *he* knew *something*, but then he weaseled out of telling me. I didn't mean to upset you."

"You didn't upset me, Essie." I chewed my lip as tears blurred my vision *again*. I wiped frantically under my glasses with the cuff of my sweater. "I don't know what's wrong with me. We weren't even together that long, really."

Essie's expression went from worried to murderous. "I'm going to kill him," she announced. "And I can do it, too. My brother showed me how."

I laughed as I dabbed at my eyes. "Please don't kill him. He's really..." I didn't have words for what he was. Wonderful? That about summed him up. "It wasn't him. I ended it."

"Why?" Essie still looked deeply suspicious. "What did he do? Did you find out he has half a dozen secret babies running around?"

"Essie!" James gave an exasperated huff and shook her head. "Don't listen to her. Zack wouldn't keep that kind of secret." She stroked my arm. "Adam and Brax are his brothers, but we're *your* friends. Whatever happened, we're on your side."

Chloe wrapped an arm around me from the other side. "You don't have to tell us if you're not ready, but it might help to talk it out."

I rolled my lips and stared at my damp sweater cuff. "There's nothing to tell, really. He said he loved me, so I thought it would be better if we went ahead and ended things."

My words were met with heavy silence. I sniffled a little and wiped my eyes.

"I'm missing something," Essie said finally. "Are you saying you *don't* have those feelings for Zack? Was he pressuring you to say it before you were ready? Because that's some high school bullshit we're not going to put up with."

"No, he didn't pressure me. I—we—" I straightened my glasses, my spine, my mind. "It's not *love*."

"Huh." Chloe took my hand and pointed at the spot

where my tears had turned the cream-colored fabric to a muddy brown. "Then why are you crying?"

Then why are you crying, Hannah? Zack's voice echoed in my brain.

My heart turned over in my chest. "I don't know. I miss him, that's all."

James hesitated. "Is it possible it *could* be love? Someday, even if you don't quite feel that way yet?"

"That's not—I don't know how to explain it." I shook my head. "I know you don't understand why I did it. Honestly, I don't entirely understand it myself. It just felt so *bad*. So terrifying. I had to get out. It felt like life or death. I know that doesn't make sense. I just...I was married once. A long time ago."

"A long time ago? You're not even thirty. It couldn't have been *that* long ago," Essie said.

"I was fourteen," I said quietly.

Stunned silence ensued.

"Oh, *shit*," James whispered.

"We need beverages," Essie announced. "*Now*."

Twenty minutes later, after Janie dropped Maya back at her parents' house, we were ensconced in a booth at Shenanigans waiting for the first round of mimosas.

And then I told them all about it.

32

HANNAH

ZACK:

Hey, any chance you're free tomorrow evening? We need to run through the rodeo schedule, and it would be better to do that here at Lodestar so you can really get a feel for how it's going to shake out.

HANNAH:

You're still helping me?

ZACK:

Come on, duchess. You know I'd never leave you high and dry.

HANNAH:

I'm off at three. I'll come by after.

ZACK:

Great! See you then,

I left brunch feeling like I had been hit by the emotional equivalent of a tsunami, if that tsunami had also hurled an eighteen-wheeler right at my feelings. I was wrung out from the conversation with my friends. My limbs felt heavy, and I was so tired I could barely keep my eyes open.

But it had been good.

Chloe had been right. It did help to talk it out. Everything with Zack had happened so fast. One minute I was lying in his arms, blissed out on post-sex endorphins, and in the next I was fourteen again, fighting for my very survival.

PTSD, Chloe had said, gently squeezing my hand. *It's not just for soldiers and firemen.*

I took a long, hot bath the second I got home and then crawled into bed. That was when I saw Zack's text message asking me to come by Lodestar tomorrow. Warmth spread through me knowing he was still going to help me. His innuendo even elicited a dry chuckle. Zack had never been able to resist an innuendo.

I slept like the dead for fourteen hours, and when I woke up, the sunlight felt brighter, somehow.

"Okay, so I was thinking that instead of handing out schedule flyers, which are all going to end up scattered in the pasture anyway, we could put a big sign here with a QR code. People can just scan it and pull the flyer up on their phone." Zack gestured as he talked.

I swallowed, watching his forearms bunch and flex. It was hard to concentrate when he looked so delicious. His maroon t-shirt clung just enough to his shoulders and pecs that I could see the shape without it being skin-tight, and the rusty red color made his eyes look bluer than ever. The worn-in Wrangler's hugged his butt and thick thighs. And the backwards baseball cap? Lord, save me.

"What do you think?" Zack asked.

I think I want to bite your clavicle.

I cleared my throat. "That's a great idea. No waste, and it will save us printing costs, too."

"Great." He grinned and my heart just about stopped beating. *Why* did his smile still do that to me? "So you're doing an opening speech, right? To welcome everyone and thank them for supporting the public library. I remembered you said something about that, so it's the first thing on the schedule."

"Right." I wasn't even nervous about it. Public speaking was never a problem for me. Gorgeous cowboys proposing marriage, on the other hand...

"I talked to Chloe," I blurted out.

He went completely still, then slowly turned to face me. "You did?"

I nodded. "She said you kept your promise."

"Yeah." He blew out a breath. "She pointed me in the direction of a few resources. I joined a support group for accident and trauma survivors. I've only been to one meeting. I'm not sure it's for me. So many of them have it much worse than I do, and I feel guilty for being there. But my therapist said it was normal to feel that way and to give it a couple months before I decide."

"You're seeing a therapist?"

"Someone Chloe suggested. He's an hour and a half from here, so I guess it's good that he thinks I only need six sessions. He had the audacity to say I'm one of his easier cases." Zack laughed. "I was mightily offended, let me tell you."

"You're ridiculous," I said, but I was laughing, too. Then I stopped laughing and really looked at him. Not ogled. *Looked*. He had always hid his darker feelings behind a smile or a laugh, but I had the feeling he wasn't doing that now. "You look good, Zack. How do you feel?"

He thought it over. "I'm okay," he said at last. "The first session was hard. Fucking *heavy*."

I nodded, remembering how I had felt yesterday after talking to my friends. How I had felt years and years ago after intense therapy sessions. "It gets easier."

"I feel..." He searched for the word. "Hopeful. Almost. Like I can maybe see a time in the not-so-distant future when I *will* feel hopeful. I think it has something to do with my therapist being so damn sure I'll make it out of this, but also it's Hurricane Red." He paused. "Ever since the accident, I've felt like our fortunes were aligned, you know? Like if things were going to be bad, then they'd be bad for both of us. When we went to rescue him, it was like I was rescuing myself in a way. That probably sounds stupid."

"No," I said. "No, it doesn't sound stupid at all."

We headed toward the arena, where the events would take place. His pinky brushed mine as we walked and then he pulled back like the touch scalded him. I had to stop myself from reaching for him.

"Sorry." His voice came out rough around the edges. "I don't know how holding your hand became such a habit."

"It's all right," I said quickly. "I don't mind."

He stopped. "You don't mind that it's a habit, or you don't mind holding my hand?"

I wanted to hold his hand. I wanted to so badly it made my chest ache. I couldn't breathe around it. I twisted my hands together, not answering.

"Hannah." He tucked an errant lock of hair behind my ear. His eyes swept over my face like he was trying to memorize every feature. "I keep thinking about that moment when everything went sideways and I...Do you think it would have gone differently, if I hadn't asked you to marry me?"

My brows drew together in confusion. Wasn't that obvious? "Yes, of course."

"That's what I thought, too. I kept running it through my head, and I realized, you didn't have a particularly good experience with marriage. And maybe the way I sprung it on you out of the blue like that—which, to be fair, duchess, it was out of the blue for me, too—but maybe the shock of it was kind of...triggering for you?"

I bit back a smile. Why did I feel like smiling right now? This was serious. "Maybe a little," I admitted.

"What do you think would have happened if I hadn't?"

I wrinkled my nose. Honestly, I hadn't really considered that. "I don't know. I suppose we would have had coffee together and then gone to work. Maybe I would have gone to Lodestar after work. We probably would have had sex again."

"No." Zack looked at the sky for a moment. His throat bobbed on a swallow. "No, I mean, what do you think would have happened if I had told you I loved you without first scaring the ever-living fuck out of you with an accidental marriage proposal?"

All the air left my lungs in an audible *whoosh*. I tried to speak, but all I managed was an embarrassing, mouse-like squeak.

But he didn't jump in with more words of his own. He stayed silent, his eyes never leaving mine, patiently waiting for me to get there.

And finally, I did.

"I don't know," I said. "Those sex hormones are pretty strong."

His eyes narrowed. "Don't you dare say this is just sex again. I swear to god, Hannah, I'll turn you over my knee right now."

I stared at him slack jawed. Gracious. Was that supposed to be a threat? Because my body wasn't reacting to it like a threat. I shifted and pressed my thighs together. "I wasn't going to say that. I was going to say, the hormones might have buffered the fear a little. Not enough to get past an accidental marriage proposal, obviously, but maybe a little thing like *I love you* would have been okay."

He dipped his chin, then tilted his head sideways and peeked at me. "I could say it now. Just to test it."

My heart slammed against my ribs. "No!" I shouted.

His brows winged up and one corner of his mouth twisted in an amused smirk.

"I mean, no," I said in a normal voice, despite my pulse galloping frantically. I needed to think about this. It was happening too fast again, and I hadn't expected it. I couldn't—

"Are you scared, duchess?" he asked.

It was almost a taunt, except his eyes crinkled at me in a smile that hadn't made it to his mouth yet. I loved that look. I didn't deserve that look, not when I had just shouted at him *not* to tell me he loved me. But he looked at me like that, and suddenly I wasn't scared, not really.

And still I said, "Yes." Because that fear...it would come back. That clawing panic would return. I didn't want to hurt him.

"Good," he said.

"Good?"

"Yeah. I'm glad you're scared. I'm counting on it. Because here's the thing, Hannah Bell." He tilted my chin up to look at him. "You're really fucking good at doing the thing that scares you."

33

HANNAH

I didn't sleep that night. Stab, pull, stab, pull, stab, pull. My needle made stitch after stitch, my brain whirling with all the things Zack had said.

I love you, Hannah Bell.

Stab, pull, stab, pull, stab, pull.

You're really fucking good at doing the thing that scares you.

Stab, pull, stab, pull, stab, pull.

I want you to win, Hannah.

Stab, pull, stab, pull, stab, pull.

My fingertips were red and sore when I finally put the pillow aside. I crawled into bed just as the first light of dawn peeked over the ridge line. My eyes drifted closed with his voice still in my head.

I want you to win, Hannah.

THE PAINTED Cat was its usual self on Saturday night. Which was to say, it was busy, but not so busy that a person making a spectacle of herself wouldn't be noticed.

Butterflies took flight in my stomach. Oh, heck. I squished the pillow against my abdomen, hoping it would smother them. It did not.

"He's not here." I looked around again, just to be certain. "Are you sure he's coming?"

James squeezed my bicep comfortingly. "Adam promised he and Brax would get him here. They'll get it done."

"Great," I said mutely. "That's great."

Essie burst out laughing. "Oh, honey. You look like you're going to hurl."

"I can't deny that's a possibility."

Janie poured a shot of tequila and pushed it across the bar top. "Here. For courage."

I downed it in two swallows. I doubted I'd ever make it in one. "Thank you."

"Do you want another one?" Janie asked.

I shook my head. "I don't want to do this drunk."

"You don't have time, anyway," Chloe said. "He just walked in."

I spun on my toes and there he was, flanked by his brothers. Looking edible, as always. His gaze snagged on mine and everything else faded away. The people, the noise, the smells. He came closer and my heart lodged itself in my throat, which made it impossible to say anything at all when he said, "Hannah."

Chloe elbowed me in the back, but that didn't do any good.

"Hi, Zack," James chirped. Then she rolled up on her toes to give Adam a kiss on the cheek. "Hi, honey."

Brax had already captured Essie by the waist and dragged her into his side. "What are you ladies up to tonight?"

I had the feeling he already knew. Or at least he knew as much as Essie knew. But Essie didn't know what I was going to say to Zack. She couldn't, because I didn't know myself, despite having thought about literally nothing else all day.

Oh, goodness. This was going to be a disaster.

The conversation swirled around us, but I kept staring at Zack and he kept staring right on back at me. His gaze dipped to the pillow I held protectively against my body and he quirked an eyebrow at me.

"You planning on taking a nap?" he asked, bemused.

I shook my head.

He looked at me like he was waiting—hoping—for more, but when I said nothing, he gave me a sad little smile then turned to the bar. "Can we get three beers, Janie?"

"You got it."

Their beers in hand, the Hale brothers headed for their

usual booth in the corner. Panic clawed at my chest as I watched Zack walk away.

No. No.

I swallowed my heart and found my voice.

"I owe you a grovel, Zack." The words rang out loud and clear above the din.

Zack froze. Slowly he turned around, his expression completely blank. "What—what did you say?"

Suddenly it was so quiet you could hear a pin drop. I licked my lips nervously. "I owe you a grovel. Because you're wonderful and patient and made me believe..." I swallowed hard. "You made me believe I could win."

He stared at me. It was...well, it should have been unnerving.

And yet I wasn't nervous at all. Because I knew—I *knew* —that if I jumped, he would catch me. So I was going to jump.

"I'm not apologizing." I straightened my spine and tilted my chin. A faint smirk ghosted his lips. "I didn't do anything I need to apologize for. We all have broken pieces inside us. Sometimes those pieces have sharp edges that only time can soften. That's where I'm at now. I need time to soften some of those sharp pieces. But I think...I think I can do it. I know I hurt you, and I wish I hadn't. I do. I wish I could say it will never happen again, but I don't want to make a promise I can't keep."

I didn't look left. I didn't look right. If I looked anywhere but Zack, at all those people I knew were staring at me, wondering what the heck was wrong with me, I'd freak out.

Zack…he was my safe haven.

So I kept my eyes on his, and pressed on.

"But I will promise you this," I continued. "I promise that when I hurt you, I will do everything in my power to fix it. I promise I will do the scary thing, whatever it is. Because I love you, Zack. I love you so much. I—" A sob rose in my throat. Oh, *no.*

"Stop," he said hoarsely. Three strides and he was taking my glasses off my face and wiping the wetness from my eyes. "Oh, god, stop. Don't cry, Hannah. I can't stand it. You don't need to grovel. You had me at Mr. Hale."

"What?" I tried to make out his face, but it was so blurry. "I didn't say Mr. Hale."

"Yes, you did. You walked into the Painted Cat, and you said, *Mr. Hale, I presume?* And I said—"

"You said *no.*" I half sobbed, half laughed, remembering. "You said, *you know damn well who I am, Hannah Bell, so you don't need to presume shit.*" I gave him a watery smile. "I'm paraphrasing, of course."

"I think that's spot on, actually."

"I love you, Zack Hale."

"Yeah?" He settled my glasses back on my face and I blinked at him. "Well, thank fuck, because I love you too, Hannah Bell."

"Kiss her, you fool!" James hollered.

"I'm getting to it!" Zack shouted back.

I grinned. "Did you like my grovel?"

He snorted. "Sure did. Especially the part where you said you had nothing to apologize for. Put a whole new spin on the concept of groveling."

"Well, I made you a pillow. Doesn't that count for something?"

"That's for me?" An odd expression crossed his face, like he was remembering something.

My grin widened. "Sure is." I turned it around, showing him the embroidery on the other side.

Zack Hale's Magic Dick Gave Me the Best Sex of My Life.

And then I was very glad that he had returned my glasses, because I had the pleasure and privilege of watching his face turn beet red from the base of his throat to the tips of his ears.

Zack Hale, my wild, wild cowboy, was blushing like a school girl.

And then he finally kissed me.

ZACK:

Everyone clear on what they're doing today?

ADAM:

What's today, again?

BRAX:

Family trip to Disney Land, remember?

ZACK:

You both suck.

TED:

Ignore them. I've been looking forward to this rodeo all month. It's going to be great.

ADAM:

We're just screwing with you. We'll be there.

Hannah was wearing a skirt. She didn't always, these days. In the month we'd been back from our road trip, she occasionally wore the jeans she'd brought home with her. It would be a waste not to, she'd explained, like she needed an excuse to do whatever the hell she wanted. But today she was wearing a skirt. Dark blue denim with a slit up to her knee. Her ankles and calf came in and out of view like a kinky game of peek-a-boo.

That, paired with her hair in pigtail braids and a cowgirl hat, gave me all kind of ideas about throwing her over my shoulder and taking her back to my cabin. Which would have been awkward, since she was standing in the middle of the arena, giving the opening speech of the rodeo.

"Libraries are a vital part of the community," Hannah said into the wireless mic. "Thank you all so much for coming out today to support the library that supports you. The money we earn today will go to new computers, new books, and new programming."

She twisted as she talked so she could address the whole audience. Every time she changed direction, a glimpse of her ankle appeared. Once I even saw her knee.

"Zack, you need to stop looking at that girl like you're

going to take a bite out of her," Dad muttered next to me. "This is a family event, son."

"*Dad.*"

He held up his hands. "Hey, I'm not the problem here. I'm just pointing it out."

I groaned under my breath, applauding with everyone else as Hannah wrapped up her pitch for the library.

"She's a good one," Dad said. "And you did good helping her pull this thing together. The two of you make a good team."

I pushed away from the fence and lifted my hand to get Hanna's attention. We needed to get the contestants lined up for the calf-roping event. She nodded and started across the arena. But of course she got waylaid by folks offering their help at the library.

"I was thinking your cabin might be a tad small for you now, if you're planning on being at Lodestar for good." He rubbed the back of his neck and pretended to be interested in the weeds poking out by the fence post. "Think you'll be sticking around?"

It was a good question. We hadn't really discussed what my role at Lodestar Ranch would be. Right now, I did the same job as the other ranch hands. I took a smaller paycheck, but I also had a cut of the ranch profits and my own cabin on the property. I had never said it was temporary, but I had never said it wasn't, either.

I still missed the rodeo, but with the season starting in earnest, I'd already been sought out by a couple of the big events looking for guest commentators. I had lined up two rodeos for later this summer, and I was looking forward to it. Maybe Hannah would come along for a road trip. And in the meantime, I was having a good time with Hurricane Red. Some day he might even be ridable.

The truth was, I still didn't entirely know what I wanted to do with the rest of my life. I knew that Hannah was in Aspen Springs, so I wanted to be here, too. I knew I was happiest outdoors. I knew I enjoyed variety and tended to get restless doing the same thing every day. Outside of that...fuck, I didn't know a damn thing.

But I was okay with that. The not knowing.

As long as I had Hannah, the Colorado Rockies, and a horse, the rest would work itself out.

"Yeah, Dad," I said, after a pause so long Dad started to look nervous. "I'm back for good."

He grinned at the weeds. "In that case, there's a quarter parcel set aside for you to build on." He tipped his hat to Hannah, who had almost reached us, and his grin turned sly. "I suggest four bedrooms. You can grow into it."

THE SUN SLUNG low in a pink sky by the time the last outhouse was loaded up on the truck. The driver thumped his horn and that was it. The rodeo was officially done. We wouldn't know the final dollar amount for another week, probably, but right now, we had a sense of accomplishment. After a day full of raucous animals, loud music, and happy people, Lodestar felt oddly quiet now that was all over.

The whole lot of us had ended the day on the front porch of the big house for a round of much-deserved beers. Eventually, the group disbanded, pair by pair. First Dad walked Essie's mom to her car. Brax and Essie were the next to go, opting to crash at Brax's old cabin instead of making the drive back to their house in Aspen Springs. When Adam, James, and Ben headed inside, Hannah and I decided to sit on my front step and watch the stars come out.

"Stay the night?" I asked.

She yawned. "If you want me to."

"I always want you to."

"Then I'll always stay."

I sat motionless, as though the slightest change would make her take it back. But all she did was rest her head on my shoulder and snuggle closer.

"I could build us something bigger," I said carefully. "And then maybe you *could* always stay."

She lifted her head and looked at me. There was hope in her eyes, but also a hint of apprehension. "Are you...are you saying we should live together?"

"I think it makes sense. But we'd have to keep going as we are for a while yet. Building a house takes time, and I want to do it right. Four bedrooms. Maybe a library with a rolling ladder."

Her eyes bugged out. "*Four* bedrooms?"

"Yes, four bedrooms. I don't care what you say, Hannah Bell, five cats is a *lot* of cats. We need the space."

She laughed. "They don't need four bedrooms!"

I shrugged. We both knew those bedrooms weren't really for the cats, but neither one of us was ready to say it out loud. For now, it was enough to think about it. Hope for it, some day in the hazy future. We knew where we were headed, even if we didn't know the precise timeframe.

"So? What do you think?" I asked. "Should I start making plans?"

"I think..." She stared at the toes of her cowboy boots and rolled her lips together. I couldn't breathe. When she looked up at me again, her eyes were suspiciously shiny. "I think I would love to live with you in a four-bedroom house full of cats, and a library with a rolling ladder. Someday."

"Someday." I gently pushed up her glasses. "I'll get to work on it."

"Thank you."

The sky deepened to a dark, dusky blue and the first stars popped out like flecks of silver. I breathed in the scent of the mountains, the horses, and Hannah.

Yeah. This was what I wanted.

"You know," I said casually, like it hadn't been on my mind for a month, "this would be the perfect moment for a marriage proposal, if we were so inclined."

She stiffened next to me. "Oh?" she said cautiously.

I laughed. "It's cute how hard you're trying not to freak

out right now, duchess, but I know you're *not* so inclined. And that's fine. Hell, it's fine if you're *never* so inclined. As long as you tell me we can share a home together, then I'll live my life a very happy man. But I'm not going to ask you to marry me. Not now, and not ever." I laced our hands together.

There was a long pause, but I didn't look at her, just ran my thumb over the bones on the back of her hand.

"Not *ever*?" she ventured.

"Not ever. That's my promise to you. Now, that's not to say I won't marry you. I just won't propose. If you ever decide you want to marry me, you'll have to do the asking."

She stared at me a long time, chewing her lip. Her head tilted. "What do you think you'd say, if I asked you?"

My heart pounded hard in my chest, even though I knew she wouldn't. Not tonight, anyway. But she was thinking about it without having a panic attack, and that was progress.

I laughed. "I've never said no to you, Hannah Bell, and if you ever ask me that question, it sure as hell won't be when I start."

She smiled and leaned into me. "Someday."

"Someday," I agreed.

Someday was a beautiful dream. But right now we had today, and today was pretty damn perfect.

So together we watched the stars.

EPILOGUE

HANNAH

don't want to spoil it for you, but James looks like a cupcake." I threaded a pearl hoop through my ear, my gaze on Zack's reflection in the mirror. All he was doing was knotting his tie, but geez. The way he looked in that suit, I was tempted to help him right back out of it.

He laughed. "You can't spoil it for me. I couldn't care less what James looks like. It's not my wedding."

He came and stood next to me, checking his reflection to see if his tie was straight. I watched him for a moment, then took us both in. My breath caught. "Well, we look like it's our wedding. I can't believe James is making the brides-maids wear white."

His eyes met mine in the mirror and for a split second all I saw was yearning. But just as quickly, it was gone again. He smiled and kissed my cheek. "You look beautiful."

Summer, with its packed schedule of rodeos and horse shows, was too busy for a wedding, so James and Adam had chosen a day in early December. James had really leaned into the "winter wonderland" theme. Adam, Brax, Zack, Blaine, and Ben were dressed in gray suits—with white cowboy hats, naturally—and James's bridesmaids wore white gowns.

"It's not snowing," I said as we left the cabin. "Dang it. James really wanted a white wedding."

Zack snorted. "Pretty sure that ship sailed a long time ago."

I rolled my eyes. "I mean *snow*. Not virginity."

He grinned. "Colorado weather can't be tamed. But those clouds look promising." He pointed to the gray sky. "She might have her winter wonderland wedding, after all."

"I hope so. I want it to be perfect for her." I kissed his cheek lightly, careful not to smudge my pink lipstick. "I need to join the bridesmaids. I'll see you out there."

The ceremony was taking place under a large, white tent that had been set up behind the big house. It was gorgeously adorned with fake snow and fairy lights. It looked like something out of the *Nutcracker*.

I squeezed James's hand. "You look beautiful."

She beamed back. "We all do."

The music started, an instrumental version of an old rock song. *Their* song. We filed down the aisle, tallest to shortest. Janie went first, then Essie, then me, then Chloe. When James appeared, I looked at Adam, not wanting to miss his reaction. And...goodness. I had never seen him smile like that. His eyes were instantly shrink wrapped.

It was too intimate, the way he looked at her. I felt like I was witnessing something I had no business seeing. I turned away quickly and my gaze landed on Zack.

Zack wasn't watching the bride like everyone else.

Zack was watching me.

That look was on his face again, the one that nearly made my heart split open. Stark, naked yearning. And I wondered...I wondered if I looked at him like that, too.

Because the way he looked at me...that was how I felt.

Like I couldn't live another second without making us forever.

The vows went by in a blur, and suddenly they were being pronounced husband and wife. Adam dipped her in a kiss and everyone cheered. They started back down the aisle.

"James!" Ben hollered. "It's snowing!"

James's eyes went wide. Then she lifted her enormous, poofy white skirts, revealing her pink cowboy boots she wore underneath, and sprinted out of the tent with Adam right behind her. The rest of us followed a little more sedately.

The snow fell in big, fluffy flakes, the kind that made you think of miracles and magic. I watched Adam pull James—his *wife*—into his arms for a kiss and my eyes welled with sudden tears. I blinked them back furiously. Of course I was wearing waterproof mascara, but I didn't want to risk it.

Zack's arms circled my waist from behind and I leaned back against his warm, broad chest. "Hey," he said against my temple. "What are you thinking about?"

You. Forever.

"They look so happy." I turned in his arms to face him. Snowflakes fell between us and I caught one on my index finger. "Oh, I get to make a wish! No, wait, it melted."

He laughed. "I don't think you're supposed to wish on snowflakes, darlin'. They're too..."

"Ephemeral?" I suggested.

"I was going to say melty."

I laughed. "That's the magic of it, I suppose. I just wasn't quick enough."

He straightened my glasses for me and smiled. "Tell me what you'd wish for. Maybe I can make it come true."

"Well." I hesitated, testing it out. The fear didn't come. Only love. "You could marry me."

He stared down at me.

"Zack?"

"Hannah..." His voice came out hoarse. "Don't tease me. Not about this. Not today."

"I'm not teasing you, Zack. I'm perfectly serious. I want to spend the rest of our lives together. I know this isn't the right place to ask you. It's James's wedding day, I don't have a ring to give you, and I'm sorry, but I'm not kneeling on the ground in this dress. But once I realized how much I wanted that to be us, it seemed impossible to wait even another hour without telling you." I looked up at him, feeling nothing but certainty. "Will you marry me, Zack?"

"Will I?" He touched his forehead to mine. "You tamed this wild cowboy a long time ago, duchess. I've been yours since you strutted into the Painted Cat and flashed your ankles at me. I was yours then. I'm yours now. I'm yours forever. Of course I'll fucking marry you. I thought you'd never ask."

I pulled back just enough to look at him. "Really? Never?"

He laughed. "Nah, I knew you couldn't resist me forever. I just thought someday might still be a ways off yet. But, Hannah." His eyes were bright and shiny, crinkling at the corners in that way I loved. "I'm really glad someday is today."

ACKNOWLEDGMENTS

Every time I sit down to write the acknowledgments, I am overwhelmed with gratitude and the sheer number of people it takes to get a book out of my head and into a reader's hands.

Lori and Nicole, who have cheered me on since the very first book in 2017.

Jonathan, who always understands that when I'm staring off into space, that counts as writing.

My daughters, who remind me to put on real pants before I leave the house.

Liana and Lisa, who keep me sane in this increasingly crazy publishing world.

Debra and Colby, who create amazing graphics and videos so readers can actually find me.

The bookstagrammers and booktokkers and reviewers who have shouted about my books—no one would know who I am without you!

Maybe—a BIG maybe—I could have done this without you, but good lord, that would have sucked. Thank you all.

ABOUT THE AUTHOR

Elizabeth Bright is a USA Today bestselling author of romance with heart, humor, and heat. She lives in Washington, D.C., with her two daughters and very needy dog. When she's not dreaming up fictional characters, she loves to go hiking and backpacking.

Sign up for Elizabeth's newsletter at www.elizabethbrightauthor.com